MARINA

MARINA

CARLOS RUIZ ZAFÓN

TRANSLATED BY
LUCIA GRAVES

LITTLE, BROWN AND COMPANY
New York · Boston

Text copyright © 1999 by Dragonworks, S.L.
English translation copyright © 2013 by Lucia Graves

Little, Brown and Company

Hachette Book Group
237 Park Avenue, New York, NY 10017
Visit our website at lb-teens.com

Little, Brown and Company is a division of Hachette Book Group, Inc.
The Little, Brown name and logo are trademarks of Hachette Book Group, Inc.

The publisher is not responsible for websites (or their content)
that are not owned by the publisher.

First U.S. Edition: July 2014

Library of Congress Cataloging-in-Publication Data

Ruiz Zafón, Carlos, 1964– author.
[Marina. English]
Marina / Carlos Ruiz Zafón ; translated by Lucia Graves. — First U.S. edition.
pages cm
Originally published in Spanish in Barcelona by Edebé, 1999.
Summary: "When boarding-school student Oscar Drai meets Marina, she promises him a mystery and takes him to a secret graveyard deep in Barcelona, where they witness a woman dressed in black lay a single rose atop a gravestone etched with a black butterfly. Their curiosity leads them down a dangerous path, and they discover a decades-old conspiracy that puts their lives in the hands of forces more sinister and mystical than they could have believed possible"— Provided by publisher.
ISBN 978-0-316-04471-4 (hardcover) — ISBN 978-0-316-32017-7 (e-book) — ISBN 978-0-316-32020-7 (e-book—library edition) [1. Mystery and detective stories. 2. Supernatural—Fiction 3. Love—Fiction. 4. Barcelona (Spain)—History—20th century—Fiction. 5. Spain—History—20th century—Fiction.]
I. Graves, Lucia, translator. II. Title.
PZ7.R8868Mar 2014 [Fic]—dc23 2013016666

10 9 8 7 6 5 4 3 2 1

RRD-C

Printed in the United States of America

A NOTE FROM THE AUTHOR

Dear Reader,

I've always believed that all writers, whether they will admit it or not, have a few favorites among their published books. These preferences are seldom related to the intrinsic literary value of the work or the success it might have achieved, if any. The naked truth is, one just tends to feel closer to some of one's offspring than to others. Of all the books I've published ever since I picked up this odd business of the novelist trade back in prehistoric 1992, *Marina* remains one of my favorites.

I wrote the novel in Los Angeles between 1996 and 1997. I was then in my early thirties and was beginning to suspect that what romantics used to refer to as my "first youth" was, slowly but surely, starting to slip through my fingers. By then I had already published three novels for young adults, but soon after embarking on *Marina* I knew that this would be the last I'd write in the genre. As the writing advanced, everything in the story began to acquire a shade of farewell, and by the time I'd finished it, I sensed that something inside me—something that even today I cannot explain but that I still miss every single day—was forever left among its pages.

Maybe, as Marina once told Oscar, we are doomed to remember what never really happened.

Safe passage,
CRZ

Marina once told me that we only remember what never really happened. It would take me a lifetime to understand what those words meant. But I suppose I'd better start at the beginning, which in this case is the end.

In May 1980 I disappeared from the world for an entire week. For seven days and seven nights nobody knew my whereabouts. Friends, companions, teachers, and even the police embarked on a futile search for a fugitive whom they suspected dead, or at best lost in the wastelands of the wrong side of town, suffering from amnesia or something worse.

By the end of that week a plainclothes policeman

thought he had recognized the boy: He seemed to fit my description. The suspect was spotted wandering around Barcelona's Estación de Francia like a lost soul in a cathedral hammered out of iron and mist. The policeman ambled up to me just like a character of his ilk would in a crime novel. He asked me whether my name was Oscar Drai and whether I was the boy from the boarding school who had vanished without a trace. I nodded but didn't say a word. I still remember the reflection of the station's vaulted ceiling on his spectacle lenses.

We sat on one of the platform benches. The policeman lit a cigarette, taking his time, and let it continue to burn without once raising it to his lips. He informed me that there were a whole lot of people waiting to ask me a load of questions for which I'd better have some good answers. I nodded again. Then he looked me straight in the eye, scrutinizing me, and said, "Sometimes telling the truth is not such a good idea, Oscar." He handed me a few coins and suggested I call my tutor at the boarding school. So I did. The policeman waited for me to finish my call, gave me money for a cab, and wished me luck. I asked him how he knew I wasn't going to disappear again. After observing me for a while, he replied, "People only disappear when they have somewhere to go." He walked with me as far as the street and said good-bye without asking me where I'd been. I watched him saunter up Paseo Colón, the smoke from his untouched cigarette following him like a faithful dog.

That day Gaudí's ghost had sculpted impossible clouds across the shimmering blue skies of Barcelona. I took a taxi to the school, where I expected to be met by the firing squad.

For the next four weeks an army of teachers, clueless counselors, and child psychologists bombarded me with questions, trying to pry out my secret. I lied like the best of them, giving each exactly what they wanted to hear or what they were able to accept. In due time they all made an effort to pretend they'd forgotten the whole episode. I followed suit and never told anyone the truth about where I had been during those seven days.

I didn't realize then that sooner or later the ocean of time brings back the memories we submerge in it. Fifteen years on, the remembrance of that day has returned to me. I have seen that boy wandering through the mist of the railway station, and the name *Marina* has flared up again like a fresh wound.

We all have a secret buried under lock and key in the attic of our soul. This is mine.

ONE

In the late 1970s Barcelona was a mirage of avenues and winding alleys where one could easily travel thirty or forty years into the past by just stepping into the foyer of a grand old building or walking into a café. Time and memory, history and fiction merged in the enchanted city like watercolors in the rain. It was there, in the lingering echo of streets that no longer exist, that cathedrals and age-old palaces created the tapestry into which this story would be woven.

I was then a fifteen-year-old boy languishing in a boarding school named after some half-forgotten saint, on the lower slopes of the hill to Vallvidrera. In those days the district of Sarriá still looked like a small village stranded on the shores of an art nouveau metropolis. My school stood at the top end of a narrow street that climbed up from Paseo de la Bonanova. Its monumental façade was more reminiscent of a castle than a school, and its angular redbrick silhouette formed a dark maze of turrets, arches, and wings.

The school was surrounded by a sprawling citadel of gardens, fountains, muddy ponds, courtyards, and shadowy pinewoods. Here and there somber buildings housed swimming pools enveloped in a ghostly vapor, eerily silent gyms, and gloomy chapels where images of long-fingered angels grinned in the flickering candlelight. The main building was four stories high, not counting the two basements and an attic set apart as an enclosed residence for the few aging priests who still worked as teachers. The boarders' rooms were located along the cavernous corridors of the fourth floor. These endless galleries lay in perpetual darkness, always shrouded in a spectral aura.

I spent my days lost in hopeless reverie in the cold classrooms of that huge castle, waiting for the miracle that took place every afternoon at twenty minutes past five. At that magical hour, when the setting sun drenched the tall windows with liquid gold, the bell announcing the end of lessons rang and we boarders were allowed almost three free hours before dinner was served in the vast dining hall. The idea was that we should devote this time to studying and to meditation, but in all honesty I don't remember having applied myself even once to either of those noble pursuits the whole time I was there.

It was my favorite moment of the day. Slipping past the porter's lodge, I'd go out and explore the city. I made an art of getting back to the school just in time for dinner, having wandered through old streets and avenues in the darkening twilight. During those long walks I felt an exhilarating sense of freedom. My imagination would take wing and soar high above the buildings. For a few hours the streets of Barcelona, the boarding school, and my gloomy room on the fourth floor seemed to vanish. For those few hours, with just a couple of coins in my pocket, I was the luckiest person in the world.

My route would often take me through what in those days was still known as the Desert of Sarriá—no sandy dunes or anything remotely desert-like about it; it was, in fact, just the remains of a forest lost in a no-man's-land. Most of the old mansions that had once populated the top end of Paseo de la Bonanova, though still standing, were in an incipient state of ruin, and all the streets surrounding the boarding school were developing the eerie atmosphere of a ghost town. Ivy-clad walls blocked the way into wild gardens where huge residences loomed: derelict weed-choked palaces through which memory seemed to drift like a perpetual mist. Some of these decaying properties awaited demolition; others had been ransacked over the years. Some, however, were still inhabited.

Their occupants were members of dying dynasties, long forgotten—families whose names had filled entire pages of the local papers in the old days when trams were still regarded with skepticism as a modern invention. Now they were the hostages of a rapidly fading era who refused to abandon their sinking ships. Fearing perhaps that if they dared step outside their withered homes they might turn to ashes and be blown away in the wind, they wasted away like prisoners entombed in the relics of their lost glory. Sometimes, as I hurried past rusty gates and ghostly gardens peopled by worn, faceless statues, I could sense their owners' suspicious looks from behind faded shutters.

One afternoon, toward the end of September 1979, I decided to venture down a street I hadn't noticed before, one of those roads studded with art nouveau mansions. It curved around, and at the end of it stood an ornate iron gate, no different from many others in the area. Beyond this entrance lay the remains of a garden marked by years of neglect. Through the weeds I glimpsed the outline of a two-story home, its somber façade rising behind a fountain with a stone mermaid whose face time had covered with a veil of moss.

It was beginning to get dark and I thought the place looked rather sinister, even for my taste. A grave silence enveloped it; only the breeze seemed to whisper a wordless warning. I realized I'd walked into one of Sarriá's "dead" spots and decided I'd better retrace my steps and return to the boarding school. I was hovering between my morbid fascination with that forgotten place and common sense when I noticed two bright yellow eyes in the shadows, fixed on me like daggers. I swallowed hard.

The motionless silhouette of a cat with velvety gray fur stood out against the gate of the old manor. In its mouth it held a tiny half-dead sparrow, and a silver bell hung from its neck. The cat studied me coldly for a few seconds, then turned and slid under the metal bars of the gate. I watched as it disappeared into the immensity of that lost paradise, carrying the sparrow on its last journey.

I was struck by the sight of the haughty, defiant little beast. Judging by its shiny fur and its bell, I surmised that it had an owner. It looked well fed. Perhaps this building was home to something more than the ghosts of a Barcelona long gone. I walked up to the gate and put my hands on the iron bars. They felt cold. The last gleam of sunset lit up the shiny trail of blood left by the sparrow through that jungle. Scarlet pearls marking a path through the labyrinth. I swallowed again. Or rather,

I tried to swallow. My mouth was dry. I could feel my pulse throbbing in my temples as if it knew something I didn't know. Just then I felt the gate yielding under my weight and realized it was open.

As I stepped into the garden, the moon lit up the veiled face of the mermaid emerging from the black waters of the fountain. She was observing me. I stood there, transfixed, expecting her to slither out of the pond and spread a wolfish grin, revealing a serpent's tongue and long fangs. None of that happened. Taking a deep breath, I considered reining in my imagination or, better still, giving up my timid exploration of the property altogether. Once again, someone made the decision for me. A celestial sound wafted through the shadows of the garden like a perfume. I could make out traces of its soft tones carving out the notes of an aria to the accompaniment of a piano. It was the most beautiful voice I had ever heard.

The melody was familiar, though I couldn't put a name to it. It came from inside the house. I followed its hypnotic trail. Sheets of diaphanous light filtered through the half-open door of a glass conservatory, above which I recognized the cat's eyes, fixed on mine from a windowsill on the first floor. I drew closer to the illuminated sunroom and its alluring sound. It was a woman's voice. The faint halo of a hundred candles twinkled inside, revealing the golden horn of an old gramophone spinning a record.

Without thinking what I was doing, I found myself walking into the conservatory, bewitched by the music from the gramophone. Sitting next to it on the table was a round, shiny object: a pocket watch. I picked it up and examined it in the candlelight. The hands had stopped and the dial was cracked. It looked like gold and as old as the house itself. A bit farther away a large armchair had its back to me, facing a fireplace above which hung an oil portrait of a woman dressed in white. Her large gray eyes, sad and profound, presided over the room.

Suddenly the spell was shattered. A figure rose from the armchair and turned to look at me. A head of long white hair and eyes burning like red-hot coals shone in the dark. The only other thing I managed to see were two huge pale hands reaching out toward me. As I scrambled off in a panic, heading for the door, I bumped into the gramophone and knocked it over. I heard the needle scratch the record and the heavenly voice broke off with a hellish scream. Those hands brushed my shirt as I rushed out into the garden with wings on my feet and fear burning in every pore of my body. I didn't pause for a moment. I ran and ran without looking back, until a sharp pain tore through my side and I realized I could hardly breathe. By then I was bathed in cold sweat and could see the school lights shining some thirty meters ahead.

I slipped in through one of the kitchen doors that was rarely guarded and crept up to my room. The other boarders must have gone down to the dining room a good while earlier. I dried the sweat from my forehead and slowly my heart recovered its normal rhythm. I was beginning to feel calmer when someone rapped on my door.

"Oscar, time to come down to dinner," chimed the voice of one of my tutors, a freethinking Jesuit named Seguí who disliked having to play the policeman.

"I'll be right down, Father," I replied. "Just a second."

I hurriedly put on the jacket required for dinner and turned off the light. Through the window the moon's specter hovered over Barcelona. Only then did I realize that I was still holding the gold watch in my hand.

TWO

For the next few days that damned watch and I became inseparable companions. I took it everywhere with me; I even slept with it under my pillow, fearful that someone might find it and ask me where I'd got it. I wouldn't have known what to answer. *That's because you didn't find it; you stole it,* whispered the accusing voice in my head. *The technical term is "breaking and entering leading to grand larceny"—and goodness knows what other malfeasance you may be liable for,* the voice added. For some odd reason, it sounded suspiciously like the voice of Perry Mason on the old TV series.

Each night I waited patiently for my friends to fall

asleep so that I could examine my forbidden treasure. When silence reigned, I studied the watch with my flashlight. All the remorse in the world could not have diminished the fascination produced by the booty of my first adventure in "disorganized crime." It was a heavy watch and appeared to be made of solid gold. The crack in the glass was probably the result of a knock or a fall. The same impact must have ended the life of its mechanism, I imagined, freezing the hands at six twenty-three for all eternity. On the back was an inscription:

FOR GERMÁN, THROUGH WHOM LIGHT SPEAKS.
K.A.
19 JANUARY 1964

It occurred to me that the watch must be worth a fortune, and soon I was assailed by pangs of guilt. Those engraved words made me feel that I'd become not just a thief of other people's valuables, but one who also stole their most precious memories.

One rainy Thursday I decided to unload my guilty conscience and share my secret. My best friend at school was a boy with penetrating eyes and a nervous temperament who insisted on being called JF, though those initials had little or nothing to do with his real name. JF had the soul of an avant-garde poet and such a sharp wit he often cut his own tongue on it. He suffered from a weak constitution and had only to hear the word *germ* mentioned within a one-kilometer radius to think he was coming down with some deadly infection. Once I looked up *hypochondriac* and copied out the definition for him.

"You might be interested to know you've been mentioned in the *Dictionary of the Royal Academy*," I'd announced.

JF glanced at the note and threw me a scathing look.

"Try looking under *i* for *idiot* and you'll see I'm not the only famous one," he replied.

That Thursday, during our lunch break, JF and I sneaked into the gloomy assembly hall. Our footsteps down the central aisle conjured up the echo of tiptoeing shadows. Two harsh shafts of light fell on the dusty stage. We sat in a pool of light, facing rows of empty seats that melted away into the darkness. Rain scratched at the first-floor windows.

"Well," JF spat out, "what's all the mystery about?"

Without saying a word, I pulled out the watch and showed it to him. JF raised his eyebrows and appraised the object carefully for a few moments before handing it back to me with a questioning look.

"What do you think?" I asked.

"I think it's a gold watch," replied JF. "Who is this fellow Germán?"

"I haven't the foggiest."

"How typical of you. Spill the beans."

I went on to recount in detail my adventure of a few days earlier in the old dilapidated mansion. JF listened to my story with his characteristic patience and quasi-scientific attention. When I finished, he seemed to weigh the matter before offering his first impressions.

"In other words, you've stolen it," he concluded.

"That's not the point," I objected.

"I'd like to know what this Germán person thinks the point may be," JF replied.

"This Germán person probably died years ago," I suggested without much conviction.

JF rubbed his chin.

"I wonder what the penal code has in store for those juvenile miscreants inclined to the premeditated theft of personal objects and watches engraved with a dedication...."

"There was no premeditation, or anything of the sort," I protested. "It all happened suddenly—I had no time to think. By the time I realized I had the watch, it was too late. You would have done the same in my place."

"In your place I would have had a heart attack," remarked JF, who was more a man of words than a man of action. "Supposing I'd been crazy enough to go into that old house, following a feral cat with a bleeding bird in its jaws. God knows what germs you could catch from that kind of animal."

For a while we just sat there without saying a word, listening to the faraway sound of the rain.

"Well," JF finally concluded, "what's done is done. You're not thinking of returning to the scene of the crime, are you?"

I smiled meekly. "Not on my own."

My friend's eyes opened wide. "Don't even think about it."

That afternoon, once classes were over, JF and I slipped out through the kitchen door and headed for the mysterious street leading to the mansion. The cobble-stones were spattered with puddles and dead leaves, and a threatening metallic sky hung over the city. JF, who wasn't at all sold on the merits of our outing, looked paler than usual. The sight of that remote corner trapped in the past must have made his stomach shrink to the size of a marble. The silence was eerie.

"I've seen enough. Let's call it a day—let's turn around and return to our boring but safe lives at school," he mumbled, taking a few steps back.

"Don't be a chicken."

"I won't even respond to that...."

Just then the tinkle of a bell drifted on the wind. JF went quiet. The cat's yellow eyes were watching us. All of a sudden the cat hissed like a serpent and showed us its claws. The fur on its back stood on end and it opened its jaws to reveal the fangs that had taken the life of the sparrow a few days earlier. A distant flash of lightning illuminated the sky like a cauldron of light. JF and I exchanged glances.

Fifteen minutes later we were sitting on a bench next to the pond in the boarding school cloister. The watch was still in my jacket pocket, feeling heavier than ever.

There it remained for the rest of that week, until the early hours of Saturday morning. Shortly before dawn I awoke with the vague feeling of having dreamed about the voice captured in that old gramophone. Outside my window Barcelona was coming alive in a canvas of scarlet shadows. I jumped out of bed and looked for the wretched watch that had been cursing my existence for the past few days. We stared at each other. Finally, arming myself with a determination one can summon only when having to face some ridiculous task, I decided to put an end to the matter: I was going to return it.

I dressed quietly and tiptoed along the dark fourth-floor corridor. Nobody would notice my absence until ten or eleven o'clock. By then I hoped to be back. Or else.

Outdoors, the streets still lay beneath that mantle of

purplish brightness tingeing the dawn skies of Barcelona. I walked down to Calle Margenat. Sarriá was waking up around me as low clouds swept through the district, capturing the first light in a golden halo. Here and there the front of a house was just visible through gaps in the haze and the swirling dry leaves.

It didn't take me long to find the street. I paused for a while to take in the silence and the strange peace that filled that lost corner of the city. I was beginning to feel that the world had stopped, like the watch in my pocket, when I heard a sound behind me.

I turned around and beheld a vision straight out of a dream.

THREE

A bicycle was slowly emerging out of the mist. A young girl clad in a vaporous white dress was pedaling up the hill toward me. In the early sunlight I could almost make out her silhouette through the cotton. Her long, straw-colored hair waved about, concealing her face. I stood there, immobile, watching her as she approached, rooted to the ground like a fool. The bicycle stopped a couple of meters away. My eyes, or my imagination, spied the shape of slim legs as she stepped down. Slowly, I took in every part of that dress—which looked like something out of a Sorolla painting—until my eyes came to rest on the girl's deep gray eyes, so deep you could fall straight into them.

They were riveted on mine with a sarcastic look. I gaped at her, smiling stupidly.

"You must be the watch thief," said the girl in a tone that matched the strength of her expression.

I reckoned she must be about my age, perhaps a year or two older. Guessing a woman's age was, for me, an art or a science, never a pastime. Her skin was as pale as her dress.

"Do you live here?" I stammered, pointing to the gate.

She didn't even blink. Those eyes drilled into me with such intensity that it took me a long while to realize she was the most stunning creature I had ever seen, or hoped to see, in my entire life. Full stop.

"And who are you to ask?"

"I suppose I'm the watch thief," I improvised. "My name is Oscar. Oscar Drai. I've come to return it."

Without waiting for a reply, I pulled the watch out of my pocket and handed it to her. She held my gaze for a few seconds before taking it. When she did, I noticed that her hand was strikingly pallid and that she wore a plain gold band on her ring finger.

"It was already broken when I took it," I explained.

"It's been broken for fifteen years," she murmured without looking at me.

When at last she raised her eyes, she did so to examine me from head to toe, like someone sizing up an old piece of furniture or a bit of junk. Something in the way she looked at me made me realize she didn't really believe I was a thief; she was probably categorizing me as your run-of-the-mill imbecile. My beguiled expression surely didn't help. The girl arched an eyebrow and smiled mysteriously as she handed the watch back to me.

"You took it; you return it to its owner."

"But—"

"It isn't my watch," she explained. "It belongs to Germán."

The mere mention of that name conjured up the image of the towering figure with white hair that had surprised me in the conservatory a few days earlier.

"Germán?"

"My father."

"And you are?" I asked.

"His daughter."

"I meant, what's your name?"

"I know exactly what you meant," replied the girl.

She climbed back onto her bike and rode through the entrance gate, looking back briefly before disappearing into the garden. Those eyes seemed to be ridiculing me with their laughter. I sighed and followed her. An old acquaintance welcomed me in: the cat, staring at me with its usual disdain. I wished I were a Doberman.

The cat escorted me as I negotiated my way through

the tangled garden. By the time I reached the fountain with the mermaid, the bicycle was leaning against it while its owner unloaded a bag from the basket fixed over the handlebars. There was a smell of freshly baked bread. The girl pulled a bottle of milk out of the bag and kneeled down to fill a bowl that was lying on the ground. The animal rushed to its breakfast. It looked like a daily ritual.

"I think he prefers to kill his food before he eats it," I said.

"He only hunts for fun. He doesn't eat what he catches," she explained as if she were talking to a child. "It's a territorial thing."

"What an adorable little beast," I remarked.

"What he likes is milk. Don't you, Kafka? You love milk, don't you?"

The Kafkaesque cat licked her fingers in agreement. The girl smiled warmly and stroked his back. Through the folds of her dress, I could see the muscles flex on the side of her body. Just then she looked up and caught me watching her and licking my lips.

"How about you? Have you had breakfast?" she asked.

I shook my head.

"Then you must be hungry. All dimwits are hungry," she said. "Here, come in and have something to eat. It will do you good to have a full stomach if you're going to tell Germán why you stole his watch."

The kitchen was a large room at the back of the house. My condemned-man's breakfast consisted of delicious buttery croissants the girl had bought at the Foix patisserie in Plaza Sarriá, along with a very large cup of white coffee. She sat down facing me while I avidly devoured my feast, eyeing me with a mixture of curiosity, pity, and suspicion, as if she'd taken in a starving beggar. She didn't eat a thing herself.

"I've seen you around here before," she remarked without taking her eyes off me. "You and that little guy who looks like he's just seen a ghost. You often cross over the street behind this one when they let you out of the boarding school. Sometimes it's just you, humming absentmindedly. I bet you have a great time in that dungeon of a school...."

I was about to make some witty reply when an enormous shadow spread over the table like a cloud of ink. My host looked up and smiled. I sat there, stock-still, my mouth full of croissant, my heart beating like castanets.

"We have a visitor," she announced gleefully. "Dad, this is Oscar Drai, an amateur watch thief. Oscar, this is Germán, my father."

I gulped down my food and slowly turned my head. Standing above me was an impressively tall figure wearing an alpaca wool suit with a waistcoat and a bow tie. The man's white hair, neatly combed back, fell to his shoulders. His face, finely chiseled around dark sad eyes, displayed a gray mustache. But what really defined him were his hands. The white hands of an angel, with slender and unusually long fingers. Germán.

"I'm not a thief, sir...." I stated nervously. "Let me explain. I only ventured into your house because I thought it was uninhabited. Once I was inside, I don't know what happened to me, I listened to that music, well, no, well, yes, the thing is, I came in and saw the watch. I wasn't going to take it, I swear, but I got scared and by the time I realized I'd taken the watch, I was already quite a distance away. That is to say, I'm not sure whether I've explained this properly...."

The girl was smiling mischievously. Germán's eyes rested on mine. They were unfathomable. I rummaged about in my pocket and handed him the watch, expecting that at any moment he'd start shouting and threatening to call the police, the civil guard, and the juvenile court.

"I believe you," he said amiably, taking the watch and sitting down next to us at the table.

His voice was gentle, almost inaudible. His daughter served him two croissants on a plate and a cup of coffee just like mine. As she did so she kissed her father on the forehead and he put his arm around her. I gazed at them against the light that strayed in through the windows. Germán's face—which I'd expected to be the face of an ogre—became delicate, almost frail. He was extraordinarily thin. Smiling at me kindly, he brought the cup to his lips, and for a moment I noticed that the affection flowing between father and daughter went beyond words and gestures. A silent bond, a look in their eyes, seemed to draw them together in the shadows of that house at the end of a forgotten street, where they took care of each other, far from the world.

Germán finished his breakfast and thanked me for having taken the trouble to return his watch. So much kindness made me feel doubly guilty.

"Well, Oscar," he said in a tired voice, "it's been a pleasure to meet you. I hope to see you around here again, whenever you wish to pay us another visit."

I couldn't understand why he insisted on speaking to me so politely. There was something about him that made me think of another age, of other times when his gray hair shone and the old mansion was a palace halfway between Sarriá and heaven. He shook my hand and said good-bye to me before disappearing into what seemed like an impenetrable maze. I saw him walk away down the corridor, limping slightly. His daughter watched him, trying to conceal the sadness in her eyes.

"Germán isn't very well," she murmured. "He gets tired easily."

But she quickly put on a cheerful expression.

"Would you like anything else?" she asked.

"It's getting late," I replied, struggling against the temptation to seize any excuse for prolonging my stay. "I think I'd better be going."

She accepted my decision and went with me into the garden. The morning light had scattered the mist and the onset of autumn tinged the trees with copper. We walked toward the gates; Kafka purred in the sun. When we reached the exit the girl remained inside and opened the gate for me. We looked at each other without saying a word. She put out her hand and I shook it. I could feel her pulse beneath her velvety skin.

"Thanks for everything," I said. "And I'm sorry about—"

"It doesn't matter."

I shrugged.

"All right."

I set off down the street, feeling the magic of the house leaving me with every step I took. Suddenly, I heard her voice behind me.

"Oscar!"

I turned around. She was still there, behind the gates. Kafka lay by her feet.

"Why did you come into our house the other night?"

I looked around, as if I were trying to find the answer written on the cobblestones.

"I don't know," I admitted finally. "The mystery, I suppose..."

The girl gave me an enigmatic smile. "Do you like mysteries?"

I nodded. I think if she'd asked me whether I liked arsenic or cyanide on toast I would have given her the same answer.

"Are you by any chance busy tomorrow?"

I shook my head, still unable to speak. If I did have anything to do, I'd think of an excuse. I may have been useless as a thief, but I confess I've always had a real talent for lying.

"Then I'll be waiting for you here, at nine," she said, disappearing into the shadows of the garden.

"Wait!"

My shout stopped her.

"You haven't told me your name...."

"Marina. See you tomorrow."

I waved at her, but she'd already vanished. I waited in vain for Marina to reappear. The sun had almost attained its full height and I guessed it must be close to noon. When I realized that she was not going to return, I made my way back to the school. Along the way, the old doorways of Sarriá seemed to smile at me conspiratorially. Although I could hear the echo of my footsteps, I could have sworn I was walking a few centimeters above the ground.

FOUR

I don't think I'd ever been so punctual in my entire life. The city was still in pajamas when I crossed Plaza Sarriá. As I did so, the church bells rang for nine o'clock mass and sent a flock of pigeons flying across the square. A picture-book sun lit up the traces left by the night's drizzle. Kafka had come down to greet me at the bottom of the road leading up to the mansion, while a group of sparrows, perched on a wall, kept a safe distance. The cat watched them with professional indifference.

"Good morning, Kafka. Have we committed any murders this morning?"

The cat replied with a simple purr and, like a

self-possessed butler, led me through the garden as far as the fountain. I could see Marina sitting on the edge, clad in an ivory-colored dress that left her shoulders bare. She was holding a leather-bound book, writing in it with a pen. Her face showed great concentration and she didn't even notice my presence. She seemed to be miles away, so I was able to stare at her for a few moments. I decided that Leonardo da Vinci must have designed those collarbones; there was no other explanation. A jealous Kafka broke the spell with a meow. The pen stopped suddenly and Marina's eyes looked up toward mine. She immediately closed the book.

"Ready?"

Marina led me through the streets of Sarriá to some unknown destination. The only clue to her intentions was an inscrutable smile.

"Where are we going?" I asked a few minutes later.

"Be patient. You'll see."

I followed her obediently, although I suspected I was the butt of a joke I couldn't yet figure out. We walked downhill until we reached Paseo de la Bonanova and from there turned left, passing by the black hole of Bar Víctor. A group of posh kids, ensconced behind dark glasses and trying too hard to look cool, sat lazily holding beers and warming the seats of their Vespas. When they saw us walk by, some of them slid their Ray-Bans down their noses in order to take a closer look at Marina. *Drool away, suckers*, I thought.

When we reached Calle Doctor Roux, Marina took a right turn. We then walked downhill for a couple of blocks until we came to a narrow, unpaved path that led off the street at the corner beside number 112. The same mysterious smile still sealed Marina's mouth.

"Is it here?" I asked, intrigued.

That path didn't seem to lead anywhere, but Marina walked straight on. She guided me to another lane that rose toward a portico flanked by cypress trees. Beyond it, pale beneath bluish shadows, lay an enchanted garden populated by tombstones, crosses, and moldy mausoleums. The old graveyard of Sarriá.

The Sarriá cemetery is in one of Barcelona's best-hidden corners. If you look for it on the map, you won't find it. If you ask locals or taxi drivers how to get there, they probably won't know, although they've all heard about it. And if, by chance, you try to look for it on your own, you're more likely than not to get lost. The lucky few who know the secret of its whereabouts suspect that this old graveyard is in fact an island lost in the ocean of the past, which appears and disappears at random.

This was the setting to which Marina led me that Sunday in September, to reveal a mystery that intrigued me almost as much as she did. Following her instructions, I seated myself next to her on a raised platform situated unobtrusively in the northern part of the enclosure. From there we had a good view of the lonely graveyard. We sat in silence, gazing at tombs and withered flowers. Marina didn't utter a word, and after a while I began to grow restless. What the hell were we doing there? That was the only mystery I could see.

"This is a bit on the dead side," I suggested, aware of the irony.

"Patience is the mother of all virtues," she responded.

"And the godmother of madness," I replied. "There's nothing here. Nothing at all."

Marina gave me a look I could not fathom.

"You're wrong," she said. "The memories of hundreds of people lie here. Their lives, their feelings, their expectations, their absence, the dreams that never came true for them, the disappointments, the deceptions and the unrequited loves that poisoned their existence... All that is here, trapped forever."

I observed her, feeling both intrigued and rather uncomfortable, although I wasn't quite sure what she was getting at. Whatever it was, it mattered to her.

"Nothing in life can be understood until you understand death," Marina added.

I tried to look as if I fully captured the morbid subtlety of it all—whatever it was she was talking about. Unsuccessfully, if her blank stare was any indication.

"To be honest, I don't often think about that sort of thing," I admitted. "I mean, about death. Not seriously, at least…"

Marina shook her head like a doctor who recognizes the symptoms of an incurable disease.

"In other words, you're one of those poor naïve little simpletons…." she remarked knowingly.

"Naïve?"

Now I was really lost. One hundred percent.

Marina's eyes wandered and her face took on a serious expression that made her look older. I was hypnotized by her.

"I don't suppose you've heard of the legend," she began.

"The legend?"

"I thought so," she pronounced. "Well, you see, they say death has messengers who roam the streets in search of dimwits and numbskulls, people who never think about things like death and mortality."

At this point she fixed her pupils on mine.

"When one of those unfortunate souls runs into a messenger of death, as he inevitably will sooner or later," Marina continued, "he is led unwittingly into a trap. A door into hell. These messengers cover their faces to conceal the fact that they don't have eyes, only two black holes full of live worms. When it's too late for any possible escape, the messenger reveals his face and the victim realizes the horror that awaits him...."

Her words seemed to hang in the air while my stomach tightened.

Only then did Marina let slip that malicious smile. A cat's smile.

"You're pulling my leg," I said at last.

"Obviously."

Five or ten minutes went by in silence, perhaps more. An eternity. A light breeze caressed the cypress trees. Two white doves fluttered about between the tombs. An ant climbed up my trouser leg. Very little else was happening. Soon one of my legs started to fall asleep and I feared my head would follow suit. I was about to protest when Marina raised a hand, signaling me to be quiet before I'd even said a word. She pointed toward the cemetery entrance.

Someone had just come in. The someone in question seemed to be a woman, wrapped in a black velvet cloak with a hood covering her face. Her hands were crossed over her chest and she wore gloves, also black. The cloak was so long we couldn't see her feet. From where we sat it looked as if the faceless figure were gliding along without touching the ground. For some reason I felt a shiver.

"Who...?" I whispered.

"Shhh..." warned Marina.

We hid behind the columns of the long platform we'd been sitting on, and spied on the lady in black. She was advancing through the graves carrying a red rose between her gloved fingers: It looked like a fresh knife wound. The woman walked over to a tombstone just beneath our observation point and stopped with her back to us. For the first time I noticed that, unlike all the other graves, this one had no name on it. All I could see was a shape engraved on the marble: a symbol that looked like an insect, a black butterfly with open wings.

The lady in black stood silently at the foot of the grave for almost five minutes. Finally she leaned forward, left the red rose on the tombstone, and walked away slowly, just as she had come. Like an apparition.

Marina looked at me nervously and drew closer to whisper something. When her lips touched my ear I felt a tingling on the nape of my neck, like a centipede dancing the bossa nova.

"I discovered her by chance three months ago," Marina explained, "when I came here with Germán to lay flowers on his aunt Reme's grave. This lady comes here on the last Sunday of every month at ten o'clock in the morning, and every time she leaves an identical rose on that grave. She always wears the same cloak, gloves, and hood. And she always comes alone. I never see her face. She never speaks to anyone."

"Who is buried there?" The strange symbol engraved on the tombstone intrigued me.

"I don't know. There's no name for it in the cemetery registry."

"And who is that lady?"

Marina was about to reply when she glimpsed the lady's figure disappearing through the cemetery gates. She took my hand and rose hurriedly.

"Quick. Or we'll lose her."

"Are we going to follow her?" I asked.

"You wanted action, didn't you?" she said in a tone halfway between pity and irritation, as if I were even dumber than I looked.

By the time we reached Calle Doctor Roux, the woman in black was heading for the Bonanova area. Although it was raining softly again, the sun seemed unwilling to hide. We followed the lady through that curtain of golden tears, crossing Paseo de la Bonanova and walking up toward the lower slopes of the hills, past mansions and small palaces that had known better times. The lady made her way into the web of deserted streets, which were blanketed with shiny leaves, like scales shed by a giant serpent. Then she stopped at a crossroads, not moving, a living statue.

"She's seen us," I whispered, hiding with Marina behind a thick tree trunk carved with initials.

For a moment I was afraid she was going to spin around and notice us. But no. After a while she took a left turn and disappeared. Marina and I glanced at each other and resumed our pursuit. The trail led us to a narrow cul-de-sac crossed by the exposed tracks of the railway that climbed up to the hilltop village of Vallvidrera. We stopped there. There was no sign of the woman in black, although we'd seen her enter the alleyway. The turrets of my boarding school could be seen in the distance, high above roofs and treetops.

"She must have gone into her home," I said. "She must live around here."

"No. These houses are all deserted. Nobody lives here."

Marina pointed to the façades hidden behind iron gates and walls. All that remained standing were a couple of abandoned warehouses and a large old stately residence that looked as if a fire had raged inside it decades ago. The lady had vanished before our very eyes.

We ventured farther up the alley. On the ground a puddle reflected the sky; raindrops distorted our reflections. At the end of the narrow lane a wooden gate swung to and fro in the breeze. Marina looked at me but didn't say anything. We approached it quietly and I leaned over to have a quick look. The gate, set in a redbrick wall, opened onto a courtyard. What had once been a garden was now entirely choked by weeds. Peering through the undergrowth, we could just make out the front of an odd-looking building covered in ivy. It took me a few seconds to realize I was staring at a greenhouse built on a metal frame. The plants hissed, like a swarm of bees lying in wait.

"You first," Marina said, waving me in.

I plucked up some courage and stepped into the mass of weeds. Without warning, Marina took my hand and followed me. As my feet sank into a blanket of rotting vegetation, I had a fleeting vision of dark snakes coiling around my ankles. We pressed ahead through a jungle of sharp branches, getting scratched in the process, until we came to a clearing in front of the greenhouse. Marina let go of my hand to gaze at the building. The ivy had spread like a cobweb over the whole structure, making it look like a palace submerged in a deep lake.

"I'm afraid she's given us the slip," I said. "No one has set foot in here for years."

Marina agreed with me reluctantly. She took one last look at the greenhouse. She seemed disappointed but didn't say anything else. *Silent defeats taste better*, I thought.

"Come on, let's go," I suggested, offering her my hand in the hope that she would take it again for our walk back through the undergrowth.

Marina ignored me, frowned, and started to walk around the greenhouse. I sighed and followed her half-heartedly. That girl was as stubborn as a mule.

"Marina," I began. "Not here..."

I found her at the back of the building, facing what looked like the entrance. She turned toward me, then raised a hand to touch the glass pane and wipe off the dirt that covered an inscription. I recognized the same black butterfly I'd seen on the anonymous grave in the cemetery. Marina placed her hand on it. Slowly, the door opened. A foul, sweet odor issued from within, like the stench of poisoned reservoirs and wells. Ignoring what little common sense I had left, I stepped into the darkness.

FIVE

The ghostly aroma of perfume and old wood wafted through the air. The unpaved floor oozed with moisture. Plumes of vapor danced up and the resulting condensation dripped down in warm drops that we could feel and hear but barely see. A strange sound throbbed in the darkness. A metallic murmur, like the sound of a venetian blind quivering.

Marina kept advancing slowly. It was hot and damp. My clothes were clinging to me and beads of sweat covered my forehead. I turned to look at Marina and in the half-light saw that the same was happening to her. That eerie sound was still stirring in the shadows. It seemed to come from every corner.

"What is that?" Marina whispered, a pang of fear in her voice.

I shrugged. We moved farther into the greenhouse, stopping at a point where a few shafts of light filtered down from the dome. Marina was about to say something when again we heard the weird rattling. Close to us, about two meters away. Directly above our heads. We exchanged a glance and slowly raised our eyes to look at a shadowy area in the roof of the greenhouse. I felt Marina's hand clasp mine tightly. She was trembling. We were both trembling.

We were surrounded by angular figures dangling in the void. I could see a dozen of them, perhaps more. Legs, arms, hands, and eyes shining in the dark. A whole pack of lifeless bodies swung over us. When they brushed against one another they produced that soft metallic sound. We took a step back, and before we knew what was happening Marina caught her ankle on a lever connected to a pulley system. The lever gave way. In a tenth of a second the army of frozen figures dropped into the space below. I threw myself over Marina to protect her and we both fell flat on our faces. The whole place shuddered violently and I heard the roar of the old glass structure as it vibrated. I was afraid that the glass panes would shatter and a rain of shards would skewer us to the ground. Just then something cold touched the back of my neck. Fingers.

I opened my eyes. A face was smiling at me. Bright yellow eyes flashed. They were lifeless. Glass eyes in a face carved out of lacquered wood. I heard Marina stifle a scream next to me.

"They're dolls," I said, almost breathless.

We stood up to have a closer look at the beings. Dummies. Figures made out of wood, metal, and clay, suspended from hundreds of cables attached to a piece of stage machinery. The lever Marina had unwittingly activated had released the pulley mechanism holding them up. They had stopped falling about half a meter from the ground and looked like hanged men performing a gruesome dance.

"What the hell...?" cried Marina.

I studied the group of dolls. One figure was dressed as a magician, another as a policeman; there was a dancer, an elegant lady in a maroon gown, a strongman.... They were all built to human scale and wore luxurious fancy-dress costumes that time had turned to rags. But something bound them together, lending them a strange quality that betrayed their common source.

"They're unfinished," I discovered.

Marina immediately understood what I meant. Each of the beings lacked something. The policeman had no arms. The ballerina had no eyes, only two empty sockets. The magician had no mouth, or hands.... We stared at the figures as they swung in the spectral light. Marina approached the ballerina, observing her carefully. She pointed to a small mark on the doll's forehead, just beneath the hairline. The black butterfly again. Marina reached out to touch it, and as she did so her fingers brushed against the doll's hair. She pulled her hand back in disgust.

"The hair...it's real," she said.

"Impossible."

We examined each of the sinister marionettes and found the same mark on all of them. I activated the lever and the pulleys began hoisting the bodies up again. As they rose, limply, I thought they looked like mechanical souls about to join their maker.

"There seems to be something over there," said Marina from behind me.

She was pointing at an old desk in one corner of the greenhouse. A fine layer of dust covered its surface. A spider scurried over it, leaving a trail of minute footprints. I kneeled down and blew the dust off the table, making it swirl into a gray cloud. On the desk was a leatherbound book, open at the middle. An old sepia-colored photograph had been glued to the page, with the caption "Arles, 1903" in neat handwriting below. The picture showed a pair of conjoined twin girls connected at the torso. Dressed in all their finery, the two sisters gave the camera the saddest smile in the world.

Marina turned the pages. The book was an ordinary photo album, but there was nothing ordinary about the old images it contained. The picture of the conjoined twins was just the beginning. As Marina's fingers turned page after page she gazed at the photographs with a mixture of fascination and repulsion. I had a quick look and felt a strange chill down my spine.

"Freaks of nature…" murmured Marina. "Human beings with deformities who used to be banished to the circus…"

The disturbing power of those images hit me like the lash of a whip. The cruel side of nature displayed its monstrous face: innocent souls imprisoned within bodies that were horribly deformed. For a few minutes we leafed through the pages of the album without uttering a word. One by one, the photographs showed us what I can only describe as nightmarish creatures. But such physical abominations didn't mask the expressions of grief, horror, and loneliness burning in those faces.

"My God…" whispered Marina.

The photographs were all identified by the year and the place they were taken. Buenos Aires, 1893. Bombay, 1911. Turin, 1930. Prague, 1933…I found it difficult to understand who would have made such a collection, or why. A catalog straight out of hell. At last Marina looked away from the book and walked off into the shadows.

I tried to do the same but felt incapable of detaching myself from the pain and the horror conveyed by the pictures. If I lived a thousand years I'd still remember the faces of each one of those poor souls. I closed the book and turned toward Marina. I heard her sigh in the gloom and I felt useless, not knowing what to do or say. The images had distressed her profoundly.

"Are you all right?" I asked.

Marina nodded, her eyes half-closed. Suddenly something made a noise. I scanned the blanket of shadows enveloping us. Again I heard the strange sound. Hostile. Evil. Then I noticed the stench of rot, nauseating and powerful. It came from the darkness like the breath of a wild animal. I realized we were not alone. There was someone else there. Watching us. Marina stared at the wall of blackness, petrified. I took her hand and led her toward the doorway.

SIX

When we emerged, the light rain had coated the streets with silver. It was one o'clock. We began walking back without exchanging a single word. Germán was expecting us for lunch at the house.

"Don't mention any of this to Germán, please," Marina begged me.

"Don't worry."

I realized that in any case I wouldn't have known how to explain what had happened. As we continued on our way, the memory of the photographs and everything we'd seen in that macabre greenhouse began to fade. When we reached Plaza Sarriá, I noticed that Marina was pale and seemed out of breath.

"Are you feeling okay?" I asked.

Marina said she was, rather unconvincingly. We sat down on a bench in the square. She took a few deep breaths, her eyes closed. A flock of pigeons scuttled around our feet. For a moment I thought Marina was going to faint. Then she opened her eyes again and smiled at me.

"Don't worry. I'm just a bit dizzy. It must have been that smell."

"Probably. There must have been a dead animal. A rat or..."

Marina agreed with my theory. After a while the color came back to her cheeks.

"What I need to do is eat something. Come on. Germán will be tired of waiting for us."

We got up and made our way back to the house, where Kafka was sitting expectantly by the gate. The cat gave me a spiteful look and ran over to rub his back against Marina's ankles. I was weighing the pros and cons of being a cat when I recognized that heavenly voice on Germán's gramophone. The music flowed through the garden like a high tide.

"What is that music?"

"Léo Delibes," Marina replied.

"No idea."

"Delibes. A French composer," Marina explained,

perceiving my ignorance. "What do they teach you at school?"

I shrugged.

"It's a piece from one of his operas. *Lakmé*."

"And that voice?"

"My mother."

I looked at her in astonishment.

"Your mother is an opera singer?"

Marina gave me an inscrutable look.

"She was," she replied. "She died."

Germán was waiting for us in the large, oval-shaped dining room. A glass chandelier hung from the ceiling. Marina's father seemed dressed for a formal occasion, in a suit with a waistcoat and with his long silvery hair neatly combed back. He looked like a gentleman from the late nineteenth century. We sat at the table, which was set with a linen tablecloth and silver cutlery.

"It's such a pleasure to have you with us, Oscar," said Germán. "Not every Sunday do we enjoy such good company."

The plates were china, genuine antiques. The menu seemed to consist of a soup that smelled delicious, and bread. Nothing else. While Germán dished out the soup—serving me first—I realized that the entire display was in my honor. But despite the silver cutlery, the museum crockery, and the Sunday-best clothes, there was no money in that house for a second course. In fact, there wasn't even any electric light. The place was always lit with candles. Germán must have read my thoughts.

"You must have noticed we don't have electricity, Oscar. To be honest, we don't really believe in the advances of modern technology. After all, what sort of technology is this that can send a man to the moon but can't put a piece of bread on every human being's table?"

"Perhaps the problem doesn't lie in the technology, but in those who decide how to make use of it," I suggested.

Germán considered my idea and nodded solemnly— I'm not sure whether out of politeness or conviction.

"You seem to be a bit of a philosopher, Oscar. Have you ever read Schopenhauer?"

I noticed Marina looking at me, as if to suggest that I should play along with whatever her father said.

"I'm afraid I've barely scratched the surface," I improvised.

We ate our soup without speaking. Germán smiled kindly every now and then and gazed at his daughter with affection. Something made me think that Marina didn't have many friends and that Germán approved of my presence, even if I was unable to tell the difference between Schopenhauer and a brand of orthopedic products.

"Tell me, Oscar. What's happening in the world these days?"

He asked the question in such a way that I thought I'd cause a stir if I told him that World War II had ended.

"Nothing much, frankly," I said, under Marina's watchful eye. "There are elections coming up...."

This awoke Germán's interest. He stopped moving his spoon about and considered the matter.

"And, if I may ask, on what side do your sympathies lie, Oscar? The right or the left?"

"Oscar is a nihilist, Dad," Marina cut in.

The piece of bread I was eating got stuck in my throat. I didn't know what the word meant, but it sounded like an anarchist on a bike. Germán eyed me carefully, intrigued.

"The idealism of youth..." he murmured. "I understand, I understand. At your age I also read Bakunin. It's like the measles: until you've had it..."

I glared at Marina, who was licking her lips like a cat. She winked at me, then looked away. Germán was observing me with a benevolent curiosity. I nodded in agreement and went back to sipping my soup. At least that way I wouldn't have to speak, and I'd avoid putting my foot in it. We ate in silence. I soon noticed that, on the other side of the table, Germán was falling asleep. When the spoon finally slipped from his fingers, Marina stood up and, without saying a word, loosened his silvery silk bow tie. Germán sighed. One of his hands shook a little. Holding her father's arm, Marina helped him up. Germán nodded with resignation and gave me a faint, almost embarrassed smile. He seemed to have aged fifteen years in the space of a breath.

"Please excuse me, Oscar," he said in a tiny voice. "Despite all my good intentions, I don't seem to be getting any younger...."

I stood up as well and glanced questioningly at Marina. She refused my help, asking me to stay in the dining room. Her father leaned on her and I watched them both leave the room.

"It's been a pleasure, Oscar," came Germán's tired voice, fading into the shadowy corridor. "Come and visit us again, come again...."

I heard his footsteps disappearing inside the house and waited in the candlelight for Marina's return. Half an hour elapsed, and the atmosphere in the house was starting to get to me. When I felt certain that Marina wasn't coming back, I began to worry. I wondered whether I should go and look for her, but I didn't think it was right for me to nose around the house without having been invited. I thought of leaving a note, but didn't have anything to write with. It was beginning to get dark, so the best thing for me to do was to leave. I'd come by the following day, after lessons, to make sure everything was all right. I was surprised to realize that after only half an hour of not seeing Marina, I was already searching for excuses to return. I went out through the kitchen door and walked across the garden to the gate. Over the city the sky was growing darker with passing clouds.

As I made my way slowly back to the boarding school, the events of the day filed through my mind. By the time I walked up the steps to my room on the fourth floor I was convinced that this had been the strangest day of my life. But had I been able to buy a ticket to relive it all over again, I would have done so without a second thought.

SEVEN

That night I dreamed that I was trapped inside an enormous kaleidoscope. A diabolical creature—of which I could see only a large eye through the lens—was making it turn. All around me the world splintered into a twisting maze of optical illusions. Insects. Black butterflies. I woke up with a start, as if undiluted caffeine were coursing through my veins instead of blood. That feverish state of mind stayed with me all day. Monday lessons filed past like trains that weren't stopping at my station. JF noticed immediately.

"You're usually in the clouds," he said, "but today you're in outer space. Are you ill?"

I reassured him with a vague gesture, then checked the clock above the blackboard. Half past three. Lessons finished in just under two hours. An eternity. Outside, the rain pattered on the windowpanes.

———

When the bell rang I slipped out as fast as I could, standing up JF—in other circumstances, I would have gone on one of our usual strolls with him into the real world. I hurried down endless corridors to the exit. The gardens and the fountains at the front of the school paled under a gathering storm. I didn't have an umbrella with me, not even a hood. The sky was a leaden slab. The street lamps burned like matchsticks.

I started to run, dodging puddles and overflowing drains until I reached the school gates. Outside, water gushed down the road in rivulets. Soaked to the skin, I ran down narrow, silent streets. The sewers roared beneath my feet. The city seemed to be slowly sinking into a black ocean. It took me ten minutes to reach the gates of Marina and Germán's house. By then my clothes and shoes were hopelessly sodden. On the horizon twilight faded into a curtain of grayish marble. I thought I heard something snap behind me at the bottom of the road, and I turned around, startled. For a second I felt as if somebody had been following me. But there was nobody there—just the rain pelting down furiously into the puddles.

I slid through the gate. Bright flashes of lightning guided me to the house, where I was greeted by the grinning mermaid in the fountain. Trembling with cold, I reached the kitchen door at the back of the old mansion. It was open. I went in. The house lay in almost complete darkness. Then I remembered what Germán had said about the absence of electricity.

Until that moment it hadn't occurred to me that I hadn't even been invited. This was the second time I was slipping into that house for no reason. I thought of leaving, but the storm was howling outside. I sighed. My hands were aching with cold and I could barely feel the tips of my fingers. I coughed like a dog and felt my heartbeat hammering in my temples. My damp clothes were stuck to my body. I was frozen. *My kingdom for a towel*, I thought.

"Marina?" I called.

The echo of my voice died away inside the large old house. I became acutely aware of the blanket of shadows spreading around me. They seemed to be moving. Only the flashes of lightning penetrating the windows afforded brief glimpses of my surroundings, like the flash of a camera, too quick for the eye.

"Marina?" I called again. "It's me, Oscar...."

Timidly, I stepped farther into the house, my sodden shoes squelching as I walked. I stopped when I reached the dining hall where we'd had lunch the day before. The table was empty, the chairs deserted.

"Marina? Germán?"

No answer came. In the deepening gloom I spied the outlines of a candlestick and a box of matches resting on a dresser. With my wrinkled, numb fingers, it took me five attempts to light the flame.

When I raised the flickering light an eerie glow filled the room. I set off down the corridor I'd seen Marina and her father disappear into the day before.

The passage led to another large room, also crowned by a chandelier, whose crystals gleamed in the dark like a diamond merry-go-round. The house was peopled with slanting shadows projected by the storm through the windowpanes. Old pieces of furniture and armchairs lay under white sheets. A marble staircase led to the next floor. I walked over to it, feeling like an intruder. Two yellow eyes shone at the top of the stairs. I heard a meow. Kafka. I let out a sigh of relief. A second later the cat withdrew into the shadows. I stopped and looked around me: I'd left a trail of footprints in the dust.

"Anyone home?" I called out again. There was no reply.

I imagined how the large room must have appeared

some decades ago, in all its finery and splendor, with an orchestra and dozens of dancing couples dressed to the nines. Now it looked like the ballroom of a sunken ship. The walls were covered with oil paintings—all of them portraits of a woman. I recognized her: She was the same woman who appeared in the painting I'd seen the first night I'd sneaked into the house. The perfection and artistry evident in each brushstroke and the ethereal luminosity exuding from those pictures were uncanny. I wondered who the artist might be. Even *I* realized that they were all painted by the same hand. The lady seemed to be watching me from every angle. It wasn't hard to notice the striking resemblance between her and Marina. The same lips on a pale, almost transparent face. The same build, slender and fragile, like a porcelain figurine. The same sad, deep, ash-colored eyes. I felt something brush against my ankle. Kafka was purring at my feet. I crouched down and stroked his silvery coat.

"Where's your mistress, killer boy?"

Kafka replied with a sad meow. There was nobody in the house. I listened to the rain scratching at the roof. It sounded like thousands of water spiders scuttling through the attic. I imagined that Marina and Germán must have gone out, though I couldn't think what for. Anyhow, it was none of my business. I stroked Kafka and decided I had to leave before they returned.

"One of us shouldn't be here," I murmured to Kafka. "And that's me."

Suddenly the fur on the cat's back stood on end. I felt his muscles tense like steel cables under my hand, and he meowed with panic. I was wondering what could have frightened the animal like that when I noticed it. The smell. The same stench of animal rot I had smelled in the greenhouse. I felt nauseous.

I looked up. A curtain of rain veiled the windows, but I was able to make out the blurred shape of the mermaid in the fountain outside. Instinctively I knew something was wrong. There was another figure keeping her company. I stood up and moved closer to the French windows. The silhouette turned round. I stopped, petrified. I couldn't make out its face, just a dark figure wrapped in a cloak. The stranger was watching me—I was quite sure—and he knew I was watching him. I stood there unmoving for an instant that felt endless. Seconds later the figure retreated into the shadows. When the next flash of lightning broke over the garden, the stranger was no longer there. It took me a while to realize that the stench had disappeared with him.

All I could think to do was to sit and wait for Germán and Marina's return. The thought of venturing outside was not tempting—and it wasn't just the storm I was concerned about. I dropped into a huge armchair. Slowly the tapping of the rain and the faint glow floating around the large room lulled me to sleep. At some point I heard the sound of the main door opening, and then footsteps inside the house. I awoke from my trance and my heart skipped a beat. I heard voices coming from the corridor. Saw a candle. Kafka ran toward the light just as Germán and his daughter stepped into the room. Marina threw me an icy look.

"What are you doing here, Oscar?"

I mumbled an incoherent reply. Germán smiled and looked at me with curiosity.

"Goodness gracious, Oscar. You're soaking! Marina, go and fetch some clean towels for Oscar.... Come here, Oscar, let's light a fire. It's a dreadful night...."

I sat facing the fireplace, holding a cup of hot broth Marina had prepared for me. I made up some dubious explanation for my presence and was careful to leave out the part about the figure I'd seen through the window and the dreadful stench that had accompanied it. Germán readily accepted my unlikely account and didn't seem the least bit annoyed by my intrusion; on the contrary. Marina was another matter. Her eyes smoldered. I was afraid that by stupidly slipping into her home again, as if I was making a habit of it, I might have harmed our friendship beyond repair. She didn't utter a single word during the half hour we sat in front of the fire. When Germán excused himself and wished me good night, I feared that my ex-friend was going to kick me out unceremoniously and tell me never to come back again.

Here it comes, I thought. *The kiss of death.*

At last Marina smiled sarcastically. "You look lousy, by the way," she said.

"Thanks," I replied. I had been expecting worse.

"I'm being generous. So, are you going to tell me what the hell you are doing here?"

Her eyes shone in the light of the fire. I sipped the rest of my broth and looked down.

"The truth is, I don't know," I said. "I suppose...I don't really know."

My awful appearance must have helped, because Marina drew closer to me and tapped my hand.

"Look at me," she ordered.

I did as I was told. She was gazing at me with a mixture of concern and affection.

"I'm not angry at you—do you understand?" she said. "It's just that I was surprised to find you here, like that, without warning. Every Monday I take Germán to the doctor, at the Sant Pau Hospital—that's why we weren't in. It's not a good day for visiting."

I felt ashamed of myself.

"It won't happen again," I promised.

I was on the verge of telling Marina about the strange apparition I thought I'd seen when she gave a gentle laugh and leaned over, kissing me on the cheek. The touch of her lips was enough to dry my clothes instantly. My words were left unspoken. Marina noticed my mute mumbling.

"What?" she asked.

I stared at her, speechless, and shook my head. "Nothing."

She raised an eyebrow as if she didn't believe me, but didn't insist.

"A bit more broth?" she asked, standing up.

"Please."

Marina took my soup bowl and went to the kitchen to fill it again. I remained by the fireplace, fascinated by the portraits hanging on the walls. When Marina returned, she followed my eyes.

"The woman in all these paintings..." I began.

"She's my mother," said Marina.

I felt I was on slippery ground.

"I've never seen portraits like these. They're like... like photographs of the soul."

Marina nodded but didn't say anything.

"They must be by some famous artist," I insisted. "I've never seen anything like them."

Marina took a while to reply.

"And you never will. The artist hasn't produced a single painting for almost fifteen years. This group of portraits was his last work."

"He must have known your mother really well to be able to portray her like this," I remarked.

Marina gazed at me. She gave me the same look that was captured in the paintings.

"Better than anyone," she replied. "He married her."

EIGHT

That night, by the fire, Marina told me the story of Germán and the Sarriá mansion.

Germán Blau had been born into a wealthy family of the flourishing Catalan bourgeoisie. The Blau dynasty were the proud owners of a sprawling industrial colony on the banks of the River Llobregat, an exclusive box at the Liceo Opera House, and a peerless list of spicy yet discreet society scandals that was the envy of the respectable set. It was said that little Germán was not the son of the great Blau patriarch but the fruit of an illicit liaison between his mother, Diana, and a colorful individual named Quim Salvat. A man for all seasons, Salvat paid homage to three noble callings: the enlightened libertine, the confident portrait artist, and the consummate philanderer—in that order. He scandalized respectable clients and at the same time immortalized their improbable good looks in somewhat unremarkable oil paintings for which he charged a fortune. Whatever the truth may have been, the fact was that Germán, among other blessings, bore no physical or character resemblance to any known member of his family. To make matters worse, since early childhood his only interests were painting and drawing, which seemed suspicious to everyone. Especially to his official father.

On Germán's sixteenth birthday Blau *père* informed him that there was no room for layabouts in the family. If the boy persisted in his ambition of becoming a so-called artist, his father was prepared to find him gainful employment in his factory as a night porter, provide him with an entry-level job as a quarry worker, or just send him off to the Foreign Legion or any other institution that would contribute to strengthening his character and turning him into a useful member of society. Faced with that formidable array of options, the young Germán decided to run away from home— but returned twenty-four hours later, escorted by civil guards.

Desperate and utterly disappointed with his alleged

firstborn, the head of the Blau dynasty decided to place his hopes on his second son, Gaspar, a more pliable soul who was keen to learn the textile business and showed a greater willingness to continue the family traditions. For all his fury, however, the captain of industry was not one to let resentment prevail over good form or appearances. Thus, fearing for Germán's financial future, Blau put the Sarriá mansion, which had been semi-abandoned for years, into his eldest son's name.

"Even if you shame us all," he informed Germán, "I haven't worked like a slave to have a son of mine end up without a roof over his head." In its heyday the mansion had been one of the most talked-about residences among the carriage-driven upper class, but nobody took care of it any longer. It was cursed, some said, even if the curse was a touch prosaic: Rumor had it that the clandestine meetings between Diana and the libertine Salvat had taken place there. And so, by one of those ironies of fate, the house in which he had supposedly been conceived passed into Germán's hands and became his residence. A short time later, once he was liberated from the ambitions and hopes his father had placed upon him, his mother secretly intervened and Germán became apprenticed to none other than Quim Salvat. On the first day Salvat looked Germán straight in the eye and pronounced the following words:

"One, I'm not your father, and I know your mother only by sight. Two, an artist's life is a life of risk, of uncertainty, and, almost always, of poverty. You don't choose it; it chooses you. If you have any doubts about either of these points, you'd better leave through that door right now."

Germán stayed.

His years of apprenticeship under Quim Salvat provided Germán with the keys to another world and, most important, to another self. For the first time in his life he realized that someone actually believed in him, in his talent and worth. For the first time ever he thought he really had a chance of becoming something more than a pale copy of his father, a man who had in turn devoted his life to becoming an even paler copy of his own father. Once he stepped into Salvat's studio, Germán felt like a different person. During the first six months he learned and improved his skills more than in all his preceding years combined. Before long he had begun to understand the nature of light and what it was trying to tell him.

Despite his frivolous reputation, Salvat was just a rather extravagant but truly generous man who happened to love the most exquisite things in life. He only painted at night, and although he was not good-looking by any standards (other than those of a grizzly bear), he was deemed a real heartbreaker, touched by an uncanny gift for seduction, which he handled with rather more ability than his paintbrush.

Breathtaking models and nubile ladies of high society paraded through his studio eager to shed their clothes, their modesty, and any other qualms to pose for him— and, Germán suspected, for something more. Salvat knew about obscure wines, obscurer poets, legendary lost cities, and newly imported amorous techniques from Bombay. He'd lived his forty-seven years with enviable panache and intensity, maintaining that human beings foolishly allowed their existence to drift by as if they were going to live forever: *That* was their undoing. He laughed at life and at death, at the divine and at the human, and mostly at himself. He cooked better than the great chefs in the Michelin Guide and ate as much as they all did put together. During the time Germán spent by his side, Salvat became his best friend. Germán would always appreciate that everything he achieved in his life, both as a man and as a painter, he owed to Quim Salvat.

Salvat was one of the privileged few who knew the secret of light. Light, he said, was like a whimsical ballerina fully aware of her charms. In Quim's hands, light was transformed into wondrous lines that lit up the canvas and opened doors into the soul. At least, that is what was written in the promotional prose of his exhibition catalogs.

"To paint is to write with light," Salvat would say. "First you must learn its alphabet; then its grammar. Only then will you be able to possess the style and the magic."

It was Quim Salvat who widened Germán's vision of the world, taking him along on his travels. Together they went to Paris, Vienna, Berlin, Rome....It didn't take long for Germán to realize that Salvat was as good a promoter of his art as he was an artist, if not better. That was the key to his success.

"Out of every thousand people who purchase a painting or a work of art, only one of them has the remotest idea of what it is they're buying," Salvat would say, a sly smile on his lips. "The rest don't buy the work; they buy the artist, what they've heard, and, more often than not, what they imagine about him. This business is no different from selling a quack's remedies or love potions, Germán. The only difference lies in the price."

Quim Salvat's big heart stopped on July 17, 1938. Some said it was due to his manifold excesses. But Germán always thought that what truly killed his mentor's faith and his will to live were the horrors of the civil war.

"I could go on painting for a thousand years," Salvat murmured on his deathbed, "but that wouldn't change men's folly, bigotry, and savagery in the slightest. Beauty is a breath of air that blows against the wind of reality, Germán. My art makes no sense. It's entirely useless...."

An endless list of lovers, creditors, friends, and colleagues, the dozens of people he'd helped without asking for anything in return, mourned him at his funeral. They knew that a light had gone out in the world, and from that day on they'd all feel lonelier. Emptier.

Salvat left Germán a very modest sum of money and his studio. He asked him to distribute the rest (which wasn't much because Salvat spent more than he earned, before he earned it) among his lovers and friends. The solicitor dealing with the will handed Germán a letter that Salvat had entrusted to him when he felt his end approaching. Germán was to open it once Salvat had died.

With tears in his eyes and a shattered soul the young Germán spent a whole night wandering aimlessly through the city. Dawn found him walking along the breakwater in the port, and it was there, in the first light of day, that he read the last words Quim Salvat had reserved for him.

Dear Germán,

I didn't tell you this when I was alive because I thought I had to wait for the right moment. But I'm afraid I won't be there when that moment comes.

This is what I have to tell you. I've never known a painter with more talent than you, Germán. You don't know it yet, nor can you understand it, but you possess that talent, and my only merit has been to recognize it. I've learned more from you than you have from me, without you realizing. I wish you could have had the teacher you deserve, someone who could have guided your talent better than this poor apprentice. Light speaks through you, Germán. The rest of us only listen. Don't ever forget this. From now on, your teacher will be your pupil and your best friend, always.

SALVAT

A week later, fleeing from unbearable memories, Germán traveled to Paris. He had been offered a post as a teacher in an art school. He wouldn't set foot in Barcelona for the next ten years.

In Paris Germán quickly earned himself some renown as a portraitist and discovered a passion that would never abandon him: the opera. His paintings were beginning to sell, and an art dealer who knew him from his days with Salvat decided to take him on. Apart from his teaching salary, he made enough from his paintings to lead a simple but dignified life. By carefully managing his income, and with the help of the director of the art school, who seemed to have well-placed relatives all over Paris, Germán managed to obtain a seat at the Opéra for the entire season. Nothing grand: dress circle, row six, a little to the left. Twenty percent of the stage was not visible, but the music could be heard just as gloriously as from the highly priced stalls and boxes.

That is where he first saw her. She looked like a creature who had stepped out of one of Salvat's paintings, but not even her beauty could do justice to her voice. Her name was Kirsten Auermann; she was nineteen and, according to the program, one of the most promising young talents in the opera world. That same evening Germán was introduced to her at a reception held by the opera company after the performance. Germán managed to sneak in, saying he was the musical critic for *Le Monde*. When he shook her hand, he was lost for words.

"For a critic, you speak very little, and you even do that with a strong accent," Kirsten joked.

Germán decided there and then that he was going to marry that woman, if it was the last thing he did in his life. He tried to conjure up all the arts of seduction he'd seen Salvat use over the years. But there was only one Salvat, and he had been in a class of his own. A long game of cat and mouse ensued. It went on for six years and ended in a small chapel in Normandy on a summer afternoon in 1946. On their wedding day the specter of the war still wafted through the air like the stench of hidden carrion.

Kirsten and Germán returned to Barcelona shortly afterward and settled in Sarriá. The house had become a ghostly museum during Germán's years of absence. Kirsten's luminosity and three weeks of vigorous cleaning did the rest.

The old mansion now experienced an era of unprecedented splendor. Germán worked without pause, possessed by an energy even he couldn't understand. His works began to be prized among the well-to-do, and soon, owning "a Blau" became an essential requirement for those who aspired to join, or remain, in polite society. In yet another ironic twist of fate his long-estranged father saw his parental pride rekindled and took to praising Germán in public. "I always believed in his talent and knew he would triumph," "It's in his blood, like all Blaus," and "I'm the proudest father in the world" became his favorite phrases, and, repeating them so often, he ended up believing them. Art dealers and gallery owners who years ago hadn't had the time of day for Germán were now bending over backward to gain his attention. Yet for all the flatterers courting his favor, and even though Vanity Fair was claiming him as one of its own, Germán never forgot what Salvat had taught him.

Kirsten's musical career was also moving along splendidly. In the days when the new 33 rpm long-play records were beginning to conquer the market, she was one of the first voices to immortalize her repertoire. Those were years of happiness and light in the Sarriá villa, years when everything seemed possible and there was not a hint of a shadow on the horizon.

Nobody thought anything of Kirsten's dizzy spells and fainting fits until it was too late. Success, travel, first-night nerves explained it all. The day Kirsten was seen by Dr. Cabrils, two bits of news changed her world forever. The first: She was pregnant. The second: An irreversible illness in her blood was slowly stealing her life. She had a year left. Two at most.

That same day, when she left the doctor's office, Kirsten ordered a watch from the General Relojera

Suiza—a venerable shop on Vía Augusta—with an inscription dedicated to Germán:

For Germán, through whom light speaks.

K.A.

19 January 1964

That watch would mark the hours they had left together.

—————

Kirsten abandoned the stage and her career. The farewell gala took place at the Liceo in Barcelona and featured *Lakmé* by Delibes, her favorite composer. Nobody would ever again hear a voice like hers. During the months of her pregnancy Germán painted a series of portraits of his wife that surpassed any of his previous work. Despite receiving many exorbitant offers, he refused to sell them.

On September 24, 1964, a baby girl with fair hair and ash-colored eyes, identical to her mother's, was born in the Sarriá house. She would be called Marina, and her face would always bear her mother's image and radiance. Kirsten Auermann died six months later, in the same room where she'd given birth to her daughter and where she'd spent the happiest hours of her life with Germán.

Her husband held her pale, trembling hand in his. She was already cold when dawn took her away as quietly as a sigh.

A month after her death Germán went back to his studio in the attic of the family home. Little Marina played at his feet. Germán picked up his brush and tried to draw a line over the canvas. His eyes filled with tears and the brush fell from his hands. Germán Blau never painted again. The light inside him had gone out forever.

NINE

For the rest of that autumn my visits to Germán and Marina's house turned into a daily ritual. I counted the hours as I daydreamed in the classroom, waiting for the moment when I could escape to that secret alleyway. My new friends were waiting for me there, except of course on Mondays, when Marina took Germán to the hospital for his treatment. We drank coffee and chatted in the somber rooms. Germán agreed to teach me the rudiments of chess. Despite his lessons, Marina always checkmated me within five or six minutes, but I didn't lose hope.

Bit by bit, almost without my noticing it, the world of Germán and Marina became my world. Their house, the memories that seemed to haunt those walls, became mine. I discovered that Marina didn't go to school so that she could care for her father and didn't leave him alone. She told me that Germán had taught her to read, write, and think.

"All the geography, trigonometry, and arithmetic in the world are useless unless you learn to think for yourself," Marina would argue. "No school teaches you that. It's not on the curriculum."

Germán had opened her mind to the world of art, literature, history, and science. The vast library in their house had become her universe. Each of its books was a door into new worlds and new ideas. One afternoon toward the end of October we sat on a windowsill on the second floor and gazed at the faraway lights on Mount Tibidabo. Marina confided in me that her dream was to become a writer. She had a trunk full of stories she'd been writing since she was nine. When I asked her to show me one of them, she looked at me as if I were drunk and refused point-blank. *This is like chess*, I thought. *Just give it time.*

Often, when they weren't aware of it, I'd watch Germán and Marina bantering playfully, reading, or facing each other silently across the chessboard. To feel the invisible bond that joined them, the self-contained world they had built far from everything and everyone, was like being under a magical spell. An enchantment that sometimes I feared might break with my presence. There were days when, as I walked back to school, I felt like the happiest person in the world simply because I was able to share it.

Without quite knowing why, I kept the friendship hidden. I hadn't told anyone about them, not even my friend JF. In just a few weeks Germán and Marina had become my secret life, and in all honesty the only life I wished to live. I remember the time when Germán went to bed early, excusing himself as usual with the impeccable manners of an old-fashioned gentleman. I was left alone with Marina in the room with the portraits. She smiled enigmatically and told me she was writing something on me. I found the very idea terrifying.

"On me? What do you mean, writing something on me?"

"I mean about you, not on top of you, as if you were a desk."

"That much I understand."

Marina was enjoying my sudden nervousness.

"Well, then?" she asked. "Do you have such a low opinion of yourself that you don't think there's any point in writing about you?"

I couldn't think of a good answer to that question. I decided to change my strategy and go on the offensive. It was something Germán had taught me in his chess lessons. Basic strategy: When you're caught with your pants down, start screaming and attack.

"Well, if that's the case, you have no choice—you'll have to show it to me," I remarked.

Marina looked hesitant. She raised an eyebrow.

"I have a right to know what is being written about me," I added.

"You might not like it."

"Perhaps. Perhaps I will."

"I'll think about it."

"I'll be waiting."

That winter the cold weather struck Barcelona in its usual fashion: like a meteorite. In barely twenty-four hours thermometers began to plunge. Armies of coats were released from their wardrobes, replacing light autumn raincoats. Leaden skies and lashing winds that bit one's ears took possession of the streets. Germán and Marina surprised me by giving me a wool cap that must have cost them a fortune.

"It'll keep your ideas warm, my friend," said Germán. "We don't want your brain to go into hibernation."

Halfway through November Marina announced that she and Germán had to travel to Madrid for a week. A doctor at La Paz Hospital, a leading authority in his field, had agreed to put Germán on a treatment that was still in an experimental phase and had only been used a couple of times in all of Europe.

"They say this doctor can perform miracles. We'll see...." said Marina.

The thought of spending a week without them fell on me like a stone slab. All my efforts to hide it were in vain. Marina, who by then could see inside my head as if I were transparent, patted my hand.

"It's just a week, okay? Then we'll see each other again."

I nodded but found no consolation in her words.

"I spoke to Germán yesterday about the possibility that you might keep an eye on Kafka and the house while we're away," Marina proposed.

"Of course. I'll do whatever you need."

Her face lit up.

"I hope this doctor is as good as they say," I said.

Marina looked at me for a long while. Behind her smile those ash-colored eyes radiated a sadness that disarmed me.

"I hope so, too," she said.

———

The train to Madrid departed from the Estación de Francia at nine o'clock in the morning. I'd slipped out at daybreak. An appraisal of my meager savings had shown them insufficient, so I arranged a loan from my friend and occasional lender JF, who knew better than to ask me what I needed the money for—"I only hope it's for something our dear Jesuit fathers wouldn't approve of," he remarked. Freshly funded, I booked a taxi to collect Germán and Marina and take them to the station. That Sunday morning had arrived wrapped in bluish streaks of mist that slowly faded in the amber of dawn. We spent a good part of the taxi ride in silence. The meter of the old SEAT 1500 clicked away like a metronome, relentlessly increasing my principal and interest.

"You shouldn't have bothered, dear Oscar," Germán said.

"It's no bother," I replied. "It's freezing cold, and we don't want your spirits to ice over, eh?"

When we reached the station, Germán sat down in a café while Marina and I went to the ticket office to collect the prebooked tickets. When it was time for them to leave, Germán hugged me so tightly I nearly burst into tears. A porter helped him into the train, and he left Marina and me alone to say good-bye. The echo of a thousand voices and whistles swirled around the monumental vault. We looked at one another quietly, barely daring to meet each other's eyes.

"Well…" I said.

"Don't forget to warm up the milk, because—"

"Kafka hates cold milk, especially after a murder spree, I know. He'll be in seventh heaven, don't worry."

The stationmaster was about to wave his flag to signal the departure.

"Germán is really proud of you," she said.

"I can't see why."

"We're going to miss you."

"That's what you think. Go on, off you go."

All of a sudden Marina bent over and let her lips touch mine. Before I could even blink she'd climbed into the carriage. I stood there, watching the train move off into the gaping mouth of the mist. When the rumble of the engine faded, I set off toward the exit. As I did so, I realized I'd never got around to telling Marina about the strange vision I'd witnessed that stormy night in her house. Some time had passed since then and I'd decided to forget it. I'd even ended up convincing myself that I'd imagined it all. Just then, as I was walking into the entrance hall, a porter rushed up to me.

"This . . . Here, I was given this for you."

He handed me an ocher-colored envelope.

"I think you're mistaken," I said.

"No, no. That lady told me to give it to you," the porter insisted.

"What lady?"

The porter turned to point at the covered entrance facing Paseo Colón. Plumes of mist swept across the entrance steps. There was nobody there. The porter simply shrugged and walked away.

Mystified, I hastened toward the exit and went out into the street just in time to spot her: The lady in black we'd seen in the Sarriá graveyard was climbing into an old-fashioned horse-driven carriage. She turned to look at me for a second. Her face was hidden under a dark veil, like a steel spider's web. A second later the carriage door closed and the coachman, wrapped in a gray coat that covered him completely, whipped the horses. The carriage set off at great speed through the traffic of Paseo Colón, heading toward the Ramblas, until it was out of sight.

I was so disconcerted I forgot that I was still holding the envelope the porter had handed me. When I remembered, I opened it. Inside was an old visiting card, with an address written on it:

MIJAIL KOLVENIK
CALLE PRINCESA 33, 4TH FLOOR, DOOR 2

I turned the card over. On the back the printer had reproduced the symbol stamped on the nameless grave in the cemetery and on the abandoned greenhouse. A black butterfly with open wings.

TEN

On my way to Calle Princesa I realized I was starving. I still had a few coins left in my pocket, courtesy of JF's financial services, so I decided to stop at a bakery opposite the basilica of Santa María del Mar and treat myself to a creamy hot pastry that tasted deliciously sinful. There was a lazy Sunday morning feeling as the aroma of sweet bread filled the air and the church bells rang. Calle Princesa climbed through the old quarter, forming a narrow valley of shadows. I walked past old palaces and buildings that seemed as ancient as the city itself until I glimpsed the number thirty-three, barely visible on one of the façades, and stepped into an entrance hall that made me think of a cloister in an abandoned chapel. A set of rusty, faded mailboxes hung on a wall of cracked enamel paint. I was trying in vain to find the name Mijail Kolvenik when I heard heavy breathing behind me.

I turned around with a start and saw the wrinkled face of an old woman. She was sitting in the porter's lodge and looked like the wax figure of a widow dressed in mourning. A ray of light touched her face. Her eyes were as white as marble. They had no pupils. She was blind.

"Who are you looking for?" she asked in a broken voice.

"Mijail Kolvenik, ma'am."

The empty white eyes blinked a couple of times. The old woman shook her head.

"I've been given this address," I said. "Mijail Kolvenik. Fourth floor, door two..."

The old woman shook her head again and then returned to her motionless state. As she did so, I noticed something moving on the table inside the lodge: A black spider was crawling over her wrinkled hands. Her white eyes stared into space. I edged away toward the stairs.

———

The gloom inside the building was so thick you could almost cut through it. I would have bet all the money I owed JF that nobody had changed a lightbulb in that stair-case for at least thirty years. The steps were chipped and slippery. The landings were wells of darkness and silence. A tremulous light peeped through a skylight in the attic, where a trapped pigeon was flapping about. The second apartment on the fourth floor had a carved wooden door with a solid knocker that looked like something out of a railway carriage. I rang the bell a couple of times and heard it echoing inside the flat. A few minutes went by. I rang again. Two more minutes. I began to think that I'd come to a tomb, one of hundreds of ghost buildings that haunted the heart of Barcelona.

Suddenly the grid in the spyhole slid open, and threads of light cut through the darkness. The voice I heard seemed to be made of sand. A voice that hadn't spoken in weeks, perhaps months.

"Who's there?"

"Señor Kolvenik? Mijail Kolvenik?" I asked. "Could I speak to you for a moment, please?"

The spyhole slammed shut. Silence. I was about to ring the bell again when the door of the flat opened.

A figure was silhouetted against the doorway. The sound of a dripping tap in a sink could be heard inside the apartment.

"What do you want, son?"

"Señor Kolvenik?"

"I'm not Kolvenik," the voice cut in. "My name is Sentís, Benjamín Sentís."

"I'm sorry, Señor Sentís, but I've been given this address, and..."

I handed him the visiting card given to me by the porter at the station. A rigid hand grabbed it, and the man, whose face I couldn't see, examined it in silence for a good while before handing it back to me.

"Mijail Kolvenik hasn't lived here for years."

"You know him?" I asked. "Perhaps you could help me?"

Another long silence.

"Come in," Sentís said at last.

Benjamín Sentís was a hefty man who inhabited a wine-colored flannel dressing gown. He held an unlit pipe in his mouth and sported one of those mustaches that joined up with his sideburns, Jules Verne style. The flat stood above the jungle of flat roofs of the old quarter and seemed to float in an ethereal light. The cathedral towers could be seen in the distance, and far away rose the mountain of Montjuïc. A piano sat collecting layers of dust, and boxes with old newspapers populated the floor. There was nothing in that house that spoke of the present. Benjamín Sentís lived in the past tense.

We sat in the room facing the terrace and Sentís had another look at the card.

"Why are you looking for Kolvenik?" he asked.

I decided to tell him everything from the start, from our visit to the cemetery to the strange sight of the lady in black in the Estación de Francia. Sentís stared absently as he listened to me, showing no emotion. At the end of my story an uncomfortable silence arose between us. Sentís looked at me carefully. He had wolfish eyes, cold and penetrating.

"Mijail Kolvenik lived in this flat for four years, shortly after he arrived in Barcelona," he said. "There are still some of his books in the back somewhere. It's all that's left of him."

"Would you happen to have his present address? Do you know where I could find him?"

Sentís laughed. "Try hell."

I looked at him without understanding.

"Mijail Kolvenik died in 1948."

According to what Benjamín Sentís told me that morning, Mijail Kolvenik had arrived in Barcelona toward the end of 1919. Just twenty, a native of Prague, Kolvenik was fleeing from the ruins left behind by the Great War. He didn't speak a word of Catalan or Spanish, although he was fluent in French and German. He had no money, friends, or acquaintances in that difficult and hostile city and spent his first night in a prison cell after being caught sleeping in a doorway to shelter from the cold. In the prison two of his cellmates, who were accused of assault and battery—as well as arson—decided to give him a beating on the grounds that the country was going to the dogs because of filthy foreigners. The three broken ribs, the bruises, and the internal injuries would heal over time, but he lost the hearing in his left ear forever. "Permanent nerve damage," the doctors diagnosed. An inauspicious beginning. But Mijail Kolvenik always said that what starts badly can only end better. Ten years later he would be one of the richest and most powerful men in the city of Barcelona.

In the prison sick bay he met the man who, over the years, would become his best friend, a young doctor of English descent named Joan Shelley. Dr. Shelley spoke a little German and knew from personal experience how it felt to be a foreigner in a strange country. Thanks to him, Kolvenik got a job at a small company called Velo-Granell Industries after he was discharged from the hospital. Velo-Granell manufactured orthopedic supplies and artificial limbs. The war with Morocco and the Great War in Europe had created a huge market for such products. Legions of men, butchered for the greater glory and the profit margins of bankers, chancellors, generals, stockbrokers, and other fathers of the nation, had been maimed and ruined for life in the name of freedom, democracy, the Empire, the race, or the flag.... Take your pick.

The Velo-Granell workshops were located near the Borne Market. Inside, glass cabinets displaying artificial arms, eyes, legs, and joints reminded visitors of the fragility of the human body. With his modest pay and a good reference from his company, Mijail Kolvenik found accommodation in a flat on Calle Princesa. An avid reader, Kolvenik learned to speak Catalan and Spanish reasonably well in a year and a half. His talent and ingenuity soon earned him a reputation as one of the key employees at Velo-Granell. Kolvenik had extensive medical, surgical, and anatomical knowledge. He designed a revolutionary pneumatic mechanism that enabled the movement of joints in artificial arms and legs. The device reacted to muscular impulses, providing the patient with unprecedented mobility. This invention placed the Velo-Granell business at the forefront of the industry. And that was just the beginning. Kolvenik's drawing table endlessly produced innovations, and it wasn't long before he was named chief engineer of the design and development workshop.

Months later, an unfortunate incident put young Kolvenik's talent to the test. The son and heir of Velo-Granell's founder suffered a terrible accident in the factory: A hydraulic press like the jaws of a dragon severed both his hands. For weeks Kolvenik worked tirelessly to create new hands made of wood, metal, and porcelain, with fingers that responded to the commands of muscles and tendons in the forearm. Kolvenik's solution made use of electric currents from the arm nerves to produce the movements. Four months after the accident the victim began to use mechanical hands that enabled him to pick up an object, light a cigarette, or do up his shirt buttons without any help. Everyone agreed that this time Kolvenik had surpassed everything imaginable. Not being very fond of praise and jubilation, Kolvenik stated that this was only the dawn of a new science. To reward him for his work, the founder of Velo-Granell Industries named Kolvenik director general of the company and offered him a package of shares that virtually turned him into one of the owners—next to the man who had been given new hands thanks to his inventiveness.

Under Kolvenik's management, Velo-Granell took on a new direction. It expanded its market and diversified its products. The company adopted the symbol of a black butterfly with open wings, an icon that was dear to Kolvenik's heart but whose significance he never fully explained. The plant expanded to launch new mechanisms: articulated limbs, circulatory valves, artificial bone tissue, and no end of novel devices. The Tibidabo funfair was peopled with automatons created by Kolvenik as a pastime and testing ground. Velo-Granell exported its products all over Europe, America, and Asia. The value of its shares and Kolvenik's personal fortune shot up, but he refused to leave the modest flat on Calle Princesa. He said there was no need for him to change. He lived alone, led a simple life, and that apartment was quite enough for him and his books.

The situation was about to change with the arrival of a new piece on the chessboard: Eva Irinova, the star of a highly successful new show in the Teatro Real. The young diva, Russian by birth, was only nineteen. People said that her beauty had driven gentlemen to suicide in Paris, Vienna, and other capital cities, once they realized they would never spend another night in her arms. No doubt this was part of the publicity legend orchestrated by some shady stage impresario, but the public will always choose a warmed-up lie over the cold truth. Eva Irinova traveled in the company of two strange characters, the twins Sergei and Tatiana Glazunow. The Glazunow siblings acted as agents and tutors for Eva Irinova. It was rumored that Sergei and the young diva were lovers and that the fiendish Tatiana slept inside a coffin beneath the stage of the Teatro Real; that Sergei had been one of the assassins of the Romanov dynasty; that Eva was able to speak to the spirits of the dead.... Again, all kinds of far-fetched showbiz gossip only served to increase the fame of the mysterious and beautiful siren who held Barcelona in the palm of her hand.

It was only a matter of time before Irinova's tale reached Kolvenik's ears. Intrigued, he went to the theater one night to see for himself what was causing such a stir. One evening was enough for Kolvenik to fall under the young woman's spell. After that day Irinova's dressing room became, quite literally, a bed of roses. Two months after this revelation Kolvenik decided to purchase a box in the theater. He would sit there spellbound, gazing at the object of his adoration. Needless to say, the matter soon became the talk of the town. One fine day Kolvenik called a meeting with his lawyers and instructed them to make an offer to the impresario of the theater, Daniel Mestres. He wanted to buy the old theater and take over the debts weighing it down. His idea was to rebuild it from the foundation and turn it into the greatest stage in Europe, a magnificent theater equipped with the latest technological advances and dedicated to his beloved Eva Irinova. The theater managers gave in to his generous proposal. The new project was christened the Gran Teatro Real. The following day, Kolvenik proposed to Eva Irinova in fluent Russian. She accepted.

After the wedding the couple planned to move into a dream mansion Kolvenik was having built next to Güell Park—he'd presented a preliminary design for the sumptuous building to the architectural firm Sunyer, Balcells i Baró. People claimed that nobody had ever paid such a huge sum for a private residence in the whole of Barcelona's history, which was saying something. And yet not everyone was happy with this fairy tale. Kolvenik's partner at Velo-Granell Industries didn't approve of his obsession. He was afraid that Kolvenik might make use of some of the company's funds to finance his feverish project of turning the Teatro Real into the eighth wonder of the modern world—and he wasn't far off the mark. As if this weren't enough, rumors started to circulate in Barcelona about Kolvenik's rather unorthodox habits. Doubts arose concerning his past and the image of a self-made man he liked to project. Most of these rumors died before they reached the press, thanks to Velo-Granell's implacable legal machinery. Money doesn't buy happiness, Kolvenik used to say, but it buys everything else.

For their part, Sergei and Tatiana Glazunow, Eva Irinova's sinister guardians, saw all of this as a threat to their future. No room was being built for either of them in the new mansion. Foreseeing a problem with the twins, Kolvenik offered them a generous sum to terminate their supposed contract with Irinova. In exchange they had to leave the country and promise never to return or try to get in touch with Eva. Aroused to fury, Sergei flatly refused such a proposition and swore Kolvenik would never get rid of him or his sister.

That very night, in the hours before dawn, just as Sergei and Tatiana were leaving a building on Calle Sant Pau, a burst of gunshots fired from a carriage almost ended their lives. The attack was attributed to a group of anarchists. A week later the twins signed the document whereby they undertook to release Eva and disappear forever. The date for the wedding between Mijail Kolvenik and Eva Irinova was fixed for June 24, 1935. The setting: Barcelona Cathedral.

The ceremony, which some people compared to the coronation of King Alfonso XIII, took place on a brilliantly sunny morning. Crowds filled every corner of the avenue leading to the cathedral, eager to immerse themselves in the lavishness and splendor of the occasion. Eva Irinova had never looked so dazzling. To the strains of Wagner's wedding march, played by the orchestra of the Liceo on the cathedral steps, the bride and bridegroom walked toward the waiting carriage. When they were barely three meters away from the coach, drawn by white horses, a figure broke through the police cordon and threw himself on the newlyweds. There were shouts of panic. When he turned around, Kolvenik faced the bloodshot eyes of Sergei Glazunow. Nobody present would ever forget what happened next. Glazunow pulled out a glass bottle and threw the contents in Eva Irinova's face. Like a curtain of steam, the acid burned through her veil. A shriek seemed to rip the skies open. The crowd of onlookers whirled about in confusion, and in a flash the attacker was lost among them.

Kolvenik kneeled next to the bride and took her in his arms. Eva Irinova's features were melting away under the acid like a freshly painted watercolor fading under water. The smoking skin fell off like charred parchment and the stench of burned flesh filled the air. The acid hadn't reached the young woman's eyes. They revealed all the horror and the agony. Kolvenik tried to save his wife's face by pressing his hands on it. All he achieved was to pull off bits of dead tissue as the acid burned through his gloves. By the time Eva finally lost consciousness, her face had become a grotesque mask of bone and raw flesh.

———

The renovated Teatro Real never opened its doors. After the tragedy Kolvenik took his wife to the unfinished mansion in Güell Park. Eva Irinova would never set foot outside that house again. The acid had completely destroyed her face and damaged her vocal cords. People said she communicated through notes written on a pad and that she spent entire weeks without leaving her rooms.

By then the financial problems at Velo-Granell Industries had begun to surface and were more serious than had first been suspected. Kolvenik felt cornered and soon stopped going to the office. It was rumored that he'd picked up some strange illness that kept him increasingly confined to his mansion. Numerous irregularities in the Velo-Granell management came to light, as well as a number of strange transactions carried out in the past by Kolvenik himself. Gossip and malicious accusations reared their ugly heads. Secluded in his refuge with his beloved Eva, Kolvenik slowly turned into a character straight out of a dark legend. A pariah. The government expropriated the Velo-Granell partnership and the legal authorities were investigating the case: With its one-thousand-page dossier, the investigation had only just begun.

In the years that followed, Kolvenik lost his fortune. His mansion became a shadowy, ruined castle. After months without pay, the couple's servants abandoned them. Only Kolvenik's personal chauffeur remained loyal. All kinds of horrific rumors started to spread. It was said that Kolvenik and his wife lived among rats, wandering through the corridors of the tomb in which they had buried themselves alive.

In December 1948 a fire devoured the Kolveniks' mansion. The flames could be seen from as far away as Mataró, or so the papers stated. Those who remember it swear that the skies of Barcelona turned into a scarlet canvas and clouds of ash swept through the city at dawn while the crowds gazed in silence at the smoking skeleton of the ruins. The charred bodies of Kolvenik and Eva were discovered in the attic, locked in an embrace. The image appeared on the front page of *La Vanguardia* under the headline THE END OF AN ERA.

By early 1949 Barcelona had already started to forget the story of Mijail Kolvenik and Eva Irinova. The great metropolis was changing irrevocably, and the mystery of Velo-Granell Industries belonged to a legendary past, forever condemned to oblivion.

ELEVEN

Benjamín Sentís's account stayed with me all week like a furtive shadow. The more I thought about it, the more I had the feeling that there were key pieces missing in his story. What the pieces were and why he might have left them out was another matter. These thoughts gnawed at me from dawn to dusk while I waited impatiently for Germán and Marina's return.

In the afternoons, once my classes were over, I went along to their house to make sure everything was all right. Kafka was always there, waiting for me by the main entrance, sometimes holding the spoils from a hunt between his claws. I would pour milk into the cat's bowl and we'd chat; that is to say, Kafka drank the milk while I went into a monologue. More than once I felt tempted to take advantage of its owners' absence to explore the house, but I resisted. The echo of their presence could be felt in every corner. I got used to waiting for nightfall in the rambling, empty house, feeling the warmth of their invisible company. I would sit in the room with the paintings and spend hours gazing at Germán Blau's portraits of his wife, painted some fifteen years earlier. I could see an adult Marina in them, the woman she was already becoming. I wondered whether one day I'd be able to create anything as worthy as that. Anything worthy at all.

On Sunday I turned up bright and early at the Estación de Francia. There were still two hours to go before the express train from Madrid was due. I spent them exploring the building. Under its vaulted ceiling trains and strangers gathered like pilgrims. I'd always thought that old railway stations were one of the few magical places left in the world, where ghosts of memories and farewells mingled with the start of hundreds of one-way journeys to faraway destinations. *If I'm ever lost, the place to look for me would be a railway station*, I thought.

The whistle of the Madrid express train rescued me

from my sentimental musings. The train burst into the station at full gallop, making straight for its platform. A groan of brakes flooded the air as the train gradually came to a halt with all the slow deliberation dictated by its tonnage. Soon the first passengers began to appear—nameless silhouettes. I looked down the platform with my heart pounding. Dozens of unknown faces filed past. Suddenly I hesitated, thinking I might have got the day wrong, or the train, or the city, or the planet. Then I heard an unmistakable voice behind me.

"This *is* a surprise, dear Oscar. We've missed you."

"Same here," I replied, shaking the old painter's hand.

Marina was stepping down from the carriage. She was wearing the same white dress she had on the day she left. She smiled at me silently, her eyes shining.

"How was Madrid?" I asked, taking Germán's briefcase.

"Beautiful. And seven times larger than the last time I was there," said Germán. "If it doesn't stop growing, one of these days it will spill over the plateau."

Germán's voice seemed charged with good humor and energy. I hoped this meant that the news from the doctor at La Paz was encouraging. On our way to the exit, while Germán chatted away with an astonished porter about the improvements in railway technology, I had the chance to be alone with Marina. She pressed my hand tightly.

"How did it all go?" I murmured. "Germán seems cheerful."

"Well. Very well. Thanks for coming to meet us."

"Thank *you* for coming back," I said. "Barcelona seemed very empty these last few days....I have lots to tell you."

We hailed a taxi outside the station, an old Dodge that was noisier than the express train from Madrid. As we drove up the Ramblas, Germán gazed out at the people, the markets, and the flower stalls and smiled contentedly.

"They can say what they like, Oscar, but there isn't another street like this one in any city in the world. Nothing can compare."

Marina agreed with her father's comments. He seemed revived and younger after the trip.

"Isn't tomorrow a holiday?" Germán asked out of the blue.

"Yes," I said.

"So you don't have classes."

"Technically, no..."

Germán burst out laughing and for a second I thought I could glimpse the boy he had once been, decades ago.

"And tell me, my good friend, are you very busy tomorrow?"

By eight in the morning I was already at their house, just as Germán had requested. The previous night I'd promised my tutor that I would spend twice as many hours studying every evening of that week, if—as it was a holiday—he'd allow me to go out on Monday.

"I don't know what you've been up to recently. This isn't a hotel, but it isn't a prison, either. Your behavior is your own responsibility," Father Seguí had remarked suspiciously. "I suppose you know what you're doing, Oscar."

When I reached the Sarriá villa I found Marina in the kitchen preparing a basket with sandwiches and thermos flasks with drinks. Kafka followed her movements carefully, licking his chops.

"Where are we going?" I asked, intrigued.

"Surprise," said Marina.

Shortly afterward Germán appeared, dressed like a rally driver from the 1920s, looking euphoric and jovial. He shook my hand and asked me whether I could help him in the garage. I nodded. I hadn't realized they had a garage. In fact, they had three, as I saw when I walked around the property with him.

"I'm glad you were able to join us, Oscar."

Germán stopped in front of the third garage door,

an ivy-covered shed the size of a small house. The metal bar squeaked when we lifted it to open the door and a cloud of dust filled the darkness inside. The place looked as if it had been closed up for twenty years. It contained the remains of an old motorcycle, rusty tools, and boxes piled up under a blanket of dirt as thick as a Persian carpet. Then I glimpsed a gray piece of canvas covering what looked like a car. Germán took one end of the canvas and gestured to me to do the same.

"Count to three?" he asked.

At his signal we both gave a strong tug and the canvas came off like a silk veil. When the cloud of dust had scattered in the breeze, the faint light filtering through the trees revealed a vision. A stunning wine-colored 1940s Tucker with chrome wheels slept inside that cave. I stared at Germán in astonishment. He smiled proudly.

"They don't make cars like this one anymore, Oscar."

"Will it start?" I asked, staring at what looked to me like a museum piece.

"What you see here is a Tucker, Oscar. It doesn't just start. It eases into a canter."

An hour later we were cruising along the coastal road. Germán sat in the driver's seat like a pioneer of early motoring with a million-dollar smile. Marina and I sat next to him, in the front. Kafka had the whole of the backseat to himself and slept peacefully. All the other cars overtook us, but their passengers turned around to stare at the Tucker in astonishment and admiration.

"Where there is class, speed is a minor detail," Germán explained.

We were nearing Blanes, and I still didn't know where we were going. Germán was concentrating on his driving and I didn't want to bother him. He drove with the same politeness that characterized everything he did, giving way even to crawling ants and waving to cyclists, pedestrians, and civil guard motorcyclists. After Blanes a signpost indicated the seaside village of Tossa de Mar. I turned to look at Marina and she winked at me. I thought we might be going to the old Tossa Castle perched on the cliffs, but the Tucker circled the village and took the narrow road that continued northward, following the coast: It was more like a ribbon than a road, suspended between the sky and the cliffs, curling around hundreds of sharp bends. Through the branches of the pine trees that hugged the steep slopes the sea could be seen extending like a carpet of incandescent blue. A hundred meters below, dozens of remote coves and inlets sketched a secret route between Tossa de Mar and the cape of Punta Prima, next to the port of Sant Feliu de Guíxols, some twenty kilometers ahead.

After driving on for another twenty minutes or so, Germán stopped the car by the side of the road. Marina looked at me as if to signal that we had arrived. We stepped out of the car and Kafka wandered off toward the pine trees as though he knew the way. While Germán was checking the Tucker's hand brake to make sure the car wasn't going to roll down the hill, Marina walked over to the edge of a slope that tumbled down to the sea. I joined her and gazed at the view. At our feet a cove in the shape of a crescent moon curved around an expanse of transparent blue sea. Beyond it, low rocks and beaches formed an arc as far as Punta Prima, where the country chapel of Sant Elm could be seen standing like a sentinel on the hilltop.

"Come on, let's go," Marina urged me.

I followed her through the pines. The path cut across the grounds of an old abandoned house, now entirely overgrown with bushes. From there a series of steps hollowed into the rocks led us down to a beach of golden pebbles. A flock of gulls took to the sky when they saw us, retreating to the cliffs that crowned the cove and formed what looked like a cathedral of rock, sea, and light. The water of the cove was so clear that I could see all the ripple lines of the sand beneath its surface. In the center the tip of a rock rose up like the prow of a ship that had run aground. The smell of the sea was intense and a salty breeze combed the coast. Marina's gaze was lost in the silvery mist of the horizon.

"This is my favorite place in the world," she said.

Marina insisted on showing me every nook and cranny along the cliffs. It didn't take me long to realize that I was likely to end up cracking my head open or falling head-first into the sea.

"I thrive on the plain. I'm not a goat," I remarked, trying to add a touch of sanity to our ropeless mountaineering.

Ignoring my pleas, Marina climbed up walls smoothed by the sea and slid through holes where the swells could be heard breathing like a stone whale. I knew I was in danger of losing face and kept thinking that at any moment fate would strike with the full force of the laws of gravity. My prediction didn't take long to come true. Marina jumped to the other side of a tiny islet to inspect a cave among the rocks, and I told myself that if she could do it, I'd better give it a try, too. A second later my clumsy legs were plunging into the Mediterranean Sea. I shook with cold and embarrassment. From the rocks Marina stared at me in alarm.

"I'm all right," I moaned. "I didn't hurt myself."

"Is it cold?"

"Oh no," I stammered. "It's as warm as a bath."

Marina smiled and before my astonished eyes removed her white dress and dived into the lagoon. She surfaced next to me, laughing. It was madness at that time of year, but I decided to imitate her. We swam with energetic strokes and then lay down in the sun on the warm pebbles. I could feel my heart racing, though I couldn't be sure whether it was due to the icy water or to the near-transparency of Marina's wet underwear. She caught me looking at her and got up to fetch her dress, which was lying on the nearby rocks. I watched her step over the pebbles, every muscle in her body visible under her damp skin as she jumped from rock to rock. I licked my salty lips, then realized I was as hungry as a wolf.

We spent the rest of the afternoon on that beach, hidden from the world, devouring the sandwiches from the basket while Marina narrated the peculiar story of the woman who owned the farmhouse we'd seen abandoned among the pine trees.

The house had belonged to a Dutch writer who suffered from a rare illness that was slowly making her blind. Aware of her fate, she decided to build herself a shelter atop the cliff where she could retire and spend her last days of light facing the beach and gazing at the sea.

"She lived here alone, her only companions being an Alsatian named Sacha and her favorite books," Marina explained. "When she lost her sight altogether, knowing that her eyes would never see another sunrise over the sea, she asked some fishermen who used to drop anchor in the cove to take care of Sacha. A few days later, at dawn, she took a rowboat and rowed out to sea. She was never seen again."

For some reason I suspected that the story of the Dutch writer was an invention of Marina's, and I told her so.

"Sometimes, the things that are the most real only happen in one's imagination, Oscar," she said. "We only remember what never really happened."

Germán had fallen asleep with his hat over his face and Kafka at his feet. Marina looked sadly at her father. Taking advantage of Germán's nap, I clutched her hand, and together we walked off to the other end of the beach. There, sitting on a long rock smoothed by the waves, I told her all the things that had happened during her absence. I didn't leave anything out, from the strange appearance of the lady in black at the station, to Benjamín Sentís's story of Mijail Kolvenik and Velo-Granell Industries. I even described the ominous apparition I'd witnessed during that stormy night in the Sarriá house. She listened to me in silence, absent, her eyes fixed on the small whirlpools of water at her feet. We remained there for a while, quietly gazing at the faraway outline of the hilltop chapel.

"What did the doctor at La Paz say?" I asked at last.

Marina looked up. The sun was beginning its descent and an amber glow illuminated her tearful eyes.

"That there isn't much time left."

I turned and saw Germán waving to us. I felt my heart shrink, and an unbearable knot seemed to tighten around my throat.

"He doesn't believe it," said Marina. "It's better that way."

When I turned back I noticed she was quickly drying her tears with a cheerful gesture. I realized I was looking straight into her eyes and, without knowing where I found the courage, I leaned over her, searching for her mouth. Marina placed her fingers on my lips and stroked my face, gently rejecting me. A second later she stood up and I watched her walk away. I sighed.

I got to my feet and went back to Germán. As I drew closer, I noticed that he was sketching in a small notebook. I remembered that it had been years since he'd picked up a pencil or a paintbrush. Germán looked up and smiled at me.

"See what you think of the likeness, Oscar," he said in a carefree manner, showing me the notebook.

Germán's pencil strokes had captured Marina's face with astonishing perfection.

"It's wonderful," I murmured.

"Do you like it? I'm glad."

Marina's motionless silhouette stood out against the light at the other end of the beach, as she faced the sea. Germán looked first at her, then at me. He tore the page out and handed it to me.

"It's for you, Oscar, so that you don't forget my Marina."

———

During the return journey the setting sun turned the sea into a pool of molten copper. Germán smiled as he drove, telling us endless stories about his years at the wheel of that old Tucker. Marina listened to him, laughing at his witty remarks and keeping the conversation going with invisible threads, like a sorceress. I sat in silence, my forehead against the window, my soul deep inside my pocket. When we were halfway back, Marina quietly took my hand and held it between hers.

We arrived in Barcelona at nightfall, and Germán

insisted on driving me right up to the boarding school. He parked the Tucker outside the school gates and shook my hand. Marina stepped out of the car and came in with me. Her presence seemed to burn me. I just wanted to get away.

"Oscar, if there is anything…"

"No."

"Look, Oscar, there are things you don't understand, but—"

"That's obvious," I snapped. "Good night."

I turned, ready to flee across the garden.

"Wait," said Marina from the gate.

I stopped by the pond.

"I want you to know that today has been one of the best days of my life," she said.

When I turned to respond, Marina had already left.

I climbed the staircase with leaden steps. When I walked past some of my classmates they looked at me sideways, as if I were a stranger. Rumors of my mysterious disappearances were making the rounds of the school. Little did I care. I picked up the day's newspaper from the table in the hallway and took refuge in my room, then lay down on the bed with the newspaper on my chest. I could hear voices in the corridor. I switched on my bedside light and buried myself in what to me felt like the unreal world of the newspaper. Marina's name seemed to be written on every line. *It will pass*, I thought. Soon the monotony of the news items calmed me down. Nothing better than reading about other people's problems to forget your own. Wars, swindles, murders, frauds, anthems, military parades, and football. The world remained unchanged. Feeling more relaxed, I went on reading. At first I didn't notice it. It was just a short article, a brief report to fill up space. I folded the newspaper and placed it under the light.

DEAD BODY DISCOVERED IN A SEWER TUNNEL OF THE GOTHIC QUARTER
Gustavo Berceo
Barcelona

In the early hours of Friday morning the body of 83-year-old Benjamín Sentís, a resident of Barcelona, was discovered inside one of the entrances to the fourth sewer of the Old Town network. It is not clear how the body came to be there, as that section has been closed since 1941. The cause of death seems to have been cardiac arrest. According to our sources, however, the corpse had had both hands amputated. Benjamín Sentís, who was retired, had acquired some notoriety during the 1940s in connection with the scandal of Velo-Granell Industries, of which he was a partner and shareholder. He spent his last years living as a recluse in a small flat on Calle Princesa, with no known relatives and almost bankrupt.

TWELVE

I spent a sleepless night going over every piece of the story Sentís had told me. I read the news item on his death again and again, hoping to unearth some secret meaning among the periods and the commas. The old man had conveniently forgotten to mention that at some point he had actually been Kolvenik's partner at Velo-Granell Industries. If the rest of his story was to be trusted, Sentís must have been the son of the company's founder, I concluded: the son who had inherited 50 percent of the company shares when Kolvenik was named director general. That would alter the position of all the pieces in the puzzle. But if Sentís had chosen to omit the key point in his story, he may have lied to me about all the rest. Daylight caught me by surprise as I struggled to understand the significance of it all.

That Tuesday I slipped out during the midday break to meet up with Marina.

As if she'd once again read my thoughts, she was waiting for me in the garden, holding a copy of the newspaper from the day before. Or perhaps I was just becoming predictable. A quick glance was enough for me to know that she'd read about Sentís's death.

"That man lied to you...."

"And now he's dead."

Marina glanced back at the house as if she were concerned Germán might hear us.

"We'd better go out for a walk," she suggested.

I agreed without argument, although I knew only too well that I had to be back in the classroom in less than half an hour. Our steps took us to Santa Amelia Park, an island of peace on the edge of the Pedralbes district. In the middle of the park stood an imposing mansion that had been recently restored as a civic center for its lucky neighbors after years of neglect and abandonment. One of its old halls now housed a modest café. We sat at a table next to a large window. Marina read out the news item that I could almost have recited by heart.

"It doesn't say anywhere that it was a murder," Marina ventured, sounding unconvinced.

"No need to state the obvious. An old man who has lived as a recluse for twenty years turns up dead in the sewers, and to cap it all someone took the trouble to remove both his hands before dumping the body. Surely he didn't just collapse while he was feeding the pigeons."

"Okay. It's a murder."

"It's more than a murder," I said, my nerves on edge. "What was Sentís doing in an abandoned sewer in the middle of the night?"

A waiter, sluggishly drying glasses behind the counter, was listening to us.

"Lower your voice," whispered Marina.

I nodded and tried to calm down.

"Maybe we should go to the police and tell them everything we know," said Marina.

"But we don't know anything," I objected.

"We probably know more than they do. A week ago a mysterious woman tells someone to hand you a visiting card with Sentís's address and the black butterfly symbol. You visit Sentís, who says he doesn't know anything about it, but recounts a strange story about Mijail Kolvenik and a company called Velo-Granell Industries implicated in some murky affairs over forty years ago. He conveniently forgets to tell you he was part of that story, that in fact he was the son of the founding partner, the man for whom Kolvenik created two artificial hands after an accident in the factory.... A few days later Sentís is discovered dead in the sewers—"

"Without his orthopedic hands," I replied, remembering that Sentís had been reluctant to shake hands with me when he asked me in.

When I thought of his rigid hand, I felt a shiver.

"One thing is certain: When we stepped into that greenhouse we must have got in the way of something," I said, trying to clear my thoughts. "And now we've become a part of it. The woman in black came to me with that card—"

"Oscar, we don't know if it was you she was after, or what her motives were. We don't even know who she is."

"But *she* knows who *we* are, and where to find us. And if she knows..."

Marina sighed.

"Let's call the police right now and forget about all this as soon as possible," she said. "I don't like it, and besides, it's none of our business."

"It is, from the moment we decided to follow the lady in the cemetery...."

Marina turned her head to look at the park. Two children were playing with a kite, trying to make it catch the wind. Without taking her eyes off them, she murmured slowly, "What do you suggest, then?"

She knew perfectly well what I had in mind.

The sun was setting behind the church in Plaza Sarriá as Marina and I headed down Paseo de la Bonanova on our way to the greenhouse. This time we had taken the precaution of bringing a flashlight and a box of matches with us. We turned into Calle Iradier and entered the lonely side streets bordering the railway line. The sound of the trains making their way up to Vallvidrera echoed through the woodland. It didn't take us long to find the alleyway where we'd lost sight of the lady and the gate concealing the greenhouse at the back.

A blanket of dry leaves covered the paving stones. As we penetrated the undergrowth, gelatinous shadows spread around us, the grass whistled in the wind, and the moon's face smiled through chinks in the sky. In the twilight the ivy covering the greenhouse looked like a thick tangle of snakes. We walked around the building and found the back door. The flame from a match revealed the symbol used by Kolvenik and Velo-Granell, blemished with moss. I swallowed hard and looked at Marina. Her face had a deathly glow.

"It was your idea to come back," she said.

I turned on the flashlight and its reddish brightness flooded the entrance to the greenhouse. I took a quick look before entering. In daylight the place had seemed sinister enough. Now, in the dark, it was like a nightmare come true. The flashlight's beam disclosed sinuous shapes among the debris as I walked in, followed by Marina. The damp floor crunched beneath our steps. We heard the spine-chilling hiss of the wooden figures as they rubbed against one another. For a moment, as I peered into the mass of shadows in the heart of the greenhouse, I couldn't remember whether we'd left the piece of stage machinery with the suspended figures hoisted up or fallen down when we'd abandoned the place. I looked at Marina and saw that she was thinking the same.

"Someone has been here since the last time," she said, pointing at the silhouettes hanging halfway down from the ceiling.

A sea of feet undulated in midair. I felt a cold sensation on the back of my neck as I realized that someone had lowered the figures again. Not wanting to lose any more time, I walked over to the desk and handed the flashlight to Marina.

"What are we looking for?" she whispered.

I pointed to the album of old photographs on the table. I picked it up and slipped it into my backpack.

"This album isn't ours, Oscar, I don't know if . . ."

Ignoring her objections, I kneeled down to inspect the drawers under the desk. The first one contained all sorts of rusty tools, blades, spikes, and blunt saws. The second was empty. Small black spiders ran around the bottom, looking for shelter in the cracks of the wood. I closed it and tried my luck with the third drawer. It was locked.

"What's the matter?" I heard Marina whisper, her voice full of anxiety.

I took one of the blades from the top drawer and tried to force the lock. Marina, standing behind me, held the flashlight up high, her eyes on the dancing shadows gliding along the greenhouse walls.

"Will you be long?"

"Don't worry. It won't take a minute."

I could feel the top of the lock with the blade. I worked my way around it, piercing the wood, which was dry and rotten and yielded easily under the pressure. As the wood splintered it made a loud rasping sound. Marina crouched down beside me and placed the flashlight on the floor.

"What's that noise?" she asked all of a sudden.

"It's nothing. It's the wood in the drawer cracking...."

She placed her hands on mine, stopping me. For a moment silence enveloped us. I could feel Marina's pulse racing. Then I, too, heard the sound: the snap of the wooden planks above us. Something was moving between those figures anchored in the dark. I strained my eyes just in time to perceive the outline of what looked like a sinuously moving arm. One of the figures was being unfastened. It moved like an asp sliding through the branches of a tree. Other shapes started to move at the same time. I grabbed the blade and stood up, trembling. At that very moment someone or something moved the flashlight lying at our feet. It rolled to a corner and we were left in total darkness. Then we heard that whistling sound, getting closer.

I grasped my friend's hand and we ran toward the exit. As we fled, the machinery holding the figures slowly descended, arms and legs brushing against our heads, trying to grab hold of our clothes. I felt metallic nails rub the back of my neck. Marina screamed and I pushed her forward through that tunnel of hellish creatures descending from the darkness. The moonbeams filtering through the gaps in the ivy lit up visions of broken faces, glass eyes, and enamel teeth.

I brandished the blade fiercely from side to side and suddenly felt it pierce a hard surface. A thick fluid soaked my fingers and I pulled my hand away. Something was dragging Marina into the shadows. She screamed with terror and I saw the sightless face of the wooden ballerina with its black, empty eye sockets as it circled her throat with fingers as sharp as razors. The figure's face was covered with a mask of dead skin. I threw myself against it with all the power I could muster and knocked it down. Keeping close together, Marina and I ran to the door while the now headless figure of the dancer rose again, a puppet on invisible strings wielding claws that snapped like scissors.

When we were out in the open I made out a number of shadowy forms blocking our way to the garden gate. We ran in the opposite direction, toward a shed standing next to the wall that separated the property from the railway line. The shed's glass doors were blurred with decades of dirt. They were locked. I broke the glass with my elbow and groped around for the lock inside the door. A handle gave way and the door opened inward. We rushed in. The back windows formed two stains of pale, milky light, with the mesh of the train's power lines just visible on the other side. Marina turned for a moment to look behind her. Angular shapes could be seen outlined against the door of the shed.

"Quick!" she shouted.

I looked desperately around me, searching for something with which to break the window. The carcass of an old car was rotting away in the dark. The crank handle lay on the hood. I grabbed it and used it to bang at the window repeatedly while protecting myself against the shower of glass. The night air blew on my face and

I could smell the stuffy air emerging from the mouth of the railway tunnel.

"This way!"

Marina clambered up onto the windowsill while I kept an eye on the figures, which were slowly creeping into the garage. I brandished the crank handle with both hands. Suddenly the figures stopped and took a step back. I looked without understanding, and then I heard that mechanical breathing above me. Instinctively I jumped out of the way, and toward the window, just as a body dropped from the ceiling. I recognized the shape of the armless policeman. Its face seemed to be covered with a mask of dead skin, roughly sewn together. The seams were bleeding.

"Oscar!" Marina shouted from the other side of the window.

I hurled myself through the jaws of the splintered windowpane. A tongue of glass cut through my pants leg: I felt it slice my skin cleanly. As I landed on the other side the pain hit me instantly and I felt the warm flow of blood under my clothes. Marina helped me up and we struggled across the railway tracks to the other side. At that very moment something gripped my ankle and I fell flat on my face. I turned around in a daze: The hand of a monstrous puppet was closing around my foot. I leaned on a rail and felt the metal vibrating as the faraway light of a train hit the tunnel walls. Then came the screech of wheels, and the ground trembled under my body.

Marina cried out when she realized a train was approaching at full speed. She kneeled by my feet and struggled to free me from the grip of those wooden fingers. The lights of the train fell on her. The whistle howled. The puppet lay there motionless, holding on to its prey, unshakeable. Marina was wrestling with both hands, trying to release me. When at last one of the puppet's fingers yielded, she let out a sigh. But half a second later the body of that being stood up and grabbed Marina's arm with its other hand. Using the crank handle I was still holding, I hit the face of the inert figure with all my strength until I cracked its skull, realizing with horror that what I had thought of as wood was in fact bone. There was life in that creature.

By now the roar of the train was deafening, drowning our screams. The stones on the railway tracks shook and the beam of light from the locomotive cloaked us in its halo. I closed my eyes and went on hitting the ghastly creature with all my might until I felt the head become unhinged from the body. Only then did its claws let go of us. We rolled over the stones, blinded by the light. Tons of steel sped by only centimeters from our bodies, showering us with sparks. The broken fragments of the creature were thrown outward like smoking embers leaping from a bonfire.

When the train had passed, we opened our eyes. I turned toward Marina and nodded to let her know I was all right. Slowly we got to our feet. Then I felt a sharp pain in my leg. Marina put my arm around her shoulders, and with her support I was able to reach the other side of the rails. Once we'd crossed the track we turned to look back. Something was moving between the rails, shining in the moonlight. It was a wooden hand, severed by the wheels of the train. The hand shook in spasms that slowed until they stopped completely. Without saying a word, we walked through the undergrowth toward a narrow lane that led to Calle Anglí. In the distance church bells were ringing.

Luckily, Germán was dozing in his studio when we arrived. Marina led me quietly to one of the bathrooms to clean the wound on my leg by candlelight. The walls and floor were covered in glazed tiles, reflecting the glow of the flames. In the middle of the room stood a large bathtub resting on four iron legs.

"Take your pants off," Marina said with her back to me, as she looked for the first-aid kit.

"What?"

"You heard me."

I did as I was told and stretched my leg over the edge of the tub. The cut was deeper than I'd thought and the surrounding area had acquired a purplish tone. I felt nauseous just looking at it. Marina kneeled down next to me and examined it carefully.

"Does it hurt?"

"Only when I laugh."

My impromptu nurse took a piece of cotton wool soaked in antiseptic and held it near the cut.

"This is going to sting. . . ."

When the liquid hit the wound, I grabbed the edge of the bathtub so hard I must have left my fingerprints stamped on it.

"Was that very painful?" Marina murmured, blowing on the cut.

"Barely felt it."

Taking a deep breath, I closed my eyes while she continued to meticulously clean the wound. Finally she took a bandage from the first-aid kit and placed it over the cut. She secured the tape with an expert hand, never taking her eyes off what she was doing.

"They weren't after us," said Marina.

I wasn't sure what she was referring to.

"Those figures in the greenhouse," she explained without looking at me. "They were looking for the photograph album. We shouldn't have taken it."

I felt her breath on my skin as she applied a clean piece of gauze.

"About what happened the other day, on the beach..." I began.

Marina stopped and looked up. "It's nothing."

She fixed the last piece of tape and stared blankly at me. I thought she was going to say something, but she just stood up and walked out of the bathroom.

I was left alone with the candles and a pair of useless pants.

THIRTEEN

When I got back to the boarding school, well after midnight, all my classmates were already in bed. Needles of yellowish light pierced through their keyholes, cutting across the corridor. I tiptoed to my room, closing the door carefully behind me, then checked the alarm clock on the bedside table: almost one in the morning. I switched on the lamp, picked up my backpack, and pulled out the photograph album we had taken from the greenhouse.

I opened it and delved once again into the gallery of characters that thronged its pages. One image showed a hand with fingers joined together by membranes, like an amphibian. Next to that a girl with blond ringlets, dressed in white, offered the camera an almost demonic smile, with long eyeteeth jutting over her lips like fangs. Page after page, cruel whims of nature filed past. Two albino siblings whose paper-white skin looked as if it might burst into flame if you held a candle near it. Twins joined at the head, facing each other for life. The naked body of a woman whose spinal column was twisted like a dead branch... Many of them were children or young people. Many seemed younger than me. There were hardly any adults or elderly people. I realized that the life expectancy for those unfortunate souls was bound to be short.

I recalled Marina saying that the album was not ours and we should never have taken it. Now that the adrenaline had stopped pumping through my veins, her words acquired a new significance. As I examined the book, I finally realized I was violating a collection of memories that didn't belong to me. I could see that those images of sadness and ill fortune were, in a way, a family album. Filled with remorse, I closed the scrapbook and put it back in my backpack. I turned off the light and closed my eyes. The image of Marina walking along her deserted beach filled my mind. I saw her wander off along the shore until sleep muffled the sound of the waves.

For a day the rain grew tired of Barcelona and headed north. Like a fugitive, I skipped my last class of the afternoon to meet up with Marina. The clouds had been drawn apart like a curtain, revealing a strip of blue, and a soft dusty sunlight brushed the streets. She was waiting for me in the garden, engrossed in her secret notebook. The moment she saw me she closed it hurriedly. I wondered whether she was writing about me, or about what had happened to us in the greenhouse.

"How's your leg?" she asked, hugging the notebook.

"I'll survive. Come, I have something I want to show you."

I pulled out the album and sat next to her by the fountain. I opened it and turned a few pages. Marina sighed quietly, disturbed by the pictures.

"Here it is," I said, stopping at a photograph on one of the last pages. "This morning, when I got up, it suddenly came to me. I hadn't noticed it until now, but today..."

Marina stared at the photograph I was showing her. A black-and-white image with that rare poignant sharpness that only old studio portraits possess. It was the image of a man whose skull was severely deformed and whose spine barely allowed him to stand upright. He was leaning on a young man dressed in a white coat, with round spectacles and a bow tie that matched his neatly trimmed mustache. A doctor. The doctor looked at the camera. The patient covered his eyes with his hand, as if he were ashamed of his condition. Behind, just visible, was a paneled screen in what looked like an office. There was a half-open door in one corner, and standing in the doorway a very young girl holding a doll looked shyly at the scene. The photograph seemed to be more a medical record than anything else.

"Have a good look," I insisted.

"All I can see is a wretched man."

"Don't look at him. Look behind him."

"A window . . ."

"What can you see through the window?"

Marina frowned.

"Do you recognize it?" I asked, pointing at the figure of a dragon decorating the façade of a building on the opposite side of the street from where the photograph had been taken.

"I've seen it somewhere . . . ."

"That's just what I thought," I agreed. "Here, in Barcelona. In the Ramblas, opposite the Liceo Opera House. I went through each photograph in the album, and this is the only one that was taken in Barcelona."

I pulled the photograph out of the album and handed it to Marina. On the back, in faded letters, it read,

MARTORELL-BORRÁS
PHOTOGRAPHIC STUDIO—1951
COPY—DR. J. SHELLEY
RAMBLA DE LOS ESTUDIANTES, 46–48, FIRST
FLOOR, BARCELONA

Marina handed back the photograph, shrugging her shoulders.

"The picture was taken almost thirty years ago, Oscar. It doesn't mean anything."

"This morning I looked the name up in the telephone book. A Dr. Shelley is still listed as living at 46–48 Rambla de los Estudiantes, first floor. I knew the name rang a bell. Then I remembered Sentís mentioning that Dr. Shelley had been Mijail Kolvenik's first friend when he came to Barcelona."

Marina studied me. "And you, to celebrate, have done more than just check the telephone directory. Silly of me to even ask, I imagine."

"I called," I admitted. "Dr. Shelley's daughter, María, answered. I told her it was of the utmost importance that we speak to her father."

"And did she consent to that?"

"Not at first, but when I mentioned Mijail Kolvenik's name, her voice changed. Her father has agreed to see us."

"When?"

I checked my watch.

"In about forty minutes."

We took the metro all the way down to Plaza Cataluña. It was beginning to get dark when we climbed the steps of the Ramblas exit. Christmas was approaching and the city was decked with garlands of light. The street lamps cast multicolored specters over the boulevard. Flocks of pigeons fluttered about between flower stalls and cafés, street musicians and showgirls, tourists and locals, policemen and crooks, citizens and ghosts from bygone eras. Germán was right: There wasn't another street in the whole world like it.

The outline of the Liceo rose before us. It was an opera night and a tiara of lights sparkled above the canopies. On the other side of the boulevard we recognized the green dragon from the photograph, protruding from the corner of a façade and holding a lantern in its claws as it gazed down at the crowds. When I saw it I thought that history might have reserved the altars and chapels for St. George, but the dragon had been granted the entire city of Barcelona in perpetuity.

Dr. Shelley's former office occupied the first floor of a stately turn-of-the-century building that gave off a vaguely funereal air. We ventured into its cavernous lobby to find a grand marble staircase that ascended in a spiral. On our way up I noticed that each of the door knockers was shaped like an angel's face. The skylight at the top of the stairwell, made up of stained-glass panes like those in a cathedral rose window, gave the visitor the impression of being inside the largest kaleidoscope in the world. As in most buildings of that time, the first floor turned out to be the third. We walked past the mezzanine, then the so-called main floor, before we reached the door on which an old bronze nameplate announced DR. JOAN SHELLEY. I looked at my watch. There were two minutes to go before the agreed time when Marina rang the doorbell.

The woman who opened the door looked as if she'd walked straight out of a religious painting: wraithlike and virginal, with skin so pale it was almost transparent and eyes so light they were practically colorless.

"Señora Shelley?" I asked politely.

She nodded, her unblinking eyes suddenly alight with something akin to curiosity.

"Good afternoon," I began. "My name is Oscar. I spoke to you this morning."

"I remember. Come in. Come in."

She ushered us in. María Shelley moved about like a ballerina leaping over clouds in slow motion. She had a fragile constitution and smelled of rose water. I estimated she was probably in her early thirties, but she looked younger. One of her wrists was bandaged and she wore a handkerchief tied around her swanlike neck. The entrance hall was lined with velvet and smoky mirrors. The house smelled like a museum, as if the air floating in it had been trapped there for decades.

"Thank you very much for receiving us. This is my friend Marina."

María's eyes rested on Marina. I've always found it fascinating to see how women examine one another. That occasion was no exception.

"Pleased to meet you," María Shelley said at last, dragging out each word. "My father is an elderly man. His temper is rather volatile. I beg you not to tire him."

"Don't worry," said Marina.

María Shelley asked us to follow her inside, walking ahead of us with an ethereal agility.

"And you say you have something that belonged to the late Señor Kolvenik?" she asked.

"Did you know him?" I asked in turn.

Her face lit up as she remembered past times.

"Not really. I heard a lot about him, though. As a child," she said, almost to herself.

The walls, clad in black velvet, were filled with images of saints, Madonnas, and martyrs in agony. Dark carpets absorbed what little light crept in through the cracks in the closed shutters. As we followed our host down that corridor I wondered how long she'd been living there, alone with her father. Had she married? Had she lived, loved, or felt anything outside the oppressive world within those walls?

María Shelley stopped in front of a sliding door and rapped with her knuckles.

"Father?"

———

Dr. Shelley, or what remained of him, sat in an armchair facing the fireplace under layers of blankets. His daughter left us alone with him. I tried not to look at her tiny waist as she withdrew. The elderly doctor, in whom it was hard to recognize the man in the photograph I had in my pocket, examined us in silence. His eyes oozed suspicion. One of his hands shook slightly on the arm of the chair. His body smelled of illness under a mask of eau de cologne. His sarcastic smile didn't hide the displeasure he felt at the world and at his own predicament.

"Time does to the body what stupidity does to the soul," he said, pointing at himself. "It rots it. What is it you two want?"

"We were wondering whether you could talk to us about Mijail Kolvenik."

"I could, but I don't see why I should," snapped the doctor. "Too much was said at the time, and it was all lies. If people stopped to consider even a quarter of what they say, this world would be paradise."

"Yes, but we are interested in the truth," I said.

The old man grimaced mockingly.

"Truth cannot be found, son. *It* finds *you*."

I tried to smile meekly, but I was beginning to suspect that Dr. Shelley wasn't going to say a word. Guessing at my thoughts, Marina took the initiative.

"Dr. Shelley," she said sweetly, "a collection of photographs that may have belonged to Mijail Kolvenik has accidentally come into our hands. You're in one of these pictures, standing next to one of your patients. That's why we've dared to bother you, in the hope that we'll be able to return the collection to its rightful owner or to whomever it may concern."

This time there was no scathing reply. The doctor looked at Marina without concealing his surprise. I wondered why that trick hadn't occurred to me. I decided that the more I let Marina take the lead in the conversation, the better.

"I don't know what photographs you're talking about, young lady."

"It's a medical file showing patients affected by malformations," Marina explained.

The doctor's eyes lit up. We'd touched a nerve. There was life beneath those blankets after all.

"What makes you think that the collection belongs to Mijail Kolvenik?" he asked, trying to sound indifferent. "Or that I have anything to do with it?"

"Your daughter told us you two were friends," said Marina, moving away from the subject.

"One of María's virtues is her naïveté," Shelley snapped.

Marina nodded, stood up, and signaled to me to do the same.

"I understand," she said politely. "I see we were mistaken. We're sorry to have bothered you, Dr. Shelley. Come on, Oscar. I'm sure we'll find someone else we can give the collection—"

"Just a moment," Shelley interrupted.

After clearing his throat he asked us to sit down again. "Do you still have it?"

Marina nodded, holding the old man's gaze. Suddenly Shelley let out what I thought was a laugh. It sounded like the pages of an old newspaper being crumpled.

"How do I know you're telling the truth?"

Marina gave me a knowing look. I pulled the photograph out of my pocket and handed it to Dr. Shelley. He picked it up with a trembling hand and examined it for a long time. Finally, turning his eyes toward the open fire, he began to talk.

Dr. Shelley told us he was the son of a British father and a Catalan mother. He'd specialized as an orthopedic surgeon in a Bournemouth hospital. When he settled in Barcelona, he soon realized that the fact that he was a foreigner and had no connections excluded him from the social circles in which promising careers were forged. Despite being more qualified, better trained, and more willing to work than any of his competitors, the best post he could get was in the prison's medical unit. That is where he met and treated Mijail Kolvenik after his brutal beating in jail. At that time Kolvenik didn't speak any Spanish or Catalan, but luckily Shelley spoke a little German. The fact that the two were outsiders learning the cold truth about the inner workings of the city helped to establish a bond between them. Shelley lent Kolvenik some money to buy new clothes, put him up in his house, and helped him find a job at Velo-Granell Industries. Kolvenik grew immensely fond of Shelley and never forgot his kindness. A deep friendship was born between them.

Later, that friendship would also develop into a

professional relationship. Many of Dr. Shelley's patients required complex orthopedic contraptions and custom-designed prostheses. Velo-Granell was the leading company in the field, and among its designers none was more talented than Mijail Kolvenik. In time, Shelley became Kolvenik's personal doctor. Once fortune smiled on him, Kolvenik helped his friend by funding a medical center specializing in the study and treatment of degenerative diseases and congenital deformities.

Kolvenik's interest in the subject went back to his childhood in Prague. Shelley told us that Mijail Kolvenik's mother had given birth to twins. One of them, Mijail, was born strong and healthy. The other, Andrej, came into the world with an incurable malformation of his bones and muscles that would end his life before he reached his seventh birthday. This episode marked young Mijail Kolvenik's early life and, in a way, determined his vocation. Kolvenik always believed that with proper medical attention and access to the technical advances that would have provided what nature had refused him, his brother could have reached adulthood and lived a full life. That belief was what led him to devote his efforts to the creation of mechanisms that, as he liked to say, could "complete" the bodies that fate had swept aside.

"Nature is like a careless child playing with our

lives. When it tires of its broken toys, it abandons them and replaces them with others," Kolvenik said. "It's our responsibility to pick up the pieces and rebuild them."

Some people thought these words denoted arrogance, even blasphemy; others, less fortunate in the cards life had dealt them, saw only hope in them. The tragic memory of his brother never left Mijail Kolvenik. The way he saw it, only cruel, whimsical chance had decided that he should live whereas his brother should be born with death written all over his body. Shelley explained that Kolvenik felt guilty about it, and that at the bottom of his heart felt he owed a debt to Andrej and to all those who, like his brother, were branded with the stigma of imperfection. It was around this time that Kolvenik began to collect photographs from all over the world of patients afflicted with terrible deformities and crippling disabilities. For him, those beings who had been abandoned by fate, God's forgotten children, were Andrej's invisible brothers. His family.

"Mijail Kolvenik was a brilliant man," Dr. Shelley continued. "People tend to become wary of individuals like him because their brilliance reminds them of their own mediocrity. Envy is a blind man who wants to pull out your eyes. What was said about Mijail in his later years and after his death was nothing but slander....It was most unfortunate. That accursed Inspector...Florián. He didn't understand that he was being used as an instrument to bring about Mijail's downfall—"

"Florián?" Marina interrupted him.

"Florián was the chief inspector of the fraud squad," said Shelley, with as much scorn as his vocal cords permitted. "A social climber, a worm who tried to make a name for himself at the expense of Velo-Granell Industries and Mijail Kolvenik. My only consolation is knowing that he was never able to prove anything. His obstinacy ended his career. He was the one who came up with all that scandal about the bodies...."

"Bodies?"

Shelley sank into a long silence. He looked at us and the cynical grin emerged again.

"This Inspector Florián," Marina asked. "Do you know where we might find him?"

"Probably in a circus, with the rest of the clowns," Shelley replied.

"Did you know Benjamín Sentís, Dr. Shelley?" I asked, trying to redirect the conversation.

"Of course," replied Shelley. "I used to see him regularly. As Kolvenik's partner, Sentís was in charge of the administrative side of Velo-Granell. A greedy man who didn't know his place in the world, in my opinion. Rotten with envy."

"Did you know that Sentís's body was discovered a week ago in the sewers?" I asked.

"I read the papers," he replied coldly.

"Didn't you find that strange?"

"No stranger than anything else that is printed in the papers," said Shelley. "The world is sick. And I'm beginning to get tired. Will that be all?"

I was going to ask him about the lady in black but Marina anticipated me, shaking her head with a smile. Shelley reached for the cord of the service bell and pulled it. María Shelley appeared, her eyes glued to her feet.

"These youngsters are leaving, María. Kindly show them out."

"Yes, Father."

We stood up. I made as if to take back the photograph, but the doctor's shaky hand stopped me.

"I'm keeping this, if you don't mind."

With those words he turned his back on us and gestured to his daughter to accompany us to the door. Just before we left the library I turned to have a last look at the doctor and saw him throw the picture into the fire. His glassy eyes watched it burn in the flames.

María Shelley led us quietly to the hall and then smiled apologetically.

"My father is a difficult man, but he has a good heart," she explained. "Life has dealt him many blows, and sometimes his moods get the better of him."

She opened the door for us and turned on the light on the landing. I noticed a glimmer of doubt in her eyes, as if she wanted to say something but was reluctant to do so. Reluctant or afraid. Marina also noticed this and offered her hand as a sign of gratitude. María Shelley shook it. Loneliness poured out of that woman's pores like cold sweat.

"I don't know what my father has told you," she said, lowering her voice and looking behind her fearfully.

"María?" came the doctor's voice from inside the flat. "Who are you talking to?"

A shadow fell over María's face.

"Coming, Father, coming…"

She gave us one last desolate look and stepped back inside. As she turned, I noticed a small medal hanging from a chain around her neck. I could have sworn it was in the shape of a butterfly with open wings. The door closed before I could make sure. We were left standing on the landing, listening to the thundering voice of the doctor as he vented his fury on his daughter. The light on the landing went out. For a moment I thought I detected a smell of decomposing flesh. It came from somewhere on the staircase, as if a dead animal were lying there in the dark. Then I thought I could hear footsteps fading away above us and the smell, or the impression, disappeared.

"Let's get out of here," I said.

FOURTEEN

On our way back to Marina's house I noticed that she was looking at me out of the corner of her eye.

"Aren't you going to spend Christmas with your family?" she asked.

I shrugged, staring at the traffic. "Probably not."

"Why not?"

I sighed, scrambling for words.

"You could say my family is, I don't know...complicated. We haven't spent Christmas together for years. My parents are too busy hating each other for us to get together."

"But I'm sure they love you," Marina offered.

I smiled to myself, biting my words.

"Not everybody is like you and Germán," I said at last.

My voice had sounded unintentionally harsh and hostile.

"I'm sorry, Oscar. I didn't mean to pry."

I nodded weakly, feigning indifference. "It's okay. I prefer it this way, really."

She nodded, and I avoided her eyes. We walked on in silence for a while. I accompanied Marina to the gates of the old mansion and said good-bye to her.

———

As I approached the school it began to rain. I looked up at the distant row of windows on the fourth floor. Only a couple of them had their lights on. Most of the boarders had left for the Christmas holidays and wouldn't return for another three weeks. Every year it was the same. The boarding school became almost empty, with only a couple of poor souls left behind in the tutors' care. The two previous years had been the worst, but this year it felt different. I had not lied when I told Marina I preferred it this way. The very idea of leaving her and Germán was unthinkable. As long as I was close to them I wouldn't feel lonely.

Once again I walked up the stairs to my room. The

corridor was silent. That whole wing was deserted. I imagined that the only person left would be Doña Paula, a widow in charge of the cleaning who lived by herself in a small apartment on the third floor. I thought I could hear the incessant murmur of her television set on the floor below. I walked past the row of empty bedrooms until I reached mine and opened the door. A roll of thunder roared above the city and the whole building trembled. The glow from the flash of lightning pierced through the closed shutters. I lay down on my bed without removing my clothes and heard the storm unleashing itself in the dark. Then I opened the drawer on my bedside table and pulled out the pencil sketch Germán had made of Marina the day we went to the beach. I gazed at it until fatigue bore down on me and I fell asleep holding it as if it were an amulet. When I awoke, the portrait had disappeared from my hands.

I opened my eyes with a start. I was shivering with cold and could feel the breath of the wind on my face. The window was wide open and the rain was cascading into the room. I sat up in a daze, groped around the bedside table in the dark, and pressed the light switch in vain: There was no power. It was then I realized that the portrait I was holding when I fell asleep was no longer in my hands, or on the bed, or on the floor. I rubbed my eyes, trying to understand. Suddenly I noticed it. Intense and penetrating. That stench of rot. In the air. In the room. On my own clothes, as if someone had rubbed the carcass of a decomposing animal over my skin while I slept. It made me retch, and a second later panic took hold of me. I wasn't alone. Someone or something had come in through the window while I slept.

Slowly, fumbling my way past the furniture, I reached the door. I tried turning on the main light; nothing. I peered into the corridor, but it was cloaked in shadow. I could smell the odor again, more intensely, like the trail of a wild animal. A moment later I thought I could see a figure entering the last room in the corridor.

"Doña Paula?" I called, almost in a whisper.

The door closed gently. Taking a deep breath, I stepped into the corridor and walked slowly down, my eyes trained on that last door. I was only a few meters away when I heard a chilling sound, like the hiss of a snake. It was murmuring a word. My name. I froze. The voice came from within the closed bedroom.

"Doña Paula, is that you?" I stammered, trying to control the trembling in my hands.

The voice repeated my name. It was a voice such as I'd never heard before. A broken whisper, cruel and poisoned with evil. I was stranded in the corridor, incapable of moving a single muscle. All of a sudden the bedroom door flew open. In the space of a seemingly endless second I thought the corridor was narrowing and shrinking under my feet, pulling me toward that door.

I could quite clearly distinguish something shining on the bed in the middle of the room. It was Marina's picture, the one I was clasping when I fell asleep. Two wooden hands, puppet's hands, were clutching it now. Bits of bloodstained wire protruded from the bases of the wrists. I knew then, with absolute certainty, that those were the hands Benjamín Sentís had lost in the depths of the sewers. They'd been torn off. I felt the air leaving my lungs.

The stench was becoming unbearable, corrosive. And in the lucidity that comes with panic, I noticed the figure hanging motionless on the wall. It was dressed in black, with its arms open wide. A mesh of tangled hair covered its face. As I stood by the door, I watched it raise its head with infinite slowness, displaying a smile of bright wolfish teeth in the dark. Under its gloves, claws began to move like bundles of snakes. I took a step back and once again heard that voice whispering my name. The figure was creeping toward me like a giant spider.

I let out a scream and slammed the door shut. I was trying to lock it from the outside when it shook violently as ten nails, sharp as knives, cut through the wood.

I started running to the other end of the corridor and heard the door being smashed to pieces. The corridor seemed to have turned into an endless tunnel. I could see the staircase a few meters farther on and turned my head to look behind me. The nightmarish silhouette was gliding straight toward me, the glow from its eyes piercing the darkness. I was trapped.

Taking advantage of the fact that I knew every nook and cranny of the school, I flung myself down the stairs and along the corridor leading to the kitchen. I closed the door behind me, but it was useless. The creature threw itself against it, knocking it down and tossing me to the floor. I rolled over the tiles and took shelter beneath a table. I spied a pair of legs. All around me dozens of plates and glasses were being smashed, spreading a blanket of broken glass. I glimpsed the edge of a serrated knife among the debris and frantically grabbed it. The figure squatted in front of me, like a wolf at the mouth of a warren. I wielded the knife close to its face and the blade sank in as if it were plunging into mud. I heard a muffled cry as the figure pulled away, and I was able to escape to the other end of the kitchen, looking for something else to defend myself with as I moved backward, step by step. I found a drawer and opened it. Cutlery, kitchen utensils, candles, a lighter...Instinctively I seized the lighter and tried to ignite it. I could see the shadow of the creature rising before me and smelled its foul breath. One of its claws was drawing close to my throat. Just then the lighter finally produced a flame that shone on the creature, now only a foot away. I closed my eyes and held my breath, convinced that I'd seen the face of death and all I could do was wait. The wait became eternal.

When I opened my eyes again, the creature had gone. I heard its footsteps fading away and followed it as it made its way to my bedroom. I thought I heard a groan, a sound that seemed full of pain or anger. When I reached my room, I peered around the door. The creature was rummaging through my backpack. It grabbed the photograph album I'd taken from the greenhouse, then turned. We stared at each other. The ghostly glow of the night outlined the intruder for a tenth of a second. I wanted to say something, but the creature had already leaped out the window.

I ran to the windowsill and looked out, expecting to see the body falling into the void. The figure was sliding down the drainpipe at an incredible speed, its black cloak flapping in the wind. From there it jumped onto the roof of the east wing, where it dodged through a forest of gargoyles and turrets. Paralyzed, I watched the hellish apparition move away beneath the storm, performing astonishing leaps, like a panther, as if the roofs of Barcelona were its jungle. I realized that the window frame was covered in blood. I followed the trail back to the corridor. It took me a while to understand that the blood was not mine. I'd wounded a human being with the knife. I leaned against the wall. My knees were giving way and I crouched down, exhausted.

I don't know how long I remained like that. When I managed to stand up, I decided to go to the only place where I thought I would feel safe.

FIFTEEN

I reached Marina's house and, groping my way through the garden, walked around the building and headed for the kitchen. A warm glow flickered through the shutters. I felt relieved. I rapped on the door and, finding it open, walked in. Despite the late hour, Marina was writing in her notebook, sitting at the kitchen table in the candlelight with Kafka on her lap. When she saw me the pen fell out of her hand.

"Good God, Oscar! What...?" she cried, staring at my torn, dirty clothes and feeling the scratches on my face. "What happened to you?"

———

After a cup or two of hot tea I managed to tell Marina what had just happened—or what I thought had happened, because I was beginning to question my own sanity. She listened to me, holding my hand between hers to calm me down. I probably looked even worse than I thought.

"You don't mind if I spend the night here? I didn't know where to go. And I don't want to go back to the school."

"Of course. I wouldn't let you go back there, anyway. You can stay with us as long as you need to."

"Thanks."

I could read in her eyes the same anxiety that was gnawing at me: After what had happened that night, her house was no safer than the school or any other place. The presence that had been following us knew where to find us.

"What are we going to do now, Oscar?"

"We could look for the inspector Dr. Shelley mentioned—Florián—and try to find out what's really going on. . . ."

Marina sighed.

"Listen, perhaps I'd better leave," I ventured.

"Definitely not. I'll get a bedroom ready for you upstairs, next to mine. Come."

"What . . . what will Germán say?"

"Germán will be delighted. We'll tell him you're going to spend Christmas with us."

I followed her up the stairs. I'd never been on the upper floor. A corridor with carved oak doors on either side stretched out in the candlelight. My room was at the end of the passage, next to Marina's. The furniture looked like a collection of antiques, but it was all very neat and tidy.

"The sheets are clean," Marina said, pulling back the bedspread. "There are more blankets in the wardrobe, in case you feel cold. And here are some towels. Let's see if I can find you a pair of Germán's pajamas."

"They'll look like a tent on me," I joked.

"Better to err on the side of generosity. I'll be back in a sec."

Her footsteps faded away down the corridor. I left my clothes on a chair and slipped between the clean starched sheets. I'd never felt so tired in my life. My eyelids had turned into leaden slabs. When she returned, Marina was carrying some sort of nightgown about two meters long, which looked as if it had been handpicked from Kaiser Wilhelm's collection of long johns.

"Good Lord," I whispered. "With all due respect..."

"Sorry, but it's all I could find. Give it a shot. I'm sure it will look great on you. It's the man that makes the clothes, not the other way around. Besides, Germán doesn't allow me to have naked boys sleeping here. House rules."

She threw the nightgown at me and left a couple of candles on a small table.

"If you need anything, bang on the wall. I'm on the other side."

For a moment we gazed at each other without saying a word. Finally Marina looked away.

"Good night, Oscar," she whispered.

"Good night."

When I awoke the room was bathed in soft, coppery light. My window faced east and I could see the bright sun rising over the city. Before getting up I noticed that my clothes had disappeared from the chair where I'd left them the night before. I realized what this meant and cursed so much kindness, convinced that Marina had done it on purpose. The smell of warm bread and fresh coffee filtered under the door. Having abandoned all hope of preserving my dignity, I prepared to go downstairs attired in that ridiculous nightgown. I stepped into the corridor and heard the voices of my hosts chatting in the kitchen. I plucked up my courage and walked down the stairs, then paused in the doorway and cleared my throat. Marina was pouring coffee for Germán, and she looked up.

"Good morning, sleeping beauty," she said.

Germán turned and stood up courteously, offering me his hand and a chair at the table.

"Good morning, my dear Oscar," he said enthusiastically. "It's a pleasure to have you with us. Marina has already told me about the building work in the school dormitories. You can stay here as long as you want. I mean it. Make yourself at home."

"Thank you so much."

Marina poured coffee into my cup, smiling conspiratorially as she pointed at my nightgown.

"Looks great on you."

"Divine. Where are my clothes?"

"They spent the night under the effects of soap and water. Don't worry. I left them outside to dry early this morning."

Germán passed me a tray full of croissants, fresh out of the Foix bakery and still warm. My mouth watered.

"Try one of these, Oscar," Germán suggested. "It's the Mercedes-Benz of croissants. And make sure to try that jam. Outstanding."

I wolfed down everything that was put in front of me like a castaway just rescued from a raft after weeks at sea. Germán was leafing distractedly through a newspaper. He seemed to be in good spirits, and although he'd already finished his breakfast, he didn't get up until I was full and there was nothing left for me to eat other than the cutlery and the napkins. Then he checked his watch.

"You're going to be late for your meeting with the priest, Dad," Marina reminded him.

Germán nodded, looking slightly annoyed.

"I don't know why I bother," he said. "The rogue cheats like a horse trader."

"It's the uniform," said Marina. "It gives him a sense of entitlement."

I looked at both of them, puzzled. I couldn't follow a word of what they were saying.

"Chess," explained Marina. "Germán and the priest have been sparring for years."

"Never challenge a Jesuit to chess, Oscar, my friend. Trust me. Now, if you'll excuse me…" Germán said, standing up.

"Of course. Good luck."

Germán took his overcoat, his hat, and his ebony cane and set off for his meeting with the scheming prelate. As soon as he'd left, Marina went out into the garden and returned with my clothes.

"I'm afraid Kafka slept on them."

The clothes were dry, but the cat's scent wasn't going to disappear, not even after five washes.

"Come on, get dressed."

"What's the rush?"

"This morning, when I went out to get the breakfast, I called the police station from the bar in the square. Inspector Víctor Florián is retired and lives in Vallvidrera. He doesn't have a phone, but they gave me an address."

"I'll be dressed in a minute."

The station for the Vallvidrera funicular was a few streets down from Marina's house. Walking briskly, we got there within ten minutes and bought our tickets. From the platform, at the foot of the mountain, the district of Vallvidrera looked like a balcony suspended from the sky above the city. The houses seemed to be nestling on the clouds, held aloft by invisible strings. We sat at the end of the carriage and saw Barcelona unfold at our feet as the funicular slowly crept uphill.

"This must be a good job to have," I said. "Funicular driver. Like being heaven's lift attendant."

Marina looked at me skeptically.

"What's wrong with what I said?" I asked.

"Nothing. If that's all you aspire to."

"I don't know what I aspire to. Not everyone sees things as clearly as you. Marina Blau, Nobel Prize in Literature and nightshirt curator for the Doge of Venice collection."

162

Marina looked so serious that I instantly regretted making the comment.

"If you don't know where you're going, you won't get anywhere," she replied coldly.

I showed her my ticket. "I know where I'm going."

She looked away. We continued our upward journey in silence for a couple of minutes. The outline of my school rose in the distance.

"Architect," I whispered.

"What?"

"I want to be an architect. That's what I aspire to. I've never told anyone."

At last she smiled at me. The funicular, rattling like an old washing machine, was reaching the top of the mountain.

"I've always wanted to have my own cathedral," said Marina. "Any suggestions?"

"Let's make it Gothic. Give me time and I'll build it for you."

The sun hit her face and her eyes shone, fixed on mine.

"Promise?" she asked, offering an open palm.

I shook her hand tightly. "Promise."

The address Marina had obtained led us to a small villa standing practically on the edge of an abyss. The place was overgrown with thick shrubbery. A rusty and rather ornate mailbox stood at the front among the vegetation, like a ruin from the industrial age. We slipped through the garden and made our way to the door. We could see crates containing piles of old newspapers tied together with string. The ocher paint on the façade was peeling off like dry skin, withered by the wind and the damp. Inspector Víctor Florián didn't go overboard on keeping up appearances.

"This place really needs an architect," said Marina.

"Or a demolition unit."

I knocked gently on the door. I was afraid that if I knocked any harder, I might send the house tumbling down the mountain.

"How about using the doorbell?"

The bell button was broken and the electric connections in the box seemed to date back to Edison's day.

"I'm not sticking my finger in there," I replied, knocking again.

Suddenly the door opened some ten centimeters. A security chain shone in front of two steely eyes that were scrutinizing us.

"Who's there?"

"Víctor Florián?"

"That's me. What I'm asking is who *you* are."

It was an authoritarian voice without a hint of patience. A voice that might give out parking tickets.

"We have some information regarding Mijail Kolvenik," Marina said by way of introduction.

The door opened wide. Víctor Florián was thickset and muscular. If someone had told me he was wearing the same suit as the day he retired, I would not have doubted it for a second. He had the air of a fiery old colonel with no war to wage and no battalion to command. If retirement requires a certain degree of peace of mind and an easy conscience, Víctor Florián did not appear to have much of either. He held an unlit cigar in his mouth and had more hair in each eyebrow than most people have on their entire head.

"What do you know about Kolvenik? Who are you? Who gave you this address?"

Florián didn't ask questions, he machine-gunned them. He showed us in after taking a look outside as if he thought we might have been followed. Indoors, the house was a nest of filth and smelled like a dusty storeroom. There were more papers there than in the archives of Barcelona's central library, but they were all jumbled together as if an electric fan had been used to arrange them.

"Come through to the back," he commanded.

We went past a room where we saw dozens of firearms

in a cabinet covering one of the walls. Revolvers, automatic pistols, Mauser rifles, bayonets...Revolutions had been started with less artillery than that.

"Lord almighty," I whispered.

"Shut up—you're not at mass," Florián snapped, closing the door on his arsenal.

The back he had mentioned was a small dining room facing the edge of the hill from which one could view the whole of Barcelona. Old habits never die: Even in his years of retirement the inspector continued to watch from above. He pointed to a sofa, full of holes. I wondered if he'd been chasing the cockroaches away with one of his vintage World War II guns. On the table were a half-empty tin of beans and an Estrella Dorada beer without a glass. *A policeman's pension buys you less than a prison meal*, I thought. Florián sat on a chair facing us and picked up a cheap-looking alarm clock. He placed it on the table in front of us.

"Fifteen minutes. If in a quarter of an hour you haven't told me something I don't know, I'll kick you out of here," he said, clearly meaning it.

It took us longer than fifteen minutes to recount everything that had happened to us. As he listened to our story, Víctor Florián's front seemed to crack little by little. Through the chinks I glimpsed what I guessed was a worn and frightened man who hid in that hole with his

166

old newspapers and his gun collection. When we'd finished our account Florián took his cigar and, after examining it quietly for almost a minute, decided to light it. *It must be that sort of day*, I thought.

Then, with his gaze lost in the mirage of the misty city, he began to speak.

SIXTEEN

In 1945 I was made inspector of the Barcelona fraud squad," Florián began. "I'd been considering asking for a transfer to Madrid when I was assigned the Velo-Granell case. Nobody wanted it. For three years the squad had been investigating Mijail Kolvenik, a foreigner with few friends among the new regime, but they hadn't been able to prove anything. Not that we necessarily had to prove things to make them stick back then. But this was a hard nut to crack. We didn't really know what we were looking for. My predecessor in the post had given up. The Velo-Granell company was surrounded by a wall of lawyers and a maze of financial fronts where everything got lost in a cloud. My superiors sold the job to me as a career-making move. That usually means career suicide. But there was a lot of pressure from high up. Cases like that can set you up in a ministerial office with a driver and all the free time of a lord, they told me. I was young and stupid. I believed what I wanted to believe. Ambition is a foolish thing...."

Florián paused, savoring his words and smiling sarcastically to himself. He nibbled his cigar as if it were a licorice twig.

"When I studied the case file," he went on, "I realized that what had started as a routine investigation into financial irregularities and even possible fraud had turned into a matter that nobody was quite sure which department should take on. Extortion. Theft. Attempted homicide.... And there were other things.... You must understand that until then my experience had been centered on investigating embezzlement, tax evasion, fraud... the national pastimes. Not that those irregularities were always punished in those days. It all came down to who you were, and your connections to the regime. But even when we did not act—and that happened often—we knew everything."

Florián submerged himself in a blue cloud of his own smoke. I wondered how long it had been since he had last enjoyed one of his cigars. He looked flustered.

"Then why did you accept the case?" Marina asked.

"Out of arrogance. Out of ambition and greed," Florián replied, as if to himself, in the same tone, I imagined, that he reserved for the most hardened criminals.

"Perhaps also to discover the truth," I ventured. "To deliver justice."

Florián smiled sadly at me. One could read thirty years of regrets in that look.

"By the end of 1945 Velo-Granell Industries was already technically bankrupt," Florián continued. "The three main Barcelona banks had canceled their lines of credit, and trading in the company shares had been suspended. When the capital reserves evaporated, the legal firewall and the network of shell companies collapsed like a house of cards. The glory days were over. The Gran Teatro Real, which had been closed since the tragedy that disfigured Eva Irinova on her wedding day, had become a ruin. The factory and workshops had closed down. Rumors spread like gangrene. Never one to lose his sangfroid, Kolvenik decided to organize a luxurious cocktail party in La Lonja, the old exchange building, in order to project an air of calm and normality. His partner, Sentís, was on the verge of panic. There were not enough funds in the company's coffers to cover even the appetizers ordered for the event. Invitations were sent out to all the big shareholders, the four hundred top Barcelona families.... The night of the party the rain was bucketing down. La Lonja was decked out like a dream palace. After nine o'clock servants from the city's wealthiest households—many of whose fortunes were in part due to Kolvenik—began to turn up to present their employers' excuses. By the time I arrived, around midnight, I found Kolvenik alone in the room, in his impeccable tails, smoking a cigarette of the sort he imported from Vienna. He greeted me and offered me a glass of the most expensive champagne. 'Eat something, Inspector; it's a shame to waste all this food,' he said. We had never met face-to-face. We chatted for an hour. He talked to me about books he'd read as a youngster, about journeys he'd never managed to make.... Kolvenik was a charismatic man. His eyes burned with intelligence. However hard I tried not to, I couldn't help liking him. Indeed, I felt sorry for him, although I was supposed to be the hunter and he the prey. I noticed that he limped and leaned on a carved ivory cane. 'I don't think anyone has ever lost so many friends in one day,' I said. He smiled and calmly rejected the idea. 'You're mistaken, Inspector. One never invites one's friends to events such as this.' He asked me politely whether I was planning to continue persecuting him. I said I wouldn't stop until I'd taken him to court. I remember that he asked me,

'What could I do to dissuade you, dear Florián?' 'Kill me,' I answered. 'Everything in due course, Inspector,' he replied with a smile. With those words he walked away, limping. I didn't see him again after that night. Yet here I am, still alive. Or something like it. For some reason Kolvenik didn't fulfill his last threat. Odd. He wasn't a man to leave any business unfinished."

Florián paused again and took a sip of water, relishing it as if it were the last glassful in the world. He licked his lips and continued with his narrative.

"From that day on, isolated and abandoned by everyone, Kolvenik lived secluded with his wife in the grotesque fortress he'd had built for himself by Güell Park. Nobody saw him during the following years. Only two people had access to him: his old chauffeur, Lluís Claret, a poor wretch who adored Kolvenik and refused to abandon him even when he couldn't pay him his salary; and his personal doctor, Dr. Shelley, whom we were also investigating. Nobody else saw Kolvenik. And Shelley's assurance that Kolvenik was secluded in his mansion, suffering from some illness that he couldn't explain to us, didn't convince us in the least, especially after we had a look through his files and accounts. For a time we even suspected that Kolvenik had died or fled abroad, and that it was all a sham. Shelley continued to maintain that Kolvenik had caught some rare disease that kept him confined to his house. He wasn't allowed to receive visitors or leave his refuge under any circumstances; those were the doctor's orders. Neither we nor the judge believed him. On December 31, 1948, we obtained a warrant to search Kolvenik's home, as well as an arrest warrant. A large amount of the company's confidential documents had disappeared, and we suspected that they were hidden somewhere in the mansion. We'd already gathered enough evidence to charge Kolvenik with conspiracy to commit fraud and tax evasion. There was no point in waiting any longer. The last day of 1948 was going to be Kolvenik's last day of freedom. A special unit was preparing to turn up at his address the following morning. Sometimes, when it comes to major criminals, you have to resign yourself to getting them on some minor technicality...."

Florián's cigar had gone out again. The inspector took a last look at it and then let it fall into an empty flowerpot. There were other such remains there, a sort of common grave for cigar butts.

"But of course things didn't go according to plan. That same night, just hours before we could apprehend him after years of playing cat and mouse, a terrible fire destroyed the house and ended the lives of Kolvenik and his wife, Eva. At dawn the two charred bodies were discovered in the attic, locked in an embrace.... Our hopes of closing the case had burned along with them. I never doubted that the fire had been started deliberately. For a while I thought that Benjamín Sentís and other members of the firm's board of directors were behind it."

"Sentís?" I interrupted.

"It was no secret that Sentís loathed Kolvenik for having taken control of his father's company, but both he and the other directors had further reasons to wish the case would never reach the courts. Dead dogs don't bite, and without Kolvenik the jigsaw puzzle didn't fit together. It could be said that a lot of bloodstained hands were cleansed in the fire that night. And yet, once again, just like everything related to that scandal from day one, it was impossible to prove anything. Everything ended in ashes. The investigation into Velo-Granell Industries is still our police department's greatest mystery. And the greatest failure of my life."

"But the fire wasn't your fault," I said.

"Little did that matter. My career in the department was ruined, and I knew it. I was assigned to the anti-subversion unit. Do you know what that is? The ghost hunters. That is how they were known in the department. I would have left my post, but those were hard times, and I was supporting my brother and his family on my salary. Besides, nobody was going to give a job to an ex-policeman. People were tired of spies and informers. I had nowhere to go. So I stayed there. The work consisted of midnight raids on shabby boarding-houses packed with old pensioners and disabled war veterans, where we searched for copies of *Das Kapital* and socialist leaflets hidden in plastic bags in the lavatory cistern, that sort of thing.... At the beginning of 1949 I thought everything had ended for me. Everything that could have gone wrong had turned out even worse. At least, that's what I thought. At daybreak on December 13, 1949, almost a year after the fire in which Kolvenik and his wife died, the dismembered bodies of two inspectors from my old unit were discovered at the door of the old Velo-Granell warehouse, in the Borne district. It appears that they'd gone there to investigate an anonymous tip they'd received on the case. Turned out to be a trap. I wouldn't wish the death they encountered on my worst enemy. Even the wheels of a train can't do what was done to the bodies I saw in the morgue.... They were experienced policemen. Tough men. Armed. They knew what they were doing. The report said that some of the neighbors heard shots. Fourteen nine-millimeter shell cases were found at the crime scene. They were all from the inspectors' standard-issue weapons. Yet not a single bullet mark or bullet was found on the walls."

"How do you explain that?" asked Marina.

"There is no explanation. It's quite simply impossible.

But it happened....I saw the empty cartridges myself, and inspected the scene along with a forensic team."

Marina and I looked at each other.

"Could it be that the shots were aimed at a moving object, a car or a carriage for example, which absorbed the bullets and then vanished without a trace?" Marina suggested.

"Your friend here would make a good detective," Florián said to me. "That's the hypothesis we formulated at the time, but there was no evidence to support it. Bullets of that caliber usually bounce off metallic surfaces and leave a trail of impacts, or at least traces of shrapnel. Nothing was found.

"Some days later, at my colleagues' funeral, I bumped into Sentís," Florián continued. "He seemed worried, and looked as if he hadn't slept in days. His clothes were dirty and he reeked of booze. He confessed to me that he didn't dare go back home, that he'd been wandering around for days, sleeping in public spaces. 'My life isn't worth a damn, Florián,' he said to me. 'I'm a dead man walking.' I offered him police protection. He laughed. I even proposed that he take shelter in my home. He refused. 'I don't want to have your death on my conscience, Florián,' he said before disappearing into the crowd. During the next few months all the former members of the Velo-Granell executive board met their deaths, theoretically of natural causes. Heart attack was the doctor's diagnosis in most of the cases. One of them drowned in his own swimming pool. The body was still holding a gun when they fished it out. For the rest the circumstances were similar. They'd all been alone in their beds; it was always at midnight; and they were all found in the process of dragging themselves across the floor... trying to flee from a death that left no trace. All except Benjamín Sentís. I didn't speak to him again for thirty years, until a few weeks ago."

"Just before he died..." I remarked.

Florián nodded.

"He called the police station and asked to speak to me. He said he had information on the crimes in the factory and on the Velo-Granell case. I called him and spoke to him. I thought he was delirious. But I agreed to see him. Out of pity. We arranged to meet in a bar close to his place on Calle Princesa the following day. He didn't turn up. Two days later an old friend of mine from the police station called to tell me they'd found his body in an abandoned sewer in the old quarter. The artificial hands Kolvenik had created for him had been amputated. But that was in the papers. What the press didn't say was that the police found a word written in blood on the wall of the tunnel: *Teufel*."

"*Teufel*?"

"It's German," said Marina. "It means devil."

"It's also the name of Kolvenik's symbol," Florián revealed.

"The black butterfly?"

He nodded.

"Why is it called that?" asked Marina.

"I'm not an entomologist," he said. "I only know that Kolvenik collected them."

It was getting close to midday and Florián invited us to lunch in a small café near the station. We all felt like getting out of that house.

The café owner seemed to be a friend of Florián's. He led us to a table set aside in a corner by the window.

"A visit from the grandchildren, boss?" he asked, smiling.

Florián only nodded without attempting to explain. A waiter served us three generous slices of Spanish omelet and some bread rubbed with tomato and oil and sprinkled with salt. While we enjoyed the meal, which was delicious, Florián continued with his account.

"When I started investigating Velo-Granell Industries I discovered that Mijail Kolvenik didn't have a very clear past.... There was no record of his birth or nationality in Prague. I suspect Mijail was probably not his real name."

"Who was he, then?" I asked.

"I've been asking myself that same question for thirty years. In fact, when I got in touch with the police in Prague, I did discover there was one person named Mijail Kolvenik, but he appeared in the registers of the WolfterHaus."

"What's that?" I asked.

"An asylum. But I don't think Kolvenik was ever there. He simply adopted the name of one of the patients. Kolvenik wasn't mad."

"Why would Kolvenik steal the identity of a mental-hospital patient?" asked Marina.

"It wasn't that unusual at the time," Florián explained. "When there's a war going on, changing your identity can amount to being reborn, leaving an inconvenient past behind. You're very young and you haven't lived through a war. You don't really get to understand people until you've lived through one...."

"Did Kolvenik have anything to hide?" I asked. "If the Prague police had information about him, there must have been a reason."

"Pure coincidence, matching surnames. Bureaucracy. Believe me, I know what I'm talking about," said Florián. "Supposing the Kolvenik of their files was our Kolvenik, he left only a thin trail behind him. His name was mentioned in the investigation into the death of a surgeon in

Prague, a man named Antonin Kolvenik. The case was closed and the death attributed to natural causes."

"Why did they take that Mijail Kolvenik to a mental hospital?" Marina asked.

Florián hesitated for a few moments, as if he didn't dare reply.

"It was suspected he'd done something with the dead man's body."

"Something?"

"The Prague police didn't explain what it was," Florián answered dryly, lighting a cigarette.

We fell into a long silence.

"What about the story Dr. Shelley told us? About Kolvenik's twin brother, the degenerative illness and—"

"That's what Kolvenik told him. Kolvenik could lie just as easily as he breathed. And Shelley had good reasons to believe him without asking any questions," Florián said. "Kolvenik financed his medical institute and his research, down to the last *céntimo*. Shelley was almost like an employee at Velo-Granell Industries. A henchman."

"So Kolvenik's twin brother was another invention?" I was disconcerted. "His existence might justify Kolvenik's obsession with people afflicted with deformities and—"

"I don't think the brother was an invention," Florián cut in. "In my opinion."

"I don't follow."

"I think the child he spoke about was in fact himself."

Marina and I exchanged glances.

"One more question, Inspector…"

"I'm no longer an inspector, young lady."

"Víctor then. You're still Víctor, aren't you?"

That was the first time I saw Flórian smile in a relaxed and open way.

"What's the question?"

"You've told us that when you investigated the alleged Velo-Granell fraud you discovered there was something else…."

"Yes. At first we thought it was a typical ploy: expense accounts with nonexistent payments to avoid tax—payments made to hospitals, to shelters for the homeless, and so on—until one of my men found it odd that some sets of expenses that bore Dr. Shelley's signature and approval had been invoiced by the autopsy centers of various hospitals in Barcelona. In other words, by the mortuaries," the ex-policeman explained. "The morgue."

"Kolvenik sold corpses?" Marina suggested.

"No. He was buying them. By the dozen. Tramps. People who died without family or acquaintances. Men or women who had committed suicide or drowned, old people who'd been abandoned…The city's forgotten dead."

In the background the murmur of a radio drifted through the air like the echo of our conversation.

"And what did Kolvenik do with those corpses?"

"Nobody knows," Florián replied. "We never managed to find them."

"But you have a theory, don't you, Víctor?" Marina continued.

Florián gazed at us.

"No."

Even though he was a policeman—albeit a retired one—lying didn't suit him. Marina didn't press him. The inspector looked tired, consumed by shadows that poisoned his memories. All his fierceness had collapsed. The cigarette was shaking in his hands, and it was hard to tell who was doing the smoking—Florián or the cigarette.

"As for the greenhouse you've told me about, don't go back there. Forget the whole business. Forget the photograph album, the nameless grave and the lady who visits it. Forget Sentís, Shelley, and myself—I'm only a foolish old man who doesn't even know what he's saying. This matter has already destroyed enough lives. Leave it alone." He signaled to the waiter to add the bill to his account and concluded, "Promise you'll do as I say."

I wondered how we were going to stop pursuing the

matter when in fact it was the matter that was pursuing us. After what had happened the night before, his advice sounded like wishful thinking.

"We'll try," said Marina on behalf of both of us.

"Try hard. The road to hell is paved with good intentions," Florián replied.

The inspector accompanied us to the funicular station and gave us the telephone number of the café.

"They know me here. If you need anything, call them and they'll pass on the message. Any time of day or night. Manu, the owner, suffers from chronic insomnia and spends the night listening to the BBC, to see if he can learn languages. So you won't bother him."

"We don't know how to thank you."

"Thank me by following my advice and keeping out of this mess," Florián answered.

We nodded in agreement. The funicular car opened its doors.

"What about you, Víctor?" asked Marina. "What are you going to do?"

"What all old people do: sit down and remember, and ask myself what would have happened if I'd done everything differently. Go on, off you go...."

We stepped into the car and sat by the window. It

was starting to get dark. A whistle blew and the doors closed. The funicular began its descent with a jolt. Slowly, the lights of Vallvidrera were left behind, as was the figure of Florián, standing immobile on the platform.

———

Germán had prepared a delicious Italian dish with a name that sounded like the title of an opera. We had dinner in the kitchen, listening to his account of the chess tournament with the priest, who as usual had beaten him by dubious means. Marina was uncommonly quiet during the meal, leaving the weight of the conversation to Germán and me. I even wondered whether I'd said or done something that might have annoyed her. After dinner Germán challenged me to a game of chess.

"I'd love to, but I think it's my turn to wash up," I explained.

"I'll do the washing up," said Marina weakly, from behind my back.

"No, really," I objected.

Germán was already in the other room, singing softly to himself and lining up the rows of pawns. I turned toward Marina, who looked away and started to wash the dishes.

"Let me help you."

"No. Go in there with Germán. He'll be pleased."

"Are you coming, Oscar?" came Germán's voice from the other room.

I gazed at Marina in the light of the candles burning on the windowsill. I thought she looked pale, tired.

"Are you all right?"

She turned around and smiled. Marina had a way of smiling that made me feel small and insignificant.

"Go on. And let him win."

"That's easy."

I took her advice and left her alone, joining her father in the sitting room. There, under the quartz chandelier, I sat at the chessboard ready to let him enjoy the pleasant interlude his daughter wished for him.

"Your move, Oscar."

I moved. He cleared his throat.

"May I remind you that pawns can't jump like that, Oscar?"

"I beg your pardon."

"That's all right. It's the fire of youth. Believe me, I envy you. Youth is like a fickle girlfriend. We can't understand or value her until she goes off with someone else, never to return. . . . Dear me! I don't know where all that came from. Let's see . . . pawn . . ."

At midnight a sound pulled me out of a dream. The house was in darkness. I sat up in the bed and listened.

A cough—muffled, distant. Feeling uneasy, I got up and went out into the corridor. The sound came from the ground floor. I went past the door of Marina's bedroom. It was open, and her bed was empty. I felt a pang of fear.

"Marina?"

There was no reply. I tiptoed down the cold steps. Kafka's eyes shone at the bottom of the staircase. The cat meowed softly and led me along a dark corridor. At the end of it a thread of light glowed beneath a closed door. The cough came from inside. Painful. Agonizing. Kafka walked up to the door and stopped there, meowing. I rapped gently.

"Marina?"

A long silence.

"Go away, Oscar."

Her voice was a groan. I let a few seconds go by and then opened the door. A candle on the floor barely lit the white-tiled bathroom. Marina was kneeling, her forehead leaning against the washbasin. She was trembling and her perspiration made her nightdress cling to her skin like a shroud. She covered her face, but I could see she was bleeding from her nose, and a few scarlet stains covered her chest. I was paralyzed, unable to react.

"What's the matter?" I whispered.

"Close the door," she said firmly. "Close it."

I did as I was told and went to her side. She was

burning with fever. Her hair was stuck to her face, which was drenched in ice-cold sweat. I was so scared I turned to rush out in search of Germán. But her hand gripped me with unbelievable strength.

"No!"

"But—"

"I'm fine."

"You're not fine!"

"Oscar, I beg you, don't call Germán. He can't do anything. It's over now. I'm feeling better."

The calmness in her voice was terrifying. Her eyes searched mine. Something in them forced me to obey. Then she stroked my face.

"Don't be afraid. I'm better."

"You're pale as death," I stammered.

She took my hand and placed it on her chest. I could feel her heart beating against her ribs. I pulled my hand away, not knowing what to do.

"Alive and kicking. See? You must promise you won't say anything about this to Germán."

"Why?" I protested. "What's wrong with you?"

She lowered her eyes, infinitely tired. I shut up.

"Promise."

"You must see a doctor."

"Promise, Oscar."

"If *you* promise to see a doctor."

"That's a deal. I promise."

She dampened a towel and began to clean the blood off her face. I felt useless.

"Now that you've seen me like this, you're not going to fancy me anymore."

"I don't think that's funny."

She went on wiping her face quietly, without taking her eyes off me. Her body, swathed in the damp, almost transparent cotton, looked fragile and brittle. I was surprised not to feel any embarrassment, seeing her like that. Nor did she seem at all shy in my presence. Her hands were shaking as she dried the sweat and the blood off her body. I found a clean bathrobe hanging on the door and held it out for her. She covered herself with it and sighed with exhaustion.

"What can I do?" I murmured.

"Stay here with me."

She sat in front of the mirror, picked up a brush, and tried in vain to untangle the mess of hair that fell over her shoulders. She didn't have the strength.

"Let me," I said, taking the brush from her.

I brushed her hair without uttering another word, our eyes locking together in the mirror. As I did so, Marina gripped my hand tightly and pressed it against her cheek. I could feel her tears on my skin and I didn't find the courage to ask her why she was crying.

I took Marina back to her room and helped her get into bed. She wasn't trembling now, and the color had returned to her cheeks.

"Thanks..." she mumbled.

I decided that the best thing to do was to let her rest, so I returned to my room. I lay on my bed again and tried unsuccessfully to fall asleep. I was restless, lying there in the dark, listening to the old house creaking while the wind clawed at the trees. A blind anxiety was gnawing at me. Too many things were happening too fast. My brain couldn't take them all in at once. In the darkness of the early hours everything seemed to become confused. I realized I was scared stiff. No wonder: I had seen so many disturbing things in the last few weeks. But nothing scared me more than not being able to understand my own feelings for Marina. Morning was breaking when I finally fell asleep.

In dreams I found myself walking through the halls of a shadowy, deserted palace of white marble, filled with hundreds of statues. They opened their stony eyes as I walked past them and murmured words that I didn't comprehend. Then, in the distance, I thought I saw Marina, and I ran toward her. A silhouette of white light, shaped like an angel, was leading her by the hand down a corridor whose walls were oozing blood. I was trying to catch up with them when one of the doors in the corridor opened and the figure of María Shelley emerged, floating above the floor and dragging a tattered shroud behind her. She was crying, although her tears never reached the ground. She stretched her arms out toward me, and when she touched me, her body dissolved into ashes. I was screaming Marina's name, begging her to return, but she didn't seem to hear me. I ran and ran, but the corridor kept growing longer. Then the angel of light turned toward me and revealed its true face. Its eyes were empty sockets, its hair a mass of white snakes. The hellish angel laughed cruelly and, spreading its white wings over Marina, walked away. In the dream I smelled a fetid breath touching the back of my neck. It was the unmistakable stench of death, whispering my name. I turned and saw a black butterfly resting on my shoulder.

SEVENTEEN

I awoke feeling breathless and even more tired than when I'd gone to bed. My temples were pounding as if I'd drunk two entire jugs of black coffee. I didn't know what the time was, but judging by the sun it was probably about noon. The hands of the alarm clock confirmed my guess. Twelve thirty. I hurried downstairs, but the house was empty. Breakfast—now cold—had been laid out for me on the table, together with a note.

Oscar:

We had a doctor's appointment. We'll be out all day. Don't forget to feed Kafka. See you at dinnertime.

MARINA

I reread the note, examining the writing as I ate my breakfast. Kafka deigned to make an appearance a few minutes later and I filled his bowl with milk. I didn't know what to do until dinnertime. I decided to go over to the school to pick up some clothes and tell Doña Paula not to bother cleaning my room because I was going to spend the holidays with my family. The walk to the school did me good. I went in through the main door and made my way up to Doña Paula's apartment on the third floor.

Doña Paula was a good woman who always had a kind smile for the boarders. She'd been widowed for thirty years and on a diet for heaven knows how many more. She suspected that the source of her weight issues was not related to chocolate and sponge cake, as her doctor argued, but to advanced mathematics.

"It all comes down to my metabolism not knowing how to count the calories, you see?" she would say.

"You look fine to me, Doña Paula."

"Thank you, my dear. The problem is, or so that wretched doctor says, my blood doesn't look as good as I do. But what does he know, anyway?"

She'd never had children and, even now, close to sixty-five, she still looked longingly at the babies she saw going by in strollers on her way to the market. She lived alone. Her sole companions were two canaries and a huge

Zenith television set, which she didn't turn off until the national anthem came on and the portraits of the royal family sent her to bed. Bleach had ruined her hands. It pained me just to look at the veins in her swollen ankles. The only luxuries she allowed herself were a visit to the hairdresser's once a fortnight and *¡Hola!* magazine—she loved reading about the lives of princesses and admiring the dresses worn by stars of the screen.

When I knocked on her door, Doña Paula was watching a repeat of *The Nightingale of the Pyrenees*, part of a nostalgia cycle of kitsch musicals dragged up from the hidden depths of the Franco years. It featured a forgotten child star and former official songbird of Spain's fascist days, the one and only Joselito. As if the sugar content of the epic weren't enough, she was fortifying herself with slices of buttered toast covered in condensed milk and chocolate spread.

"Hello, Doña Paula. Sorry to bother you."

"Oh, Oscar my dear, you never bother me! Come in, come in...."

On the screen Joselito was belting out an ode to a baby goat under the benevolent and charmed gaze of a couple of civil guards. Next to the TV set a collection of small Madonna figures in a glass case shared a place of honor with old photographs of Doña Paula's husband, Rodolfo, sparkling with brilliantine and sporting a resplendent

Falangist uniform. Despite her devotion to her deceased husband, Doña Paula was delighted with democracy because, she said, it meant television was now in color, and one had to keep up with the times.

"Hey, what a lot of noise the other night, eh? On the news they were telling us about the earthquake in Chile and, well, I don't know, I just got so scared...."

"Don't worry, Doña Paula: Chile is very far away. Across the ocean, on another continent."

"I'm sure it is, but as they speak Spanish there, too, I don't know, well, I just think..."

"Don't you worry; there's no imminent danger. I just wanted to let you know that I'm going to spend Christmas with my family, so you don't need to trouble yourself with my room."

"Oh, Oscar, that's wonderful!"

Doña Paula had practically watched me grow up and was convinced that whatever I did was right. "You're really talented," she'd say, although she never explained very clearly in what way. She insisted that I drink a glass of milk and eat some biscuits she herself had baked. I complied, even though I wasn't very hungry. I stayed with her for a while, watching the film and agreeing with all her comments. The kind woman talked a mile a minute when she had company, which was very seldom.

"He really was a handsome little boy, wasn't he?"

she said, pointing at Joselito. According to Doña Paula, rumor had it that once Joselito's voice had broken and he'd lost his angelic looks and popularity he'd grown up to become a mercenary and a guerrilla fighter in the distant jungles of Central America.

"I wouldn't be surprised, Doña Paula. You know what they say: There's no business like show business. Well, I'm going to have to leave you now...."

I said good-bye to her with a peck on the cheek and left. I went up to my room for a minute and hurriedly collected a few shirts, two pairs of pants, and clean underwear, packing it all into a bag without hanging around a second more than was necessary. On my way out I stepped into the secretary's office and, wearing a blank expression, repeated my story about spending the holidays with my family. I left the school wishing that everything were as easy as lying.

We had dinner in silence in the room with the portraits. Germán was uncommonly taciturn, lost in thought. Sometimes our eyes met, and he would smile at me purely out of politeness. Marina stirred her bowl of soup without once lifting the spoon to her lips. The entire conversation was reduced to the sound of the cutlery scratching the plates and the spluttering of the candles. It wasn't hard to imagine that the doctor's observations on Germán's health had not been good. I decided not to ask about what seemed evident. After dinner, Germán excused himself and retired to his bedroom. He looked older and more fatigued than ever. Since I'd met him this was the first time I'd seen him ignore the portraits of his wife, Kirsten. As soon as he'd disappeared, Marina pushed her plate away and sighed.

"You haven't touched your food," I said.

"I'm not hungry."

"Bad news?"

"Let's talk about something else, shall we?" she snapped in a dry, almost hostile tone.

The sharpness of her words made me feel like a stranger in that house. As if she'd wanted to remind me that this was not my family, this was not my home, and these were not my problems, however much I tried to hold on to that dream.

"I'm sorry," she murmured after a while, stretching a hand out toward me.

"It's okay," I lied.

I stood up to clear the dishes and take them to the kitchen. She stayed there, sitting quietly and stroking Kafka, who meowed on her lap. I took longer than I needed, scrubbing the dishes until I could no longer feel my hands under the cold water. When I returned to the room, Marina had already gone up to bed. She'd left two lighted candles for me. The rest of the house lay in darkness and silence. I blew out the candles and went out into the garden. Black clouds were spreading slowly across the sky. An icy wind stirred the trees. I turned and saw a light shining in Marina's window. I imagined her lying on her bed. A moment later the light went out. The large old house loomed darkly, like the ruin it had seemed to me on the first day I saw it. I considered going to bed myself to get some rest, but I was beginning to feel rather uneasy and foresaw a long sleepless night. I decided to go for a stroll to clear my mind, or at least exhaust my body. I'd only taken a few steps when it began to drizzle. It was an unpleasant night and there was nobody out on the streets. Thrusting my hands into my pockets, I started to walk. I wandered about for almost two hours. Neither the cold nor the rain seemed to tire me out. Something was going around in my head, and the more I tried to ignore it, the more intensely it made its presence felt.

My steps took me to the Sarriá graveyard. The rain spat on faces of blackened stone and lopsided crosses. Beyond the entrance gates I could see rows of spectral forms. The damp earth reeked of dead flowers. I pressed my head against the bars. The metal was cold, and a trickle of rust slid over my skin. I scanned the darkness, as if expecting to find an explanation for all the things that were happening. All I could perceive was death and silence. What was I doing there? If I had any common sense left, I thought, I'd return to the house and sleep for a hundred hours without interruption. It was probably the best idea I'd had in three months.

I turned around and was about to head back along the narrow corridor between the cypress trees when I noticed the glow of a distant lamp through the rain. Suddenly the halo of light vanished and a dark shape invaded the path. I heard horses' hooves on the cobblestones and saw a black carriage approaching, slicing through the curtain of rain. The jet-black horses exhaled a ghostly cloud of breath. The figure of a coachman could be seen on the driver's seat. I searched for a hiding place on one side of the path but found only bare walls. The ground vibrated beneath my feet. I had just one option: to retreat. Soaking wet and almost unable to breathe, I climbed over the gates and jumped inside the holy enclosure.

EIGHTEEN

I fell on muddy ground that was softening under the pouring rain. Rivulets of dirty water dragged withered flowers among the tombstones. My feet and hands sank into the mud. I scrambled up and ran to hide behind the statue of a mourning angel, its arms raised to heaven. The carriage had stopped on the other side of the gates. The coachman got down. He carried a lamp and wore a cloak that covered him completely. A wide-brimmed hat and a scarf protected him against the rain and the cold, masking his features. I recognized the carriage. It was the same one the lady in black had climbed into that morning outside the Estación de Francia. On one of the carriage doors I glimpsed the symbol of the black butterfly. Velvet curtains covered the windows. I wondered whether she was inside.

The coachman walked up to the gates and inspected the graveyard. I stood there without moving, glued to the statue. Then I heard the metallic tinkle of a bunch of keys and the click of a padlock. I cursed under my breath. The iron gates creaked. Footsteps in the mud. The coachman was heading toward my hiding place. I had to get out of there. I turned to look at the cemetery behind me. The mantle of black clouds parted for a moment and the moon sketched a path of shimmering light. Rows of tombs shone briefly in the darkness. I crept backward through the tombstones, toward the depths of the cemetery, until I reached the foot of a mausoleum: It was sealed with gates of wrought iron and glass. The coachman was drawing closer. I held my breath and sank into the shadows. He was only two meters away from me now, holding the lamp high. He walked straight past me and I gave a sigh of relief. I saw him making his way toward the heart of the cemetery and instantly knew where he was going.

I was probably more frightened than I cared to admit, but I followed him all the same. I hid behind one tombstone after another until I reached the north sector of the enclosure. Once there, I climbed onto a platform that afforded a good view of the whole area. A few meters farther along, the coachman's glowing lamp rested on the nameless grave. The rain bled over the butterfly figure carved in the stone. I could see the shape of the coachman as he leaned over the grave. He pulled a long object from his cloak, a metal bar, and wrestled with it. I gulped when I realized what he was trying to do. He wanted to open the grave. I wished I could get the hell out of there, but I couldn't move. Using the bar as a lever, the coachman managed to shift the stone a couple of centimeters. Slowly, the tomb's black hole opened up until the stone slab fell heavily to one side and split in two upon impact. The ground shook under my feet. The coachman took the lamp and raised it above a pit two meters deep. A passage down to hell. The surface of a black coffin gleamed below. The coachman looked up at the sky and then, all of a sudden, jumped into the grave. He disappeared from view in an instant, as if the earth had swallowed him. After a few seconds I heard heavy blows and the sound of wood breaking. I jumped down and, creeping over the mud, inched my way to the edge of the grave and peered in.

The rain was pouring down into the grave, and the bottom of it was flooding. The coachman was still there, tugging at the lid of the coffin, which finally gave way with a tremendous crash. Rotten wood and frayed cloth were exposed to the light: The coffin was empty. The man stared at it and froze. I heard him murmur something. It was time for me to rush off, but as I did so, I kicked a stone. It fell into the grave and banged against the coffin. The coachman instantly turned toward me. In his right hand he held a gun.

I ran desperately toward the exit, weaving between tombstones and statues, hearing the coachman yelling at me as he climbed out of the grave. In the distance I glimpsed the gates, and the coach on the other side of them, and I kept running in that direction. The coachman's footsteps were now close behind and I realized he would catch up with me in a matter of seconds once I was out in the open. I remembered the weapon in his hand and looked frantically around for a hiding place. My eyes alighted on the only possibility, and I prayed that the coachman wouldn't think of looking there: the trunk on the back of the carriage. I jumped onto the carriage's platform and dived into it headfirst. Seconds later I heard the coachman's hurried footsteps reach the corridor of cypress trees.

I imagined what he must be seeing: the empty path in the rain. His steps halted. He walked around the coach. I was afraid I might have left footprints that would give me away. Then I felt him climbing into the driver's seat. I didn't move. The horses neighed. The wait seemed endless. At last I heard the crack of the whip and a jolt knocked me to the bottom of the trunk. We were moving.

———

The rattling soon turned into a dry, brisk vibration that pounded my muscles, which were rigid with cold. I tried to peep over the opening of the trunk, but I found it impossible to hold myself up with the swaying.

We left Sarriá behind. I weighed the chances of breaking my neck if I tried to jump out of the moving carriage and thought better of it. I didn't feel strong enough to try any more heroics, and besides, deep down, I wanted to know where we were going, so I surrendered to the circumstances. I settled down in the bottom of the trunk as best I could. I suspected that I'd need to recover my strength for later on.

The journey seemed endless. Lying there like a piece of luggage didn't help. I felt as if we'd covered several kilometers in the rain. My muscles were stiffening under my wet clothes. From the sounds around me I could tell we'd left behind the busier avenues and were now driving through deserted streets. I sat up and raised myself as far as the opening to have a look. I saw dark, narrow streets like gaps cut into rock. Street lamps and Gothic façades in the mist. I dropped down again, disconcerted. We were in the old town, in some part of the Raval quarter.

A stench like the smell of a fetid swamp rose from the flooded sewers. We wandered through Barcelona's heart of darkness for almost half an hour before coming to a stop. I heard the coachman jump down from the driver's seat and, seconds later, the sound of a heavy door opening. The carriage advanced at a slow trot and we went into what I imagined, from the smell, must be an old stable. The door closed again.

I didn't move. The coachman unhitched the horses, murmuring a few words to them that I wasn't able to grasp. A strip of light fell through the opening of the trunk. I heard the sounds of running water and footsteps over straw. Finally, the light went out and the coachman's steps faded away. I waited a couple of minutes, until all I could hear was the breathing of the horses, and slipped out of the trunk. A bluish half-light spread through the stable. I walked stealthily to a side door and went through into a dark garage with tall ceilings supported with wooden beams. At the other end of the garage I could discern the outline of what looked like an emergency exit. I checked the door and discovered that it opened from the inside. I opened it carefully and finally was out in the street.

I found myself in a dark alleyway of the Raval quarter. It was so narrow that I could touch both sides by just stretching out my arms. A foul-smelling trickle of water ran down the middle of it. The corner was only some ten meters away. I walked toward it. A wider street glowed under the foggy light of century-old street lamps. I saw the door to the stable on one side of the building— a miserable-looking gray structure. Over the door frame was the year of its construction: 1888. From where I stood I realized that this was the annex of a much larger building, which occupied the entire block. The second structure had palatial dimensions. A wall of scaffolding and dirty tarpaulins masked it entirely: A cathedral could have been hiding beneath it. I tried, unsuccessfully, to make out what the building was. I couldn't think of any such construction in that part of the Raval district.

As I drew closer, I peered through the wooden panels covering the scaffolding. A large art nouveau canopy was buried in thick shadows. I managed to make out a few columns and a row of windows decorated with an intricate wrought-iron design. Box offices. The arches of the main entrance, visible farther along, made me think of the doorway to an enchanted castle. Everything was shrouded in a layer of debris, damp, and abandonment. Suddenly I understood where I was. This was the Gran Teatro Real, the sumptuous monument Mijail Kolvenik had rebuilt for his wife, Eva, who had never been able to grace its stage. The theater stood there, a colossal catacomb in ruins, looking like a bastard son of the Paris

Opéra and Gaudí's Sagrada Familia church, awaiting demolition.

I returned to the adjacent building housing the stables. The main entrance was little more than a black hole. The large wooden door had a smaller panel cut into it that reminded me of the doorway to a convent. Or a prison. The panel was open and I stepped through it into a hall. A ghostly interior courtyard rose up to a skylight of broken glass. A cobweb of clotheslines draped with rags flapped in the wind. The place smelled of poverty, of sewers, of disease. The walls oozed dirty water from burst pipes. The floor was covered in puddles. I noticed a row of rusty mailboxes and went over to examine them. They were mostly empty, broken, and nameless. Only one of them seemed to be in use. I read the name beneath the grime: LLUÍS CLARET I MILÁ, 3°.

The name sounded vaguely familiar, although I couldn't place it. I wondered whether this was the coachman's name. I repeated the name over and over again to myself, trying to recall where I'd heard it. Suddenly something jogged my memory. Inspector Florián had told us that during Kolvenik's last years only two people had access to him and to his wife, Eva, in the house by Güell Park: Shelley, his personal doctor, and a chauffeur named Lluís Claret, who refused to abandon his master. I felt in my pockets for the telephone number Florián had given us in case we needed to get in touch with him. I thought I'd found it when I heard voices and footsteps coming from the top of the stairs. I fled.

Once I was back in the street, I ran around the corner into the alleyway to hide. After a while, a figure stepped out of the door and set off beneath the drizzle. It was the coachman again—Claret. I waited for him to disappear and followed the echo of his footsteps.

NINETEEN

Pursuing Claret, I became a shadow among the shadows. The poverty and squalor of the forsaken Raval district could be smelled in the air. Claret's long strides took me through streets I'd never been in before. I couldn't locate where I was until I saw him turn a corner and I recognized Calle Conde del Asalto, the area's main thoroughfare. When we reached the Ramblas, Claret turned left, heading for Plaza Cataluña.

A few night owls were wandering along the boulevard. The lit-up kiosks looked like ships stranded at low tide. When we reached the Liceo Opera House, Claret crossed over to the opposite sidewalk, then stopped in front of the building where Dr. Shelley and his daughter, María, lived. Before he went in, I saw him pull a shiny object from inside his cloak. His gun.

The building's façade was a mask of reliefs and gargoyles spitting out thin rivulets of rainwater. A blade of golden light flashed in a window at the top. Shelley's study. I imagined the old doctor in his armchair, unable to get to sleep. I ran to the door. It was locked from the inside. Claret had closed it. After inspecting the front of the building, looking for some other way in, I walked around to the back. There, a narrow fire-escape ladder rose up to a cornice encircling the structure—a stone ledge that ran around to the balconies at the front of the building. The glass-covered balcony of Shelley's study was only a few meters away. I climbed the fire-escape stairs to the cornice. When I got there, I examined it again and realized it was only about a foot wide. The drop down to the street looked like an abyss. I took a deep breath and stepped onto the ledge.

Clinging to the wall, I advanced a centimeter at a time. The surface was slippery and some of the slabs underfoot were loose. I had the feeling that the ledge was getting narrower with every step I took. The wall I was holding on to was covered with figures of fauns grinning like devils and seemed to be leaning outward. I stuck my hand into the open mouth of one of the fauns, wondering whether its jaws might clamp down and snap off my fingers. Using the figures as handholds, I finally reached the wrought-iron handrail surrounding the covered balcony of Shelley's study.

I managed to climb onto the metal platform outside the French windows. The windowpanes were misted up. By pressing my face against the glass I was able to see inside. The window wasn't bolted, so I pushed it gently until it opened a fraction. A breath of warm air carrying the smell of burned wood from the fireplace hit my face. The doctor was sitting in his armchair facing the fire, as if he'd never moved from there. Behind him the study doors opened. Claret. I was too late.

"You have betrayed your oath," I heard Claret say.

It was the first time I'd heard his voice clearly. Grave, broken, like the voice of Diego, one of the gardeners at school, whose larynx had been destroyed by a bullet during the war. The doctors had reconstructed his throat, but it was ten years before the poor man was able to speak again. When he did, the sound that came out of his lips was like Claret's voice.

"You said you'd destroyed the last flask," Claret said, drawing closer to Shelley.

The other man didn't bother to turn around. I saw Claret raise his revolver and aim at the doctor.

"You're wrong about me," said Shelley.

Claret walked around the old man and stood in front of him. Shelley looked up. If he was afraid, he didn't show it. Claret pointed the gun at his head.

"You're lying. I ought to kill you right away," said Claret, forcing out each syllable as if it hurt him.

He placed the barrel of the gun between Shelley's eyes.

"Go on. You'll be doing me a favor," said Shelley calmly.

I swallowed hard. Claret cocked the hammer.

"Where is he?"

"Not here."

"Where, then?"

"You know where," replied Shelley.

I heard Claret sigh. Crestfallen, he pulled the gun away and let his arm drop.

"We're all cursed," said Shelley. "It's only a matter of time.... You never understood him, and now you understand him less than ever."

"You're the one I don't understand," said Claret. "I'll go to my death with a clear conscience."

Shelley laughed bitterly. "Death doesn't care much about consciences, Claret."

"But I do."

Suddenly María Shelley appeared in the doorway.

"Father, are you all right?"

"Yes, María. Go back to bed. It's only our friend Claret. He was just leaving."

María hesitated. Claret was staring fixedly at her, and for a moment I felt I could see a vague complicity passing between them.

"Do as I tell you. Leave."

"Yes, Father."

María left the room. Shelley's eyes were drawn to the fire again.

"You can worry about your conscience. I have a daughter to worry about. Go home. There's nothing you can do. Nothing anybody can do. You saw how Sentís ended up."

"Sentís got what he deserved," Claret pronounced.

"You're not thinking of going to meet him?"

"I don't abandon my friends."

"But they've abandoned you," said Shelley.

Claret made for the doors but stopped when he heard Shelley call out.

"Wait…"

Shelley stood up and walked over to a cupboard next to his desk. He groped around his neck for a chain with a small key hanging from it. He then opened the cupboard, took something out, and handed it to Claret.

"Take them," he ordered. "I don't have the courage to use them. Or the faith."

I strained my eyes, trying to see what he was offering Claret. It was a case; it looked as if it contained silvery capsules. Bullets.

Claret accepted them and examined them carefully. His eyes met Shelley's.

"Thank you," murmured Claret.

Shelley shook his head silently, as if he didn't want to be thanked. I saw Claret empty the gun and fill it with the bullets Shelley had given him. As he did so, Shelley watched him nervously, rubbing his hands.

"You're not...?" Shelley begged.

The other man closed the chamber and turned the drum.

"I have no choice," Claret replied, walking to the doors.

As soon as he disappeared, I slid back onto the cornice. The rain had eased. Hoping I wouldn't lose track of Claret, I hurriedly retraced my steps back to the fire escape, clambered down, then ran around the building just in time to catch sight of him walking down the Ramblas. I quickened my pace, narrowing the gap between us. He didn't turn off until he reached Calle Fernando, from where he headed toward Plaza San Jaime. I glimpsed a public telephone booth among the arches of Plaza Real. I knew I had to call Inspector Florián as soon as possible to let him know what was happening, but to stop now would have meant losing Claret.

When he entered the Gothic quarter I went in after him. Soon his silhouette was lost under bridges stretching between palaces. Elaborate arches projected dancing shadows on the walls. We had reached the enchanted Barcelona, the labyrinth of spirits, where streets had mythical names and the ghosts of time walked behind us.

TWENTY

I followed Claret until I reached an alleyway tucked away behind the cathedral. A shop selling masks stood on the corner. I sidled up to the shop window and was met by the vacant gazes of paper faces. Then I peered around the corner to have a look. Claret had stopped about twenty meters farther on, next to a manhole that led down to the sewers. He was struggling with the heavy metal lid. When at last it opened he stepped into the hole. Only then did I move closer. I heard footsteps going down the metal stairs and saw the reflection of a beam of light. I sneaked over to the mouth of the sewer and looked down. Stagnant air surged up the hole. I waited there until Claret's footsteps were no longer audible and the darkness had swallowed the light he was carrying.

It was time to phone Inspector Florián. I noticed the lights of a bar that either closed very late or opened very early. The place—a dive that stank of cheap wine—occupied the lower ground floor of a building that looked at least three centuries old. The bartender had a sour complexion and minute eyes, and sported what looked like a military cap. He raised his eyebrows and looked at me with disgust. The wall behind him was decorated with the fascist pennants of the Blue Division, postcards of Franco's Valley of the Fallen memorial, and a portrait of Mussolini.

"Get out," he snapped. "We're not open until five."

"I just need to make a phone call. It's an emergency."

"Come back at five."

"If I could come back at five it wouldn't be an emergency! Please. I need to call the police. It's important."

The bartender studied me carefully and at last pointed to a telephone on the wall. "Wait till I connect you. You've got money on you to pay me, haven't you?"

"Of course," I lied.

The receiver was dirty and greasy. Next to the phone, in a glass saucer, were matchboxes with the name of the bar and an imperial eagle printed on them. THE PATRIOT, they read. While the bartender had his back to me I filled my pockets with them. When he turned around, I smiled innocently. I dialed the number Florián had given me and heard the phone ring over and over again, but there was no answer. I was beginning to fear that the inspector's insomniac friend had fallen asleep to the sound of the BBC news bulletins when someone picked up the receiver at the other end.

"Good evening, forgive me for disturbing you at this time of night," I said. "I urgently need to speak to Inspector Florián. It's an emergency. He gave me this number in case—"

"Who's calling?

"Oscar Drai."

"Oscar who?"

I had to spell my name out patiently.

"Just a moment. I don't know whether Florián is home. I can't see any lights on from here. Can you wait?"

I looked at the owner of the bar, who was drying glasses at a military tempo beneath Il Duce's gallant gaze.

"Yes," I replied boldly.

The wait seemed endless. The bartender kept his eyes trained on me as if I were Karl Marx's grandson. I tried smiling at him. He seemed unmoved by my friendly demeanor.

"Could you serve me a white coffee?" I asked. "I'm frozen."

"Not until five o'clock."

"Could you tell me the time, please?" I asked.

"It's not five yet," he replied. "Have you really called the police?"

"The glorious civil guard, pride of the land, to be precise," I improvised.

At last I heard Florián's voice. He sounded awake and alert.

"Oscar, where are you?"

"In some kind of gestapo watering hole called The Patriot."

I gave him the essentials as fast as I could. When I told him about the sewer tunnel, his voice grew tense.

"Listen to me carefully, Oscar. I want you to wait for me where you are and not move until I get there. I'm grabbing a cab in a second. If anything should happen, just start running. Don't stop until you reach the police station on Vía Layetana. There you ask for Mendoza. He knows me, and you can trust him. But whatever happens—do you understand?—whatever happens, don't go down into those tunnels. Is that clear?"

"Crystal clear."

"I'll be there in a minute."

I was cut off.

"That's sixty pesetas," the bartender immediately announced from behind me. "Night rates."

"I'll pay you at five, my general," I shot back calmly.

The bags under his eyes turned the color of Rioja wine.

"Watch it, you little creep, or I'll smash your head in!" he threatened furiously.

I made a dash for it before he was able to get out from behind the bar with his regulation riot truncheon. I'd wait for Florián next to the mask shop. He wouldn't be long, I thought.

The cathedral bells struck four o'clock. Signs of exhaustion were beginning to haunt me like famished wolves. I walked in circles to fight off the cold and the drowsiness. After a while I heard footsteps on the cobblestones. I turned around expecting to see Florián, but the silhouette I saw didn't match that of the old policeman. It was a woman. I instinctively hid, fearing that the lady in black had come to find me. The woman's shadow fell on the street and she crossed in front of me without seeing me. It was María, Dr. Shelley's daughter.

She walked up to the mouth of the tunnel and leaned over to peer into the chasm. In her hand she held a glass flask. Her face shone in the moonlight, transfigured. She was smiling. I knew instantly that something was wrong, out of place. It even occurred to me that she was in some sort of trance and had sleepwalked to this place. It was the only explanation I could think of. I preferred that hypothesis to considering other alternatives. I thought of going up to her, calling her by name, anything. I plucked up my courage and took a step forward. No sooner had I done so than María spun around with the agility and speed of a cat, as if she'd smelled my presence in the air. She stood in the alleyway, her eyes blazing, and the grin that appeared on her face froze my blood.

"Go away," she murmured in an unknown voice.

"María?" I uttered, disconcerted.

A second later she jumped into the tunnel. I rushed over to the edge, expecting to see María Shelley's shattered body. A beam of moonlight flicked over the well and lit up her face at the bottom of the pit.

"María!" I shouted. "Wait!"

I ran as fast as I could down the steps. A penetrating fetid smell hit me after I'd covered a couple of meters. The circle of light from the street above grew smaller. I fumbled for one of the matchboxes in my pocket and struck a match. The sight it revealed was uncanny.

A circular tunnel stretched into the darkness. Damp and rot. The squeal of rats and the endless rumbling from the maze of tunnels that spread beneath the city. An inscription on the wall, covered in grime, read: SGAB/1881 COLLECTOR SECTION IV/LEVEL 2—STRETCH 66.

On the other side of the tunnel the wall had collapsed. The subsoil had invaded part of the sewage channel. I could see different layers of the city's past, piled up one on top of another.

I gazed at the corpses of older Barcelonas, over which the new city had emerged. This was the place where Sentís had met his death. I lit another match. Trying to hold back the bile rising in my throat, I advanced a few meters, following the sound of the footsteps.

"María?"

My voice became a bloodcurdling spectral echo; I decided to keep my mouth shut. I noticed dozens of tiny red spots moving like insects on a pond. Eyes. The eyes of rats observing me. The flame from the matches I kept lighting held them at a prudent distance.

I was trying to decide whether to go farther into the tunnels when I heard a faraway voice. I took one last look at the entrance to the street high above, a world away. There was no sign of Florián. I heard the voice again. With a sigh, I headed into the darkness.

———

The tunnel I was walking along made me think of the guts of an animal. A stream of fecal water covered the floor. I pressed forward with only the matches to guide me. I lit each on the previous one, never allowing the gloom to envelop me completely. As I moved deeper into the labyrinth I became used to the smell of the sewers.

I also noticed that the temperature was rising. A sticky dampness clung to my skin, clothes, and hair.

A few meters farther on I sighted a cross gleaming on the wall, painted crudely in red. There were other similar crosses drawn on the walls. Then I thought I could see something shining on the ground. I kneeled down to have a closer look and realized it was a photograph. I recognized it instantly. It was one of the pictures from the album we'd found in the greenhouse. There were more photographs on the floor of the tunnel, all from the same place. Some were torn. Twenty paces farther on I found the album, practically destroyed. I picked it up and leafed through the empty pages. It seemed as if someone had been searching for something and, when they hadn't found it, had torn up the album in anger.

I was at a crossroads, a sort of distribution chamber or hub. I looked up and saw the mouth of another passageway that began right above the spot where I was standing. I thought I could see a grating. I lifted the match toward it but a gust of swampy air from one of the sewers blew out the flame. Just then I heard something moving slowly, slithering along the walls. I felt a shiver down the back of my neck. I searched for another match in the dark and fumbled about, trying to strike it, but it wouldn't light. This time I was certain: Something was moving in the tunnels, something alive, and it wasn't the rats. I was suffocating. An overpowering stench invaded my nostrils. Finally I managed to light a match. At first I was blinded by the flame; then I saw something creeping toward me. From all the tunnels. Shapeless figures crawling like spiders. The match fell from my trembling fingers. I wanted to start running but my muscles had seized up.

Suddenly a beam of light sliced through the shadows and I thought I caught sight of an arm reaching out to me.

"Oscar!"

Inspector Florián was rushing toward me. In one hand he held a flashlight, in the other a gun. Florián reached me and swept every corner with the beam from his flashlight. We both listened to the spine-chilling sound of those shapes scuttling away, fleeing from the light. Florián held his gun up high.

"What was that?"

I wanted to reply, but my voice failed me.

"And what the hell are you doing down here?"

"María..." I managed to say.

"What?"

"While I was waiting for you, I saw María Shelley throw herself into the sewers, and—"

"Shelley's daughter?" asked Florián, disconcerted. "Here?"

"Yes."

"And Claret?"

"I don't know. I've been following a trail of footprints...."

Florián inspected the walls surrounding us. A rusty iron door closed off one end of the chamber. He frowned and approached it slowly. I stuck close to him.

"Are these the tunnels where Sentís was found?"

Florián nodded, pointing to the other end of the tunnel.

"This sewer network extends right up to the old Borne Market. That's where Sentís was discovered, but there were signs that his body had been dragged there."

"Isn't that where the old Velo-Granell factory is?"

Again Florián nodded.

"Do you think someone is using these passageways to move beneath the city, from the factory to—"

"Here, hold the flashlight," Florián interrupted me. "And this."

"This" was his revolver. I held it while he struggled with the metal door. The gun weighed more than I'd imagined. I put my finger on the trigger and examined it in the light. Florián threw me a murderous look.

"It's not a toy—be careful. Keep fooling around and a bullet will blow your head open like a watermelon."

The door gave way. The stink that issued from inside was indescribable. We took a few steps back, fighting our nausea.

"What the hell is in there?" cried Florián.

He pulled out a handkerchief and covered his mouth and nose with it. I handed him the gun and held the flashlight. Florián kicked the door open and I shone the light on what lay behind it. The atmosphere was so thick we could barely see anything. Florián cocked the gun and walked toward the open door.

"Stay there," he ordered.

I ignored his words and advanced toward the entrance to the chamber.

"Dear God..." I heard Florián whisper.

I found it hard to breathe. It was impossible to accept the sight that lay before our eyes. Trapped in the darkness, hanging from rusty hooks, were dozens of bodies, lifeless and incomplete. Two large tables were covered in a chaotic mess of strange tools: bits of metal, cogs, and mechanisms made of wood and steel. A glass cabinet on the wall held a collection of vials, a set of hypodermic syringes, and a mass of dirty, blackened surgical instruments.

"What in hell is this?" Florián muttered, visibly scared.

On one of the tables lay a sinister figure made of wood, leather, metal, and bone, like an unfinished toy: a boy with round, snakelike eyes and a forked tongue showing through black lips. Branded onto the boy's forehead, the butterfly symbol was clearly visible.

"It's his workshop.... This is where he creates them...." I let slip audibly.

And then the eyes of that hellish doll moved. It turned its head. Its guts made a clicking sound like a clock being set. I felt its black reptilian pupils settling on mine. The forked tongue licked the doll's lips. It was smiling at us.

"Let's get out of here," said Florián. "Now!"

We rushed back into the chamber and closed the metal door behind us. Florián was breathing with difficulty. I couldn't even speak. He took the flashlight from my shaking hands and inspected the tunnel. As he did so, I saw a drop fall through the beam of light. And another, and yet another. Bright scarlet drops. Blood. We stared at each other in silence. Something was dripping from the ceiling. Florián signaled to me to move back a few steps and pointed the light up. I saw Florián's face grow pale and his firm hand start to shake.

"Run," was all he said to me. "Get out of here!"

He raised the revolver after casting one last look at me. In his eyes I saw first terror and then the realization of certain death. He opened his lips to say something else, but no sound ever emerged from his mouth. A dark figure hurled itself at Florián, striking him before he was able to move a single muscle. I heard a gunshot, a deafening explosion that bounced off the walls. The flashlight landed in a stream of water. Florián's body was flung against the wall with such force that it made an indent the shape of a cross in the blackened tiles. I was sure he was dead before he peeled off the wall and fell limply to the floor.

I started to run, looking desperately for the way back. An animal howl inundated the tunnels. I turned around. About a dozen figures were crawling at me from every direction. I ran as I'd never run in my life, listening to the invisible pack howling behind me, stumbling as I ran with the image of Florián's body embedded in the wall still fixed in my mind.

I was nearing the exit when a figure leaped out before me, just a few meters ahead, barring me from the steps to the street. I stopped dead in my tracks. The light filtering down from above revealed the face of a harlequin. Two diamond shapes covered its glassy eyes, and steel fangs protruded from its lips of polished wood. I took a step back. Two hands rested on my shoulders. Nails tore my clothes. Something viscous and cold surrounded my neck. I felt the knot tightening, choking me. My sight began to fail. Then something grabbed me by the ankles. The harlequin kneeled down in front of me and stretched its hands toward my face. I thought I was going to pass out. I prayed for that to happen. A second later, the head of wood, leather, and metal burst into pieces.

The shot came from my right. The explosion drilled

through my eardrums and the smell of gunpowder filled the air. The harlequin collapsed at my feet. I heard a second gunshot. The pressure on my throat disappeared and I fell flat on my face. I was only aware of the intense smell of gunpowder. Then I noticed that someone was pulling me; I opened my eyes and thought I could see a man leaning over and lifting me up.

Suddenly I saw daylight, and my lungs filled with clean air. Then I lost consciousness. I remember dreaming about the sound of horses' hooves while bells rang endlessly.

TWENTY-ONE

The room in which I awoke looked familiar. The windows were closed and a bright light seeped through the shutters. A figure stood by my side, quietly watching me. Marina.

"Welcome to the world of the living."

I sat up with a jerk. Suddenly my vision blurred and I felt as if needles of ice were boring through my skull. Marina held me while the pain gradually abated.

"Careful," she whispered.

"How did I get here?"

"Someone brought you at dawn. In a carriage. He didn't say who he was."

"Claret," I murmured as the pieces began to fall into place in my mind.

It was Claret who had pulled me out of the tunnels and brought me back to the Sarriá mansion. I realized that I owed him my life.

"You gave me one hell of a fright. Where have you been? I've spent all night waiting for you. Don't ever do anything like that to me again, do you hear?"

My entire body ached; even moving my head to nod hurt. Marina brought a glass of cold water to my lips. I drank it in one go.

"You want more?"

I closed my eyes and heard her pouring another glassful.

"Where's Germán?" I asked.

"In his study. He was worried about you. I told him something you ate didn't agree with you."

"He believed you?"

"My father believes everything I tell him," said Marina with no malice.

She handed me the glass of water.

"What does he do in his studio for hours on end if he no longer paints?"

Marina held my wrist and felt my pulse.

"My father is an artist," she said after a minute. "Artists live in the future or in the past, rarely in the present. Germán lives from his memories. It's all he's got."

"He's got you."

"I'm his biggest memory," she said, looking straight into my eyes. "I've brought you something to eat. You've got to get your strength back."

I waved a hand in refusal. The very idea of eating made me feel sick. Marina put a hand around the back of my neck and supported me while I drank again. The clean, cold water tasted like a blessing.

"What's the time?"

"It's midafternoon. You've been sleeping for almost eight hours."

She placed a hand on my forehead and left it there for a few seconds.

"At least your fever has gone."

I opened my eyes and smiled. Marina looked pale as she gazed at me.

"You were delirious. You were talking in your sleep...."

"What did I say?

"Nonsense."

I felt my throat. It hurt.

"Don't touch it," said Marina, pulling my hand away. "You've got quite a wound on your neck. And cuts on your shoulders and back. Who did this to you?"

"I don't know."

Marina sighed impatiently.

"You scared me to death," she said. "I didn't know what to do. I went to a telephone booth to call Florián, but I was told by the barman that you'd just called and the inspector had left without saying where he was going. I rang again shortly before daybreak and he still hadn't returned."

"Florián is dead." I noticed my voice breaking as I mentioned the poor inspector's name. "Last night I returned to the cemetery—" I began.

"You're mad," Marina interrupted.

She was probably right. Without another word, she offered me a third glass of water. I gulped it down. Afterward I slowly recounted what had happened the night before. When I finished my account, Marina just stared at me in silence. It seemed as if there was something else worrying her, something that had nothing to do with what I'd told her. She urged me to eat what she'd brought for me, whether I was hungry or not. She offered me some bread and chocolate and didn't take her eyes off me until I'd swallowed almost half a chocolate bar and a roll the size of a taxi. The sugar rush soon revived me.

"While you slept, I too was playing detective," Marina said, pointing to a thick leather-bound volume on the bedside table.

I read the title on the spine.

"Are you interested in entomology?"

"Bugs," Marina clarified. "I've found our friend, the black butterfly."

"*Teufel...*"

"An adorable creature. It lives in tunnels and basements, far from the light. It has a life cycle of fourteen days. Before dying, it buries its body among rubble and, three days later, a new larva emerges."

"It resurrects?"

"That's one way of putting it."

"And what does it feed on?" I asked. "There aren't any flowers or pollen in tunnels."

"It feeds off its young," Marina explained. "It's all there. The exemplary lives of our cousins the insects."

Marina walked over to the window and drew back the curtains. Sunlight flooded the room. She stayed there, looking pensive. I could almost hear the cogs turning in her head.

"What's the point of attacking you to recover the photograph album, only to abandon it later?"

"Probably whoever attacked me was looking for something specific in the album."

"But whatever that was, it wasn't there anymore," Marina added.

"Dr. Shelley," I said, suddenly remembering.

Marina looked at me questioningly.

"When we went to see him, we showed him the picture in which he appeared in the office," I said.

"And he kept it!"

"Not only that. As we were leaving I saw him throw it into the fire."

"Why would Shelley destroy that photograph?"

"Perhaps it revealed something he didn't want anyone to see," I suggested, jumping out of bed.

"Where do you think you're going?"

"To see Lluís Claret," I replied. "He's the person who holds the key to all this business."

"You're not leaving this house for the next twenty-four hours," Marina objected, leaning against the door. "Inspector Florián gave his life so that you could have a chance to escape."

"In twenty-four hours whatever is hiding in those tunnels will have come to get us—unless we do something to stop it," I said. "The least Florián deserves is that we do him justice."

"Shelley said death cares little about justice," Marina reminded me. "Maybe he was right."

"Maybe," I admitted. "But *we* care."

As we approached the Raval quarter, mist spread through the alleyways, tinted by the lights from shabby dives and taverns. We'd left behind the friendly bustle of the Ramblas. Soon there wasn't a tourist or any other casual pedestrian in sight. Furtive glances followed us from stinking doorways, from windows cut into crumbling façades. The echo of voices and old radios rose through these canyons of poverty, but only as far as the rooftops. The voice of the Raval never reaches heaven.

Soon, through gaps between the grime-covered buildings, we caught sight of the dark monumental outline of the Gran Teatro Real ruins. Crowning the very top of the skylight dome, silhouetted against the sky, was a weather vane in the shape of a black-winged butterfly. We stopped to stare at the ghostly sight. What had once been the most fantastic building ever erected in Barcelona was now decomposing like a corpse floating in a swamp.

Marina pointed at the lit-up windows on the third floor of the adjoining building. I recognized the entrance to the stables. That was Claret's home. We walked up to the main door. The bottom of the stairwell was still flooded after the previous night's downpour. We began to climb the worn, dark steps.

"What if he won't see us?" asked Marina anxiously.

"He's probably waiting for us," it occurred to me.

When we reached the second floor I noticed that Marina was breathing heavily, and with difficulty. I stopped and saw that she was turning pale.

"Are you all right?"

"A bit tired," she replied with an unconvincing smile. "You walk too fast for me."

I took her hand and helped her up to the third floor, one step at a time. We stopped outside Claret's door. Marina took a deep breath. Her chest trembled as she did so.

"I'm all right, really," she said, guessing at my fears. "Go on. Knock. You haven't brought me all the way here just to show me around the district, I hope."

I rapped on the door. The wood was old, solid, and as thick as a wall. I knocked again. We heard slow steps approaching. The door opened and Lluís Claret, the man who had saved my life, greeted us with an inscrutable stare.

"Come in," was all he said, turning back into the flat.

We closed the door behind us. The apartment was dark and cold. Paint peeled off the ceiling in yellowish flakes. Lamps with no lightbulbs were festooned with spiders' nests, and the patterned tiles under our feet were cracked.

"This way," Claret called out from inside the flat.

We followed his voice to a room whose only source of light came from a small brazier. Claret was sitting by the burning coals, staring silently at them. The walls were covered with old portraits: people and faces from a bygone age. Claret looked up at us. His eyes were pale and penetrating, his hair silvery, and his complexion like parchment. Dozens of lines marked the passing of time on his face, but despite his advanced age he exuded an air of strength that many men thirty years younger would have envied. He looked like a music-hall star who had grown old in the sun with dignity and style.

"I didn't get the chance to thank you. For saving my life."

"It's not me you have to thank. Can I ask how you found me?"

"Inspector Florián told us about you," Marina butted in. "He explained that you and Dr. Shelley were the only two people who remained close to Mijail Kolvenik and Eva Irinova to the very end. He said you never abandoned them. How did you meet Mijail Kolvenik?"

A faint smile crossed Claret's lips.

"Señor Kolvenik came to this town during one of the worst cold spells of the century," he explained. "Alone, hungry, and beset by the icy weather, he sheltered for a night in the doorway of an old building. All he had was a few coins to buy a bit of bread and some hot coffee. Nothing else. While he was considering what to do, he discovered that there was someone else in the doorway. A boy of about five, wrapped in rags, a beggar who had taken shelter there just as he had. Kolvenik and the boy didn't speak the same language, so they could barely understand each other. But Kolvenik smiled at him and gave him all the money he had, making gestures to indicate that he should use it to buy food. Not quite believing his good luck, the child ran off to buy a large loaf of bread from a bakery that was open all night, next to Plaza Real. He returned to the doorway to share the bread with the stranger but saw the police leading him away. In prison Kolvenik's cellmates beat him savagely. During the days when he was in the prison hospital the boy waited by the door like a dog that had lost its master. When Kolvenik emerged into the streets two weeks later, he was limping. The boy was there to hold him up. He became his guide and swore he would never abandon the man who, on the worst night of his life, had given him all his worldly possessions. . . . I was that boy."

Claret stood up and told us to follow him to a door at the end of a narrow passage. He pulled out a key and opened it. On the other side was an identical door, and between the two a small chamber.

To mitigate the darkness, Claret lit a candle. Then, with another key, he opened the second door. A sudden draft invaded the passageway, making the candle hiss. I felt Marina clutch my hand as we stepped through. Then we stopped as a fabulous vision opened up before us: the interior of the Gran Teatro Real.

Tier upon tier rose toward the huge dome. Velvet curtains hung from the boxes, fluttering in the void. Above a vast expanse of empty stalls, large glass chandeliers still awaited the electricity connection that had never materialized. We were standing in a side entrance to the stage. Above us the stage machinery seemed to rise to infinity, a universe of curtains, scaffolding, pulleys, and walkways lost in the heights.

"This way," Claret said, leading us.

We crossed the stage. A few musical instruments languished in the orchestra pit. On the conductor's podium a score lay open at the first page, buried under cobwebs. Farther back, the long carpet covering the central aisle looked like a road to nowhere. Claret walked on ahead of us, toward a door with a light shining behind it, and signaled to us to wait there a moment. Marina and I looked at each other.

It was the door to a dressing room. Hundreds of dazzling costumes hung from metal rails. One wall was covered in mirrors framed with lights, and the other was taken up by dozens of old photographs of an extraordinarily beautiful woman: Eva Irinova, the woman who had entranced her audiences, the woman for whom Mijail Kolvenik had built this sanctuary.

And then I saw her.

The lady in black was gazing at herself in silence, her

veiled face looking into the mirror. When she heard our footsteps, she turned slowly and nodded her head. At this signal Claret allowed us to come closer. We walked toward her as if we were approaching an apparition, with a mixture of fear and fascination. We stopped a couple of meters away. Claret stayed in the doorway, on the alert. The woman faced the mirror again, studying her image.

Suddenly, with the utmost care, she lifted her veil. The few lightbulbs that were working showed us her face in the mirror, or what the acid had left of it. Naked bone and wrinkled skin. Shapeless lips, just a slit on the blurry features. Eyes that could no longer cry. For an endless moment she let us see the horror that was usually covered by her veil. Afterward, just as gently as she had revealed her face and her identity, she covered herself again and motioned for us to sit down. A long silence ensued.

Eva Irinova stretched out a hand toward Marina's face and stroked it, moving over her cheeks, her lips, and her neck, reading her beauty and her perfection with trembling, yearning fingers. Marina swallowed hard. The lady drew her hand back and I could see her lidless eyes flashing behind the veil. Only then did she start to speak and tell us the story she had been hiding for more than thirty years.

TWENTY-TWO

I've never seen my country, except in photographs. All I know about Russia comes from stories, gossip, and other people's memories. I was born on a barge crossing the Rhine in a Europe devastated by war. Years later I learned that my mother was already pregnant with me when, alone and ill, she crossed the Russo-Polish border, fleeing from the revolution. She died giving birth to me. I've never known her name, or who my father was. She was buried on the banks of the river in an unmarked grave, lost forever. A couple of actors from Saint Petersburg who were traveling on that barge, Sergei Glazunow and his twin sister, Tatiana, took care of me out of pity and because, according to what Sergei told me many years later, the fact that I was born with different-colored eyes was a sign of good luck.

"Thanks to Sergei's machinations we joined a circus company in Warsaw on its way to Vienna. My first memories are of those people and their animals: the circus big top, the jugglers, and a deaf and mute fakir called Vladimir who swallowed glass, was a fire-breather, and always gave me paper birds he made as if by magic. Sergei ended up becoming the manager of the company, and we established ourselves in Vienna. The circus was both my school and the home in which I grew up. By then we already knew, however, that it was doomed. Reality was becoming more grotesque than the pantomimes of clowns and dancing bears. Soon nobody would need us. The twentieth century had become the dark circus of history.

"When I was only seven or eight, Sergei said it was time I started earning my own living. That is how I became part of the show, first as an assistant for Vladimir's tricks and later with my own act, in which I sang a lullaby to a bear and made it fall asleep. The act, which had been planned as a filler to allow time for the trapeze artists to get ready, turned out to be a success. Nobody was more surprised than me. Sergei decided to extend my performance. I ended up standing on a floodlit platform singing ditties to some poor old lions, all of them starving and unwell. The animals and the audience listened to me, mesmerized. In Vienna people talked about the girl whose voice could tame beasts. And they paid to see her. I was nine years old.

"It didn't take Sergei long to realize that he no longer needed the circus. The girl with the different-colored eyes had lived up to her promise of good fortune. He completed all the formalities required to become my legal guardian and announced to the rest of the company that we were going to set ourselves up independently. He explained that a circus was not a suitable place in which to bring up a young girl. When it was discovered that for years someone had been stealing part of the box-office takings, Sergei and Tatiana accused Vladimir, adding that he had behaved improperly toward me. Vladimir was arrested by the authorities and imprisoned, even though the money was never found.

"To celebrate his independence, Sergei bought a luxury car, a dandy's wardrobe, and jewels for Tatiana. We moved into a villa Sergei had rented in the woods of Vienna. It was never clear where he'd got the funds for so much extravagance. I sang every afternoon and evening in a theater next to the Opera House, in a show called *The Angel from Moscow*—the first of many similar performances. It was Tatiana's idea to call me Eva Irinova, a name she'd taken from a popular newspaper serial of the time. At Tatiana's suggestion I was provided with a singing teacher, a dance teacher, and an acting coach. When I wasn't onstage, I was rehearsing. Sergei didn't allow me to have friends or go out for walks; I couldn't even be on my own or read books. 'It's for your own good,' he would say. When my body began to develop, Tatiana demanded that I have a room to myself. Sergei reluctantly agreed, but insisted on keeping the key. He would often return home in the middle of the night, drunk, and try to get into my room. Most times he was so intoxicated he couldn't put the key in the keyhole. Other nights he wasn't. The applause of an anonymous audience was my only satisfaction during those years. As time went by, I needed it more than the air I breathed.

"We traveled frequently. Word of my success in Vienna had reached the ears of impresarios in Paris, Milan, and Barcelona. Sergei and Tatiana always came with me. Naturally, I never saw a penny of the takings from all those concerts, nor do I know where the money went. Sergei always had debts and creditors. It was my fault, he told me bitterly. All his money was spent on my care and my keep, yet I was incapable of thanking him and Tatiana for everything they had done for me. Sergei taught me to see myself as a dirty, lazy, ignorant, and stupid girl. A miserable wretch who would never do anything of any value, and whom nobody would ever love or respect. But none of that mattered, he whispered in my ear, his breath stinking of cheap spirits, because he and Tatiana would always be there to take care of me and protect me from the world.

"On my sixteenth birthday I realized that I hated myself and could barely look at my reflection in the mirror. I stopped eating. My body disgusted me and I tried to hide it under dirty, ragged clothes. One day I found one of Sergei's old razor blades in the rubbish bin. I took it to my room and got into the habit of cutting my hands and arms with it. To punish myself. Every night Tatiana would dress my wounds without saying a word.

"Two years later, in Venice, a count who had seen me perform asked me to marry him. That night, when Sergei found out, he gave me a savage beating. He split open my lips and broke two of my ribs. Tatiana and the police restrained him. I left Venice in an ambulance. We returned to Vienna, but Sergei's financial problems were very serious. We received threats. One night someone set fire to our house while we slept. A few weeks earlier Sergei had received an offer from a Barcelona impresario for whom I'd already performed successfully in the past. Daniel Mestres—that was his name—had become the main shareholder in Barcelona's old Teatro Real and wanted to open the season with me. And so, packing our cases at dawn, we fled to Barcelona with little more than the clothes we were wearing. I was about to turn nineteen, and I kept praying that I wouldn't live to be twenty. For some time I'd been thinking about taking my own life. Nothing could make me cling to this world. I'd been dead for ages, without knowing it. It was then that I met Mijail Kolvenik....

"We'd been working at the Teatro Real for a few weeks. It was rumored in the company that a gentleman sat in the same box every night to hear me sing. At the time all sorts of stories concerning Mijail Kolvenik were circulating around Barcelona: how he'd made his fortune...tales about his personal life and identity, packed with mysteries and secrecy...His legend preceded him. One night, intrigued by this strange character, I decided to send him an invitation to visit me in my dressing room after the show. It was almost midnight when Mijail Kolvenik knocked on my door. After all the gossip, I was expecting someone arrogant and threatening. But my first impression of Mijail was of someone shy and reserved. He wore dark, simple clothes, with no other adornment than a small brooch on his lapel: a butterfly with open wings. He thanked me for my invitation and told me how much he admired me and what an honor it was to make my acquaintance. I replied that, after everything I'd heard about him, the honor was mine. He smiled and suggested that I forget the rumors. Mijail had the loveliest smile I have ever known. When he smiled, you could believe anything that came from his lips. Someone once said—and he was right—that Mijail could have convinced Christopher Columbus that the world was as flat as a pancake. That night he convinced me to take a stroll through the streets of Barcelona. He told me that he often walked through the sleeping city after midnight. I'd barely left the theater since we'd arrived, so I agreed. I knew that Sergei and Tatiana were going to be furious when they found out, but I didn't care. We slipped out incognito through the proscenium door. Mijail offered me his arm, and we walked around until dawn. He showed me the captivating city through his eyes. He spoke to me about its mysteries, its enchanted corners and the spirit that lived in those streets. He told me hundreds of legends. We walked through the secret alleyways of the Gothic quarter and the old town. Mijail seemed to know everything. He knew who had lived in every building, what crimes or romances had taken place behind every wall and every window. He knew the names of all the architects, craftsmen, and countless invisible men responsible for creating that stage set. As I listened, I had the feeling that Mijail had never shared those stories with anyone. I was overwhelmed by the loneliness that seemed to possess him, and at the same time I thought I could discern, inside him, a dark abyss into which I couldn't help peering. Morning was breaking as we sat on a bench in the port. I gazed at the stranger with whom I'd been walking for hours and felt as if I'd always known him. I told him so. He laughed, and at that moment, with that rare certainty we only experience a couple of times in our lives, I knew I was going to spend the rest of my life with him.

"That night Mijail said he believed each one of us is only granted brief moments of pure happiness. Sometimes only days or weeks. Other times years. It all depends on our luck. The remembrance of such moments stays with us forever and becomes a land of memories to which we vainly attempt to return during the rest of our existence. For me, those moments will always be found in that first night, walking through the city. . . .

"It didn't take long for Sergei and Tatiana to react. Especially Sergei. He forbade me to see or speak to Mijail. He said that if I ever left the theater again without his permission, he'd kill me. For the first time in my life I discovered that he no longer frightened me. All I felt was disdain. To infuriate him even further I told him that Mijail had asked me to marry him and that I'd accepted. Sergei reminded me that he was my legal guardian: Not only was he not going to authorize this marriage, but we were leaving for Lisbon. I sent a desperate message to Mijail through one of the dancers in the company.

That night, before the performance, Mijail came to the theater with two of his lawyers and held a meeting with Sergei. He announced that he'd signed an agreement that very afternoon with Mestres, the Teatro Real impresario, whereby he had become its new owner. Sergei and Tatiana were instantly fired.

"Soon Mijail presented Sergei with an entire file of documents, proof of the illegal activities he'd carried out in Vienna, Warsaw, and Barcelona. More than enough material to put him behind bars for fifteen or twenty years. To that Mijail added a check for an amount that exceeded anything Sergei could have obtained in his entire life through his mean and shady deals. He was given two options: If within forty-eight hours he and Tatiana abandoned Barcelona forever and promised not to get in touch with me again in any way, they could take the file and the check; if they refused to cooperate, the file would end up with the police, together with the check as an incentive to oil the wheels of justice. Sergei flew into a rage. He shouted like a madman that he was never going to let me go, that Mijail would have to step over his dead body to get his own way.

"Mijail smiled and left. That night Tatiana and Sergei arranged to meet a strange individual who offered his services as a hit man. On their way out of that meeting they were almost killed by shots fired anonymously from a passing carriage. The papers published the news item, venturing various hypotheses to account for the attack. The next day Sergei accepted Mijail's check and vanished from Barcelona with Tatiana, without saying good-bye....

"When I found out what had happened, I demanded the truth from Mijail. I wanted to know whether he was responsible for the attack. I desperately wanted him to say he wasn't. He fixed his eyes on mine and asked me why I doubted him. I felt like dying. All that happiness and hope seemed about to collapse like a house of cards. I asked him again. Mijail said no, he wasn't responsible for the attack.

" 'If I were, neither of them would be alive,' he replied coldly.

"Soon afterward he hired one of the best architects in town to build the house next to Güell Park, following his detailed instructions. The cost wasn't an issue; no expense was to be spared to realize his vision. While the house was being built, Mijail rented an entire floor in the great Hotel Colón, in Plaza Cataluña, the most luxurious hotel in Barcelona at the time. We moved there temporarily. For the first time in my life I discovered it was possible to have so many servants you couldn't remember all their names. Mijail had only one helper: his chauffeur, Lluís.

"Bagués, the jewelers, called on me in my rooms. The best couturiers took my measurements to create a wardrobe fit for an empress. Mijail opened unlimited accounts for me in the best shops in Barcelona. People I'd never seen in my life would bow to me in the streets or in the hotel lobby. I was invited to balls in palaces belonging to families whose names I'd only ever seen in the society pages of the press. I wasn't even twenty. I'd never had enough money in my hands for a tram ride. It was like a dream, but I began to feel overwhelmed by all the lavishness and waste surrounding me. When I told Mijail, he would say that money was unimportant, unless one didn't have any.

"We would spend the day together, strolling through the city, visiting the Tibidabo casino (although I never saw Mijail bet a single coin) or the Liceo. In the evening we'd go back to the Hotel Colón and Mijail would retire to his rooms. I began to notice that, quite often, Mijail would go out in the middle of the night and not return until dawn. According to him, he had business matters to deal with.

"But tongues were wagging. I felt as if everyone else knew the man I was about to marry better than I did. I heard the maids talking behind my back. In the street people would look me up and down after a hypocritical smile. Slowly I became a prisoner of my own suspicions, and an idea began to torment me. All that luxury, the extravagance that surrounded me, made me feel like one more piece of furniture. One more of Mijail's whims. He could buy anything: the Teatro Real, Sergei, cars, jewels, palaces. And me. I burned with anxiety when I saw him leave every night, in the small hours, convinced that he was running to the arms of another woman. One night I decided to follow him and put an end to the charade.

"I trailed him to the old workshop of Velo-Granell Industries, next to the Borne Market. Mijail had gone there alone. I had to creep in through a tiny window in an alleyway. The inside of the factory looked to me like the scene of a nightmare. Hundreds of feet, hands, arms, legs, and glass eyes were scattered about the premises… replacement parts for a broken and miserable humanity. I walked through the plant until I came to a large, dark room where shapeless figures were visible floating inside enormous glass tanks. In the middle of the room, in the half-light, Mijail was staring at me from a chair, smoking a cigar.

" 'You shouldn't have followed me,' he said. There was no anger in his voice.

"I argued that I couldn't marry a man of whom I'd only seen one half, a man whose days I knew, but not his nights.

" 'You might not like what you find,' he hinted.

"I said I didn't care what or why. I didn't care what he did or whether the rumors about him were true. I only wanted to share his life, completely. Without shadows. Without secrets. He nodded and I knew what that meant: It meant going through a door from which there was no turning back. When Mijail switched on the lights in that room, I awoke from the dream I'd been living in for the last few weeks. I was in hell.

"The formaldehyde tanks contained corpses that gyrated in a macabre dance. On a metal table was the naked body of a woman that had been dissected from the belly to the throat. The arms were stretched out wide, and I noticed that the joints in her arms and hands were made of pieces of metal and wood. Tubes went down her throat, and bronze cables were sunk into her extremities and hips. Her skin was translucent and bluish, like the skin of a fish. Speechless, I watched Mijail as he approached the body, gazing sadly at it.

" 'This is what nature does with its children,' he said. 'There is no evil in men's hearts, just a simple struggle to survive the inevitable. The only devil is Mother Nature....My work, all my efforts, are just an attempt to outdo the great sacrilege of creation....'

"I saw him take a syringe and fill it with an emerald-colored liquid he kept in a bottle. Our eyes met briefly, and then Mijail plunged the needle into the corpse's skull and emptied the contents. He pulled out the needle and waited, motionless, for a moment, observing the inert body. Seconds later I felt my blood curdle. The eyelashes on one of the eyelids were fluttering. I heard the sound of the mechanisms in the wood-and-metal joints. The fingers flapped. Suddenly the woman's body sat up with a violent jerk. A deafening animal scream filled the room. Threads of white froth ran over her black, swollen lips. The woman pulled off the cables perforating her skin and fell to the floor like a broken puppet. She howled like a wounded wolf, then raised her head and fixed her eyes on mine. I found it impossible to look away from the horror I saw in them, from the spine-chilling animal force they gave off. She wanted to live.

"I was paralyzed. A few seconds later the body lay once again inert, lifeless. Mijail, who had watched the whole event impassively, picked up a sheet and covered the corpse.

"He drew close to me and took my trembling hands. He looked at me as if he was trying to discover whether I would be able to remain by his side after what I'd witnessed. I tried to find words to express my fear, to tell him how wrong he was. . . . All I managed to stammer was 'Get me out of here.' He did. We returned to the Hotel Colón. He accompanied me to my bedroom, asked for a bowl of hot broth to be brought to me, and wrapped me in blankets while I drank it.

" 'The woman you saw tonight died six weeks ago under the wheels of a tram,' he told me. 'She leaped forward to save a boy who was playing on the line and couldn't avoid the impact. The wheels severed her arms at the elbows. She died in the street. Nobody knows her name. Nobody claimed her. There are dozens like her. Every day...'

" 'Mijail, you don't understand,' I said. 'You can't do God's work....'

"He caressed my forehead and smiled sadly, nodding as he did so.

" 'Good night,' he said.

"He walked over to the door and paused before leaving.

" 'If you're not here tomorrow,' he said, 'I'll understand.'

"Two weeks later we were married in Barcelona Cathedral."

TWENTY-THREE

Mijail wanted that day to be special for me. He went out of his way to deck out the entire city so that it looked like the backdrop for a fairy tale. But my reign as queen of that dream world was to come to a sudden end on the steps of the cathedral. I didn't even hear the screams of the crowd. Like a feral beast leaping out of the undergrowth, Sergei emerged from the multitude, and before we could react or even realize what was happening, he threw the acid on my face. The acid devoured my skin and my eyelids and burned deeply into my hands. It ripped my throat and severed my vocal cords. I didn't speak again for two years, until Mijail started to rebuild me as if I were a broken doll. It was the start of the horror.

"Construction on the house was discontinued and we moved into an unfinished palace on the top of a hill, which was to become our prison. It was a dark, cold place with a jumble of towers and arches, vaults, and spiral staircases leading nowhere. I hated it. The attack had left me severely impaired, and I was confined in a room at the top of the main tower to live like a recluse. Nobody had access to it except for Mijail and, sometimes, Dr. Shelley. I spent the first year under the drowsy effects of morphine, barely able to tell reality from the terrible nightmares plaguing me. I would dream that Mijail was experimenting on me just as he had been doing with the unclaimed bodies he purchased from hospitals and morgues. Reconstructing me and outsmarting nature. I just wanted to die, or to find the strength to end my own life before it was too late. When I finally recovered consciousness, I realized that my nightmares had been real. He had given me back my voice. He had rebuilt my face, my lips, and my throat so that I could feed myself and speak. He had altered my nerve endings so that I didn't feel the pain of the extensive damage caused by the acid—I had lost my sense of touch and couldn't feel anything anymore, neither heat nor cold. I was a ghost in my own body. Yes, in a way I had mocked death, but I ended up becoming one more of Mijail's accursed creatures.

"By then, of course, Mijail had lost his influence and position in society. Nobody supported him anymore. His old allies, all of them hypocrites, had turned their backs on him and abandoned him to the wolves. The police and the local authorities began to hound him. His partner, Sentís, who had never been more than an envious mediocrity, volunteered false information to implicate Mijail in matters that had nothing to do with him. He was trying to remove him from control of the business. Sentís was just another of the pack. Everyone wanted to see Mijail fall so they could devour his remains. As is usually the case, the army of sycophants had turned into a horde of hungry hyenas. None of this surprised Mijail. He'd seen it coming. From the very start he had relied only on his friend Shelley and on Lluís Claret. 'Man's meanness,' he used to say, 'is a fuse in search of a flame.' But, even though Mijail had anticipated all of this, I believe this betrayal finally broke the fragile link he had with the outside world. He took refuge in his own labyrinth of solitude. His behavior became increasingly bizarre. Down in the cellars he started breeding dozens of specimens of an insect that obsessed him, a black butterfly known as a *Teufel*. Soon the black butterflies were flying around the house. They alighted on mirrors, pictures, and furniture like silent sentries. Mijail forbade the servants to kill them, ward them off, or get close to them. A swarm of black-winged insects flew through the halls and corridors. Sometimes they would land on Mijail and cover him while he stood there without moving. When I saw him like that I thought I was going to lose him forever.

"Around that time I befriended Lluís Claret, and our friendship has lasted until today. It was Lluís who kept me informed of what was going on beyond the walls of that fortress. Mijail had been feeding me fantasies about the Teatro Real and my return to the stage. He spoke about repairing the damage the acid had caused, about my singing with a voice that no longer belonged to me.... Dreams. Lluís explained that the work at the Teatro Real had also stopped. The funds had run out months earlier. The building was now an immense carcass falling apart.... Mijail's outer calm was just a front. He would spend weeks, even months, without leaving the house. Entire days locked up in his studio, barely eating or sleeping. Joan Shelley, as the doctor admitted to me later, worried about his health, but even more about his sanity. He probably knew Mijail better than anyone else and had helped him with his experiments from the start. It was he who spoke openly to me about Mijail's obsession with degenerative diseases and his desperate attempts to discover the mechanisms by which nature allowed the human body to atrophy and decay. To him, nature was a merciless beast that fed on its young without caring about the fate of the beings it harbored. He collected photographs of strange cases of degeneration and medical freaks. What Mijail searched for in the misfortunes of those poor souls was an answer to his question: how to outwit his inner demons.

"It was then that the first symptoms of his own illness became apparent. Mijail knew that he carried it inside him, like a ticking time bomb. He had always known it, ever since he watched his brother die in Prague. It all happened very fast. His body began to destroy itself. His bones were crumbling. Mijail covered his hands with gloves. He hid his face and his body. He avoided my company. I pretended not to notice, but it was obvious: His shape was changing. One winter's day, at dawn, I was awakened by his cries. Mijail was shouting at the servants, sending them away. Nobody challenged him; in the last few months they had all grown afraid of him. Only Lluís refused to abandon us. Weeping with anger, Mijail broke all the mirrors in the house and ran to lock himself in his studio.

"One night I asked Lluís to fetch Dr. Shelley. For two weeks Mijail hadn't come out of his room or replied to my calls. I could hear him sobbing on the other side of the wall of his studio, talking to himself. . . . I no longer knew what to do. I was losing him. With Shelley and Lluís's help, I broke the door down and we managed to get him out of there. We discovered to our horror that Mijail had been operating on his own body, trying to rebuild his left hand, which was turning into a grotesque, useless claw. Shelley gave him a sedative and we spent the night at his bedside while he slept. During that long night, as he watched his old friend in the throes of death, Shelley vented his despair and broke his promise never to reveal the story Mijail had confided in him years earlier. As I listened to his words, I realized that neither the police nor Inspector Florián ever suspected they were pursuing a ghost. Mijail was never a criminal or a fraudster. Mijail was simply a man who thought his destiny was to cheat death before death cheated him."

"Mijail Kolvenik was born in the tunnels of Prague's sewage system on the last day of the nineteenth century.

"His mother was a seventeen-year-old maid who served a family of the high aristocracy. Her beauty and naïveté had turned her into her master's plaything, one among many. When she revealed she was pregnant, she was thrown out like a mangy dog into the dirty, snow-covered streets, branded for life. In those days, when winter draped the streets in a mantle of death, they say the destitute would take shelter in the tunnels of the old sewers. Legend had it that an entire city of darkness spread beneath the streets of Prague and that thousands of dispossessed spent their lives there without ever seeing the sun again. Beggars, sick people, orphans, and fugitives. These people followed the cult of an enigmatic character they called the Prince of Beggars, who was said to be ageless, with the face of an angel and blazing eyes. It was also said that his body was cloaked in black butterflies and that he welcomed into his kingdom all those whom the cruel world had denied a possibility of survival aboveground. Searching for that world of shadows, the young girl entered the underground network, hoping to survive. Soon she discovered that the local legend was true. The people in the tunnels lived in the dark and created their own world. They had their own laws. And their own god: the Prince of Beggars. Nobody had ever seen him, but they all believed in him and left offerings in his honor. Using red-hot irons, they all branded their skin with the emblem of the butterfly. It was prophesied that a messiah sent by the Prince of Beggars would come to the tunnels one day and give his life to deliver its inhabitants from their suffering. The messiah's downfall would come from his own hands.

"That is where the young mother gave birth to twins:

Andrej and Mijail. Andrej was born with a cruel, terrible illness. His bones would not solidify and his body grew with no shape or structure. One of the inhabitants of the tunnels, a doctor who was being pursued by the law, told her that Andrej's condition was incurable. The end was just a question of time. But his brother, Mijail, was a bright boy who, though timid by nature, dreamed of leaving the tunnels one day and emerging into the world aboveground. He often fantasized that he was the long-awaited messiah. He never knew who his father was, so in his mind he awarded that role to the Prince of Beggars, whom he thought he could hear in his dreams. Mijail seemed to have none of the signs of the terrible disease that would end his brother's life. Sure enough, Andrej died when he was seven without ever having left the sewers, and his body was laid to rest in the underground currents, following the rituals of the sewer world. Mijail asked his mother why this had happened.

" 'It's God's will, Mijail,' his mother replied.

"Mijail would never forget those words. But the blow of little Andrej's death was too much for his mother to bear. The following winter she caught pneumonia. Mijail remained by her side until the last moment, holding her trembling hand. She was twenty-six but had the face of an old woman.

" 'Is this God's will, Mother?' he asked her lifeless body.

"He was never given an answer. A few days later young Mijail emerged into the streets. Nothing tied him any longer to the underground world. Starving and frozen, he took shelter in a doorway. By chance, a doctor named Antonin Kolvenik, who was returning from a home visit, discovered him there. The doctor took him to a nearby tavern, where he bought him a warm meal.

" 'What's your name, son?'

" 'Mijail, sir.'

"Antonin Kolvenik paled.

" 'I once had a son with your name. He died. Where is your family?'

" 'I have no family.'

" 'Where's your mother?'

" 'God has taken her.'

"The doctor nodded gravely. He picked up his bag and pulled out a contraption that left Mijail speechless. Mijail glimpsed other instruments inside the bag. Shining, wondrous instruments.

"The doctor placed the strange object on the boy's chest and put the two ends in his ears.

" 'What's that?'

" 'It's for listening to what your lungs are saying.... Take a deep breath.'

" 'Are you a magician?' Mijail asked in astonishment.

"The doctor smiled.

" 'No, I'm not a magician. I'm only a doctor.'

" 'What's the difference?'

"Antonin Kolvenik had lost his wife and son during an outbreak of cholera some years earlier. Now he lived alone, had a modest office and a passion for the works of Dvořák. He looked at the ragged boy with curiosity and pity. He reminded him of his own lost son. Mijail brandished a winning smile.

"Dr. Kolvenik decided to take the boy home with him. Mijail spent the next ten years there. The kind doctor gave him an education, a home, and a name. Mijail was only a teenager when he began to assist his adoptive father in his practice and learn about the mysteries of the human body. God's mysterious will was revealed through that complex framework of flesh and bone, driven by a mysterious spark of magic. Mijail soaked up the lessons avidly, convinced that in all that science there was a message waiting to be deciphered.

"He wasn't even twenty when death paid him another visit. The old doctor's health had been deteriorating for some time. A cardiac arrest destroyed half of his heart one Christmas Eve while they were planning a trip for Mijail to see southern Europe. Antonin Kolvenik was dying. Mijail swore to himself that this time death would not snatch anyone away from him.

" 'My heart is weary, Mijail,' said the old doctor.

'It's time for me to go and rejoin my Frida and my other Mijail....'

" 'I'll give you another heart, Father.'

"The doctor smiled. That strange youngster and his bizarre ideas...The only reason he feared abandoning this wretched world was that he was going to leave the boy alone and helpless. Mijail's only friends were books. What would become of him?

" 'You've already given me ten years of your company, Mijail,' he said. 'Now you must think of yourself. Of your future.'

" 'I'm not going to let you die, Father.'

" 'Mijail, do you remember that day when you asked me what was the difference between a doctor and a magician? Well, Mijail, there is no magic. Our body begins to destroy itself from the moment it is born. We are fragile. We're creatures of passage. All that is left of us are our actions, the good or the evil we do to our fellow humans. Do you understand what I'm trying to tell you, Mijail?'

"Ten days later the police found Mijail covered in blood, crying next to the body of the man he had learned to call Father. The neighbors had alerted the authorities when they smelled a strange odor and heard the young man's howls. The police report concluded that Mijail, disturbed by the doctor's death, had dissected him and had tried to rebuild his heart using a mechanism of valves and cogs. Mijail was admitted to the Prague mental hospital, from which he escaped two years later by pretending to be dead. When the authorities went to the morgue to fetch his body, all they found was a white sheet with black butterflies flying around it.

"Mijail reached Barcelona carrying the seeds of madness that would manifest years later. He showed little interest in material things or in people's company and was never proud of the fortune he amassed. He used to say that nobody deserves to have a penny more than he's ready to offer those who need it more than he does. The night I met him Mijail told me that, for some reason, life usually grants us what we are not looking for. He was given wealth, fame, and power, yet his soul yearned only for spiritual peace so that he could silence the shadows in his heart...."

"During the months following the incident in his studio, Shelley, Lluís, and I worked together to keep Mijail away from his obsessions and to distract him. It was no easy task. Mijail always knew when we were lying to him, even if he didn't say so. He'd play along, pretending to be docile and resigned to his condition. When I looked into his eyes, however, I could see the darkness flooding his soul. He had stopped trusting us. The miserable conditions we lived in worsened. Creditors had seized our accounts, and the Velo-Granell assets had been confiscated by the government. Sentís, who thought his scheming was going to turn him into the sole owner of the business, discovered that he was actually bankrupt. All he managed to salvage was Mijail's worthless old flat on Calle Princesa. We were only able to hold on to the properties Mijail had put in my name: the Gran Teatro Real—a tomb in which I finally took shelter—and a greenhouse next to the Sarriá railway, which Mijail had used in the past as a workshop for his experiments.

"Lluís took care of selling my jewelry and dresses to the highest bidder so that we could buy food. My bridal trousseau, which I had never used, became our means of survival. Mijail and I barely spoke. He wandered around the mansion like a ghost while his body became increasingly deformed. Soon he wasn't able to hold a book in his hands. He had trouble reading. I no longer heard him cry. Now he just laughed. His bitter laughter in the middle of the night froze my blood. With his deformed hands he wrote in a notebook—pages and pages of illegible writing whose content we were unable to decipher. When Dr. Shelley came to visit him, Mijail would lock himself in his room and refuse to come out until his friend had left. I told Dr. Shelley about my fear that Mijail might be thinking of taking his own life. Shelley told me that he feared something even worse. I didn't know, or I didn't want to know, what he was referring to.

"It was then that I had a crazy, desperate idea. I thought it might be a way of saving Mijail, and our marriage. I decided to have a child. I was convinced that if I managed to give him a child, Mijail would find a reason to go on living and return to my side. I got carried away with that yearning. My entire body burned with longing to conceive the infant that would bring us salvation and hope. My dream was to raise a small Mijail, pure and innocent. In my heart I longed to have a new version of his father, but one free of all madness and evil. I couldn't let Mijail suspect what I was scheming or he would refuse outright. It would be difficult enough to find the opportunity to be alone with him. As I said, for a long time Mijail had been avoiding me. His deformity made him feel uncomfortable in my presence. The disease was beginning to affect his speech. He stammered, full of anger and shame. He could swallow only liquids. My efforts to show that he didn't repel me, that nobody could understand and share his suffering better than I, only seemed to make matters worse. But I was patient, and for once in my life I thought I'd fooled Mijail. I only fooled myself. That was my worst mistake.

"When I told Mijail we were going to have a baby, his reaction scared me to death. He disappeared for almost a month. Lluís found him in the old greenhouse in Sarriá weeks later, unconscious. He'd been working tirelessly. He'd reconstructed his throat and his mouth. His appearance was monstrous. He'd given himself a deep voice, metallic and malevolent. His jaws had rows of metal eye-teeth. His face was unrecognizable except for his eyes. Beneath that horror, the soul of the Mijail I loved was still burning in its own inferno. Next to him Lluís found a pile of contraptions and hundreds of plans. I asked Shelley to have a look at them while Mijail was recovering with a sleep from which he didn't wake in three days. The doctor's conclusions were horrifying. Mijail had completely lost his mind. He was planning to rebuild his entire body before the disease consumed him altogether. We shut him away in a room at the top of the main tower, an impregnable cell. I gave birth to our daughter listening to my husband's wild screams while he was locked up like a beast. I didn't share a single day with the baby. Dr. Shelley took care of her and swore he would bring her up as if she were his own daughter. She would be called María and, like me, she would never know her real mother. What little life remained in my heart left with her, but I knew I had no choice. I sensed an imminent tragedy in the air. I could feel it like poison working its way through my veins. It was just a matter of time. As usual, the final blow came from where we least expected it."

"Benjamín Sentís, whose envy and greed had led to his own downfall, had been planning his revenge. Sentís was already suspected of helping Sergei escape after he attacked me outside the cathedral. As in the dark prophecy of the sewer-tunnel people, the hands Mijail had given Sentís years earlier had only served to weave misfortune and betrayal. And then, on the last night of 1948, Benjamín Sentís, who hated Mijail with a passion, returned to deal him one final blow.

"During those years my former tutors, Sergei and Tatiana, had been in hiding. They, too, were anxious for revenge. The time had come. Sentís knew that Florián's squad was planning to search our house in Güell Park the following day, looking for supposedly incriminating evidence against Mijail. If the search took place, Sentís's lies and fraudulent claims would be exposed. Shortly before midnight Sergei and Tatiana used cans brimming with gasoline to douse the outside of our house. Sentís, always the coward in the shadows, watched from his car as the first flames appeared, and then fled the scene.

"When I awoke, blue smoke was rising up the staircase. The fire spread in a matter of minutes. Lluís rescued me and we managed to save our lives by jumping off a balcony onto the garage roof, and from there to the garden. When we turned around, we saw that the flames had completely enveloped the first two floors and were rising toward the tower where we kept Mijail locked up. I wanted to rush toward the flames to save him, but Lluís wouldn't allow me to, holding me back as I screamed and struggled. At that moment we caught sight of Sergei and Tatiana. Sergei was laughing like a madman. Tatiana was trembling silently, her hands dripping with gasoline. What happened next was a vision straight out of a nightmare. The flames had reached the top of the tower. The windows shattered into a shower of glass. Suddenly a figure emerged from the flames. I thought I saw a black angel leap out onto the walls. It was Mijail. He was crawling like a spider on the outside of the building, holding on with the metal claws he had made himself. He moved at a terrifying pace. Sergei and Tatiana were staring at him in astonishment, not understanding what they were witnessing. The shadow threw itself over them and, with tremendous strength, dragged them inside the burning house. When I saw them disappear into that inferno and heard their screams of agony as the fire peeled the flesh off their bones, I fainted.

"Lluís took me to our last remaining shelter, the ruins of the Gran Teatro Real, which has been our home ever since. The following day the newspapers announced the tragedy. Two charred bodies, clasped together, had been found in the attic. The police assumed that they belonged to Mijail and me. Only we knew that in fact they were those of Sergei and Tatiana. A third body was never found. That same day Lluís and Shelley went to the Sarriá greenhouse in search of Mijail. There was no sign of him. The transformation was about to be completed. Shelley gathered all of Mijail's papers, his plans and his handwritten notes, to remove all the evidence. For weeks he studied them, hoping to find some clue that would help him locate Mijail. We knew he was hiding somewhere in the city, waiting, finishing his metamorphosis. Thanks to the notes, Shelley discovered Mijail's plan. The diaries described a serum developed from the essence of the butterflies he had been breeding for years, the same liquid I had seen Mijail use to resuscitate the dead body of a woman in the Velo-Granell factory. At last I understood what he was planning to do. Mijail had retired to die. He needed to rid himself of his last breath of humanity so that he could cross over to the other side. Like the black butterfly, his body was going to be buried in order to be reborn out of the darkness. And when he returned, he would no longer do so as Mijail Kolvenik. He would do so as a beast."

Her words echoed through the Gran Teatro.

"For months we had no news of Mijail, nor did we find his hiding place," Eva Irinova continued. "Deep down we were hoping his plan would fail. We were wrong. A year after the fire, two police inspectors went to the Velo-Granell factory, alerted by an anonymous tip. Sentís again, of course. As he hadn't heard from Sergei and Tatiana, he suspected that Mijail was still alive. The factory premises had been sealed off and nobody had access to them. The two inspectors discovered an intruder inside the factory. They fired at him, using up all their bullets, but—"

"That's why they never found the bullets," I said, recalling Florián's words. "Kolvenik's body absorbed all the shots...."

The old lady nodded.

"The policemen's bodies were found torn to pieces," she said. "Nobody could understand what had happened. Except for Shelley, Lluís, and me. Mijail had returned. During the next few days, all the members of the old Velo-Granell board of directors who had betrayed Mijail met with their deaths under strange circumstances. We suspected that Mijail was hiding in the sewer system, using the tunnels to move about the city. It was not an unknown world to him. Only one question remained: Why had he gone to the factory? Once again his notebooks gave us the answer: the serum. He needed to inject himself with the serum to stay alive. The reserves he'd kept in the tower had been destroyed, and he must have used up all the provisions he kept in the greenhouse. Dr. Shelley bribed a policeman to allow him access to the factory. There we found a cupboard containing the last two bottles of serum. Shelley decided to keep one of them. After an entire life fighting illness, death, and pain, he was incapable of destroying that serum. He needed to study it and unveil its secrets. When he analyzed it he managed to put together a mercury-based compound with which he intended to neutralize the serum's power. He filled twelve bullets with this compound and hid them, hoping he would never have to use them."

I realized those were the bullets Shelley had given to Lluís Claret. I was still alive thanks to them.

"What about Mijail?" asked Marina. "Without the serum…"

"We found his dead body in a sewer beneath the Gothic quarter," said Eva Irinova. "Or what was left of it, because he'd turned into a hellish creature, stinking of the rotten flesh with which he had rebuilt himself.…"

The aged woman raised her eyes to look at her old friend Lluís. The chauffeur took over and concluded the story.

"We buried the body in the Sarriá cemetery, in an unmarked grave," he explained. "Officially, Mr. Kolvenik had died a year earlier. We couldn't reveal the truth. If Sentís had discovered that Señora Kolvenik was still alive, he wouldn't have stopped until he'd destroyed her as well. We condemned ourselves to a secret life in this place."

"For years I thought Mijail was resting in peace," said Eva Irinova. "I would go there on the last Sunday of every month, like the day I met him, to visit him and remind him that soon, very soon, we would be reunited. So we lived in a world of memories, and yet we forgot something essential...."

"What was that?" I asked.

"María, our daughter."

Marina and I exchanged glances. I remembered that Shelley had thrown the photograph we had shown him into the fire. The girl in that photograph was María Shelley.

When we took the album from the greenhouse, we had robbed Mijail of the only memento he possessed of the child he had never known.

———

"Shelley raised María as if she were his own daughter, but she always suspected that the story the doctor told her, about her mother dying during childbirth, was not true. Shelley never was a good liar. In time María discovered Mijail's old notebooks in the doctor's study and reconstructed the story I have told you. María was born with her father's madness. I remember that the day I told Mijail I was pregnant, he smiled. That smile worried me, even though at the time I didn't know why. Many years would pass before I understood, from Mijail's notebooks, that the black butterfly from the sewers feeds on its young, and when it buries itself to die, it takes with it one of its larvae, which it devours when it comes back to life.... When you came across the greenhouse, after following me from the graveyard, María also found, at last, what she'd been trying to discover for years: the vial of serum Dr. Shelley had been hiding. And, thirty years after his death, Mijail returned from the dead. He has been feeding off María ever since, reconstructing himself using bits from other bodies, acquiring strength, creating others like him...."

I swallowed hard as I remembered what I'd seen the night before in the tunnels.

"When I realized what was happening," the lady continued, "I wanted to warn Sentís that he would be the first to fall. In order not to reveal my identity, I used you, Oscar, with that visiting card. I thought that when he saw it and heard what little you knew, fear would make him react and he would protect himself. Once more I overestimated the evil old man....He wanted to meet Mijail and destroy him—and he dragged Florián down behind him. Lluís went to the Sarriá cemetery and saw for himself that the tomb was empty. At first we suspected that Shelley had betrayed us. We thought that he was the one who had been visiting the greenhouse, building new creatures...that perhaps he didn't want to die without understanding the mysteries Mijail had left unexplained. We were never sure about him. When we realized he was trying to protect María, it was too late. Now Mijail will come for us."

"Why?" asked Marina. "Why would he come back to this place?"

The lady quietly undid the two top buttons of her dress and pulled out a chain with a medallion. The chain also held a glass vial with an emerald-colored liquid inside it.

"For this," she said.

TWENTY-FOUR

I was examining the serum bottle against the light when I heard it. So did Marina. Something was creeping over the dome of the theater.

"They're here," said Lluís Claret from the doorway, his voice ominous.

Showing no surprise, Eva Irinova placed the chain holding the serum back around her neck. I saw Lluís Claret take out his revolver and check the cylinder. The silver bullets Shelley had given him shone inside.

"You must leave," Eva Irinova ordered us. "You now know the truth. Learn to forget it."

Her face was hidden behind the veil and her mechanical

voice lacked all expression. I found it hard to accept the true meaning of her words.

"Your secret is safe with us," I said all the same.

"Truth is always safe from people," Eva Irinova replied coldly. "Now go."

Claret signaled to us to follow him and we left the dressing room. Through the translucent glass dome the moon cast a rectangle of light over the stage. Above the dome the silhouettes of Mijail Kolvenik and his creatures stood out like swaying shadows. When I looked up I thought I could count at least a dozen of them.

"Dear God..." murmured Marina next to me.

Claret was looking in the same direction. I saw fear in his eyes. One of the shapes struck the roof fiercely. Claret cocked the gun and aimed. The creature kept punching the roof with all its might. In a matter of seconds the glass would give way.

"There's a tunnel under the orchestra pit. It crosses beneath the stalls up to the foyer," Claret informed us without taking his eyes off the dome. "You'll find a trapdoor under the main staircase. It will lead you to a corridor. Follow it until you come to a fire exit."

"Wouldn't it be easier to go back the way we came?" I asked. "Through your flat..."

"No. They've already been there."

Marina clutched my arm and tugged at me. "Let's do what he says, Oscar."

I looked at Claret. In his eyes I could see the cold serenity of a man prepared to meet death without fear or remorse. A second later the glass pane of the dome burst into a thousand pieces and a wolfish creature hurled itself onto the stage. Claret held his weapon with both hands and aimed calmly. The bullet blew off the top of the creature's skull and it slumped to its knees, dead. We raised our eyes to the opening in the dome. A dozen silhouettes loomed around the edge, looking at us with cold, angry eyes. I immediately recognized Kolvenik, standing in the middle. At his signal they slipped in and started to crawl down toward the stage.

Marina and I jumped into the orchestra pit and followed Claret's directions while he covered our backs. I heard another deafening shot. I turned to take one last look before entering the narrow passageway. A body wrapped in bloodstained rags leaped onto the stage and pounced on Claret. Claret's bullet opened a smoking hole in its chest the size of a fist. The body was still advancing when I closed the trapdoor and pushed Marina forward.

"What will happen to Claret?"

"I don't know," I lied. "Run."

We hurried down the tunnel. It can't have been more than a meter wide and a meter and a half high. We had to stoop and feel the walls with our hands to advance without losing our balance. We'd only covered a few meters when we heard heavy footsteps above us. We were being followed from the orchestra seats; someone was stalking us. The echo of the shots became more and more intense. I wondered how many shots Claret had left before being torn to shreds by the pack.

Suddenly somebody lifted a plank of wood above our heads. Light poured through, blinding us, and something fell at our feet. It was a body. Claret. His eyes were empty, lifeless. The barrel of the gun he held in his hands was still smoking. There were no apparent bruises or wounds on his body, but something looked wrong. Marina peered over my shoulder and moaned. His neck had been so brutally broken that his head was facing backward. A shadow spread over us and I noticed a black butterfly settling on Kolvenik's old friend. I was distracted for a second and wasn't aware of Mijail's presence until he plunged right through the soft, rotten wood and was clasping Marina's neck with his claws. He lifted her straight up, snatching her from my side before I was able to hold her back. I shouted his name. He turned slowly and looked into my eyes. I was paralyzed with fear. Then he spoke to me. I'll never forget his voice.

"If you want to see your friend in one piece again, bring me the bottle."

For a few seconds I was unable to think straight. Then

anguish brought me back to reality. I leaned over Claret's body and fumbled for the weapon; the muscles in his hand had stiffened with his final spasm, and his index finger was stuck in the trigger. Pulling back one finger at a time, I retrieved the gun. I opened the cylinder and saw that there was no ammunition left. I felt Claret's pockets for more bullets and found the second charge of ammunition: six silver bullets, each with a puncture in its tip. The poor man hadn't had time to reload. Maybe after so many years of fearing that meeting, Claret had been incapable of shooting at Mijail Kolvenik, or what was left of him. Little did it matter now.

Trembling, I clambered up the tunnel wall into the seats above and set off in search of Marina.

Dr. Shelley's bullets had left a trail of bodies across the stage. Others had ended up skewered on chandeliers or dangling over the boxes. Lluís Claret had rid himself of the pack of beasts, but not of the master. Gazing at the corpses, I couldn't help thinking that this was the best fate they could aspire to. Once the breath of life had left them, the monstrosity of their artificial grafts and components became more evident. One of the bodies lay stretched out in the central aisle of the floor, faceup, its jaw dislocated. I stepped over it. The emptiness in its opaque eyes sent an icy shiver down my spine. There was nothing in them. Nothing.

I approached the stage and climbed onto it. The light in Eva Irinova's dressing room was still on, but there was nobody there. There was a smell of carrion in the air. The prints of bloodstained fingers could be seen on the old photographs hanging on the walls. Kolvenik. I heard a creaking sound behind me and turned around, holding the gun up high. I could hear footsteps moving away.

"Eva?" I called.

I returned to the stage and noticed a ring of amber light in the balcony. As I drew closer I recognized Eva Irinova's silhouette. She was holding a candelabrum in her hands and gazing at the ruins of the Gran Teatro Real. The ruins of her life. She turned around and slowly raised the flaming candles until they touched the threadbare tongues of velvet hanging from the boxes. The dry material caught fire immediately. Bit by bit she sowed a trail of fire that soon spread over the walls of the boxes, the gilded enamel of the main hall, and the seats.

"No!" I yelled.

Eva ignored my call and disappeared through a door leading to the corridors behind the boxes. In a matter of seconds the flames were spreading like blood on water, creeping forward and devouring everything in their path. The glow of the fire revealed the lost grandeur of the theater. A sudden wave of intense heat swept over me and the smell of burned wood and paint made me feel nauseous.

I followed the rising flames with my eyes. I could see the stage machinery far above, an intricate system of ropes, curtains, pulleys, suspended sets, and walkways. Two blazing eyes observed me from on high. Kolvenik. He was holding Marina in one hand, as if she were a toy. I watched him move around the scaffolding with the agility of a cat. I turned my head and noticed that the flames had spread along the whole of the first floor and were beginning to lick their way up to the boxes on the second level. The air coming through the hole in the dome was feeding the flames, creating a huge chimney.

I hurried toward a flight of wooden stairs. They rose in a zigzag and wobbled under my feet. When I reached the third floor I stopped and looked up. I'd lost Kolvenik. Just then I felt claws dig into my back. I swung around to escape their mortal embrace and found that I faced one of Kolvenik's creatures. Claret's shots had almost ripped off one of its arms, but the figure was still alive. It had long hair and its face had once belonged to a woman. I pointed the gun at her, but she didn't stop. Suddenly I felt certain I'd seen that face before. The glow of the flames revealed what remained of her eyes. I felt my mouth drying up.

"María?" I stammered.

Kolvenik's daughter, or the creature inhabiting her carcass, stopped for a moment, hesitating.

"María?" I said again.

Nothing remained of the angelic aura I remembered. Her beauty had been destroyed and a pathetic, spine-chilling vermin had taken its place. Her skin was still fresh; Kolvenik had worked fast. I lowered the gun and stretched out a hand toward the poor woman. Perhaps there was still some hope for her.

"María? Do you recognize me? I'm Oscar, Oscar Drai. Don't you remember me?"

María Shelley looked at me intently. For a moment a spark of life rose to her eyes. I saw her shed tears and raise her hands. She stared at the monstrous metal claws that sprouted from her arms and I heard her moan. Again I stretched out a hand to her. María Shelley took a step back, trembling.

A wave of flames burst over one of the bars supporting the main curtain. The sheet of threadbare material fell away in a blanket of fire and the ropes that had been holding it up snapped outward like fiery whips, reaching the walkway on which we were standing. A line of fire fell between us. Again I held a hand out to Kolvenik's daughter.

"Please, take my hand."

She withdrew, shying away, her face drenched in tears. The platform under our feet creaked.

"María, please..."

The creature gazed at the flames as if she could see something in them. She gave me one last look and seized the blazing rope, which was now lying on the platform. The fire spread over her arm, her torso, her hair, her clothes and face. I watched her burn as if she were a wax figure until the wooden planks beneath her feet gave way and she fell into the abyss.

I ran to one of the third-floor exits. I had to find Eva Irinova and save Marina.

"Eva!" I yelled when at last I sighted her.

She ignored my call and continued on her way. I caught up with her on the central marble staircase, grabbed her arm, and stopped her. She struggled to free herself.

"He's got Marina. If I don't give him the serum he'll kill her."

"Your friend is already dead. Get out of here while you can."

"No!"

Eva Irinova looked around us. Plumes of smoke were creeping up the stairs. There wasn't much time left.

"I can't go without her."

"You don't understand," she replied. "If I give you the

serum he'll kill both of you and nobody will be able to stop him."

"He doesn't want to kill anybody. He only wants to live."

"You still don't understand, Oscar," said Eva. "I can't do anything. It's all in God's hands."

With those words she turned and walked away.

"Nobody can do God's work. Not even you," I said, reminding her of her own words.

She paused. I raised my gun and aimed. The click as I cocked the gun echoed through the gallery. The sound made her turn around.

"I'm only trying to save Mijail's soul," she said.

"I don't know whether you'll be able to save Kolvenik's soul, but you can still save your own."

The lady now looked at me without speaking, facing the threat of the gun in my shaking hands.

"Would you be able to shoot me in cold blood?" she asked.

I didn't answer. I didn't know the answer. The only things occupying my mind were the image of Marina in Kolvenik's claws and the few minutes remaining before the flames would finally open the doors of hell in the Gran Teatro Real.

"Your friend must mean a lot to you."

I nodded, and it seemed to me that the woman was smiling the saddest smile of her life.

"Does she know?" she asked.

"I don't know," I said without thinking.

She nodded slowly and I saw her pull out the emerald bottle.

"You and I are the same, Oscar. We're alone, condemned to love someone without hope...."

She handed me the bottle and I lowered my weapon. I put the gun on the floor and took the bottle in my hands. As I examined it I felt as if a load had been lifted from my shoulders. I was going to thank her, but Eva Irinova was no longer there. Nor was the revolver.

By the time I reached the top floor, the entire building seemed about to crumble under my feet. I ran to the end of the gallery, searching for an entrance to the area above the stage. Suddenly one of the doors burst off its frame, wrapped in flames. A river of fire flooded the gallery. I was trapped. I looked desperately around me and saw only one way out: the windows onto the street. I drew closer to the smoke-filled windowpanes and noticed a narrow ledge on the other side. The fire was coming toward me. The windowpanes splintered as if touched by an infernal breath. My clothes were smoking; I could feel the heat of the flames on my skin, and I was suffocating. I jumped onto the ledge. The cold night air hit me and

I could see the streets of Barcelona spreading out many meters below. It was an overwhelming sight: The fire had completely enveloped the Gran Teatro Real, and the scaffolding outside had collapsed, burned to cinders. The old façade rose like a cathedral of flames in the middle of the Raval quarter. Fire engine sirens howled in the distance as if bewailing their own impotence. Near the metal spire, where the dome's network of steel nerves came together, Kolvenik was holding Marina.

"Marina!" I screamed.

I took a step forward and instinctively grabbed a metal arch so as not to fall. It was scorching. I shrieked with pain and pulled my hand away. Smoke rose from my blackened palm. At that very moment a new tremor ran through the structure and I guessed what was about to happen. With a deafening blast, the theater collapsed, leaving only the naked metal skeleton intact, a spider's web of aluminum stretching over an inferno. In its center stood Kolvenik. I could see Marina's face. She was alive. So I did the only thing that could save her.

I took the bottle and raised it so that Kolvenik could see it. He pushed Marina aside, moving her close to the edge of the precipice. I heard her scream. Then he extended an open claw into the void. The message was clear. In front of me a beam stretched toward him like a bridge. I stepped forward.

"Oscar, no!" Marina begged.

I fixed my eyes on the narrow gangway and risked it. I could feel the soles of my shoes melting with every step I took. A suffocating wind rising from the fire roared all around me as I moved forward step by step, keeping my eyes on the beam like a tight-rope walker. When I looked up I discovered a terrified Marina. She was alone! I was about to put my arms around her when, suddenly, Kolvenik rose behind her. He grabbed her again and held her out over the chasm. I pulled out the bottle and mimicked his action, letting him know I would throw it into the flames if he didn't put Marina down. I remembered Eva Irinova's words: "He'll kill both of you." So I opened the bottle and threw a couple of drops into the void. Kolvenik flung Marina against a bronze statue and lunged at me. I jumped to one side to dodge him and the bottle slipped through my fingers.

The serum evaporated as it touched the red-hot metal. Kolvenik's claw caught the flask when there were only a few drops left inside. He closed his metal fist over it and crushed it to bits. A few emerald drops slid through his fingers. The flames illuminated his face, a well of irrepressible hatred and anger. Then he started to move toward us. Marina clutched my hands and pressed them hard. She closed her eyes, and I did the same. I could smell the rotten stench of Kolvenik a few centimeters away and braced myself for the impact.

The first shot whistled through the blaze. I opened my eyes and saw Eva Irinova's silhouette advancing as I had done, along the beam. She held the revolver up high. A rose of black blood spread across Kolvenik's chest. The second shot, much closer, destroyed one of his hands. The third one hit him in the shoulder. I pulled Marina away. Kolvenik staggered and turned toward Eva. The lady in black was advancing slowly, coldly aiming her weapon at him. I heard Kolvenik groan. The fourth shot opened a hole in his stomach. The fifth and last left a black hole between his eyes. A second later Kolvenik collapsed to his knees. Eva Irinova dropped the gun and ran to his side.

She took him in her arms and cradled him. Their eyes met and I saw her caress his monstrous face. She was crying.

"Take your friend away from here," she said without looking at me.

I led Marina along the walkway until we reached the ledge outside the building. From there we managed to climb onto the roof of the annex building and get safely away from the inferno. Before losing sight of Eva, we turned around. The lady in black was embracing Mijail Kolvenik. Their figures were silhouetted against the flames until the fire enveloped them completely. I thought I could see their ashes scattering in the wind, floating over the city, until dawn took them away forever.

———

The following morning the papers reported on the greatest fire in the history of Barcelona, with stories about the old Gran Teatro Real and how its disappearance had silenced the last echoes of a long-gone age. The ashes had spread a blanket over the waters of the port and would continue to fall over the city until evening. Photographs taken from the hill of Montjuïc revealed the horrific scene of an infernal pyre rising heavenward. The tragedy took a new turn when the police disclosed their suspicions that the building had been occupied by homeless beggars and that a number of them had become trapped among the debris. Nothing was known about the identity of the two charred bodies that had been found, locked in an embrace, at the top of the dome. The truth, as Eva Irinova had predicted, was safe from people.

No newspaper mentioned the old story of Eva Irinova and Mijail Kolvenik. It no longer interested anyone. I remember standing with Marina that morning in front of one of the newspaper stands in the Ramblas. The front page of *La Vanguardia* bore the headline, spread over five columns, BARCELONA BURNS!

Early risers and the merely curious hurried to buy the first edition, wondering who had painted the sky with garlands of amber and gray. Slowly we walked away toward Plaza Cataluña while the ashes continued to fall all around us like dead snowflakes.

TWENTY-FIVE

In the days that followed the fire at the Gran Teatro Real, a cold spell struck Barcelona. For the first time in many years a blanket of snow covered the city from the port to the top of Mount Tibidabo. Marina and I, together with Germán, spent a Christmas filled with long silences, our eyes rarely meeting. Marina barely mentioned what had happened, and I began to notice that she avoided my company and preferred to retire to her room to write. I killed time playing endless games of chess with Germán in the large sitting room, by the fireside. I watched the snow fall and waited for the moment when I'd be alone with Marina. A moment that never came.

Germán pretended not to notice what was going on and tried to cheer me up by making conversation.

"Marina tells me you want to be an architect, Oscar."

I would nod, not really knowing what I wanted anymore. I spent my nights awake, piecing together the story we had lived through. I tried to keep the phantoms of Kolvenik and Eva Irinova out of my mind. More than once I thought of visiting old Dr. Shelley to let him know what had happened. But I lacked the courage to face him and to explain how I'd witnessed the death of the woman he had brought up as his daughter, or how I'd seen his best friend burn to death.

On the last day of the year the fountain in the garden froze. I feared that my days with Marina were about to end. Soon I would have to return to the boarding school. We spent New Year's Eve in candlelight, listening to the distant bells of the church in Plaza Sarriá. Outside it was still snowing: It looked as if the stars had tumbled out of the sky without warning. At midnight we murmured a toast. I wanted to catch Marina's eye, but she hid her face in the shadows. That night I tried to understand what I'd done or said to deserve such treatment. I could feel Marina's presence in the next room, like an island floating away in the current. I imagined her awake. I rapped on the wall. I called her name, in vain; there was no reply.

I packed my belongings and wrote a note in which I

said my farewells to Germán and Marina and thanked them for their hospitality. Something had broken— though I couldn't explain what—and I felt that I was in the way. At daybreak I left the note on the kitchen table and set off toward the school. As I walked away I was sure Marina was watching me from her window. I waved good-bye, hoping she'd be looking. My footsteps left a trail through the snow in the deserted streets.

There were still a few days to go before the rest of the boarders were due to return. The rooms on the fourth floor were pools of loneliness. While I unpacked, Father Seguí paid me a visit. I greeted him politely and continued putting away my clothes.

"Funny people, the Swiss," he said. "While the rest of us hide our sins, they stuff theirs with liqueur, wrap them in silver paper, add a ribbon, and sell them at the price of gold. The prefect has just sent me a huge box of chocolates from Zurich, and there's nobody around to share it with. Someone is going to have to lend me a hand before Doña Paula discovers them...."

"You can count on me," I offered halfheartedly.

Seguí walked over to the window and gazed at the city, which spread out like a mirage at our feet. Then he turned and observed me as if he could read my thoughts.

"A good friend once told me that problems are like cockroaches," he said in the joking tone he used when he wanted to say something serious. "If you bring them out into the light, they get scared and leave."

"He must have been a wise friend," I said.

"Not quite," Seguí replied. "But he was a good man. Happy New Year, Oscar."

"Happy New Year, Father."

———

I spent those days, until the start of the school term, barely leaving my room. I tried to read, but the words flew off the page. I would spend hours at the window, gazing at Germán and Marina's rambling old house in the distance. A thousand times I thought of returning, and more than once I ventured as far as the alleyway that led to their front gate. I no longer heard Germán's gramophone through the trees—only the wind through the naked branches. At night I'd relive, over and over again, the events of the last few weeks until I collapsed into a restless, feverish, suffocating sleep.

Lessons began a week later. Those were leaden days, with steamed-up windows and radiators dripping in the dark rooms. My old friends and their conversations felt alien to me. They chatted about presents, parties, and memories that I couldn't and didn't want to share. The words of my teachers washed over me. I couldn't make out the importance of Hume's solemn pronouncements or see how derived equations could help turn back the clock and change the fates of Mijail Kolvenik and Eva Irinova. Or my own fate.

The memory of Marina and of the terrifying events we had shared prevented me from thinking, eating, or holding a coherent conversation. She was the only person with whom I could share my anguish, and the need for her presence began to cause me physical pain. I was burning inside. Nothing and nobody could ease the pain. I became a gray figure in the corridors. My shadow merged with the walls. Days fell off the calendar like dead leaves. I kept hoping for a note from Marina, a sign to let me know she wanted to see me again. A simple excuse to run to her side and put an end to the distance separating us, a distance that seemed to grow day by day. But the note never came. I whiled away the days by returning to the places where I'd been with Marina. I would sit on the benches in the square, hoping to see her walk by....

At the end of January Father Seguí called me to his study. Looking serious, with a penetrating gaze, he asked me what was wrong.

"I don't know," I answered.

"Perhaps if we talk about it we might find out what it is," he suggested.

"I don't think so," I said, so brusquely I was immediately sorry.

"You spent a week away over Christmas. May I ask where?"

"With my family."

A shadow fell over my tutor's eyes.

"If you're going to lie to me, we might as well not continue this conversation, Oscar."

"It's the truth," I said. "I've been with my family."

February brought the sun with it. The winter light melted the layers of ice and frost that had masked the city. That cheered me, and one Saturday I turned up at Marina's house. A chain secured the gates. Beyond the trees the old mansion looked more abandoned than ever. For a moment I thought I was losing my mind. Had I imagined it all? The inhabitants of that ghostly mansion, the story of Kolvenik and the lady in black, Inspector Florián, Lluís Claret, the creatures brought back to life...characters whom the black hand of fate had eliminated one by one...Had I dreamed up Marina and her enchanted beach?

"We only remember what never really happened...."

That night I woke up screaming, bathed in cold sweat, not knowing where I was. In my dreams I'd returned to Kolvenik's tunnels. I was following Marina without being able to reach her until I found her covered in a mantle of black butterflies; but when they flew off, only emptiness remained. Inexplicable. Cold. The destructive devil that obsessed Kolvenik. The nothingness behind the last darkness.

When Father Seguí and my friend JF heard my screams and ran into my room, it took me a few seconds to recognize them. Seguí felt my pulse while JF looked at me in dismay, convinced that his friend had lost his mind altogether. They didn't leave my side until I fell asleep again.

The following day, after two months without seeing Marina, I decided to return to the old house in Sarriá. I wasn't going to give up until I'd found an explanation.

TWENTY-SIX

It was a misty Sunday. The shadows of the trees with their dry branches conjured up skeletal shapes. The church bells rang in time to my footsteps. I stopped in front of the gate that barred my way. I noticed tire marks on the fallen leaves and wondered whether Germán had taken his old Tucker out of the garage again. I slipped in like a thief by jumping over the gate and walked into the garden.

The mansion's silhouette loomed in utter silence, darker and more desolate than ever. I noticed Marina's bike lying abandoned among the weeds. The chain was rusty, the handlebars blackened by damp. As I stared at the scene I felt I was standing before a ruin inhabited only by old bits of furniture and invisible echoes.

"Marina?" I called.

The wind carried my voice away. I walked around the house, toward the back door that led to the kitchen. It was open. An empty table, covered with a layer of dust. I walked through the rooms. Silence. I reached the large hall with the paintings. Marina's mother looked at me from them all, but for me the eyes were Marina's. It was then that I heard someone crying behind me.

Germán was curled up in one of the armchairs, still as a statue. Only his tears were moving. I had never seen a man of his age cry like that. It froze my blood. His eyes were lost in the portraits and he looked pale, haggard. He'd aged since the last time I'd seen him. He was wearing one of the formal suits I remembered, but it was creased and dirty. I wondered how many days he'd been like this. How many days he'd spent in that armchair.

I kneeled down in front of him and patted his hand.

"Germán."

His hand was so cold it scared me. Suddenly the painter put his arms around me and hugged me, trembling like a child. I felt my mouth go dry. I hugged him back and held him while he wept on my shoulder. I was afraid the doctors had given him bad news, that he'd lost all the hope of the past few months, so I let him weep while I wondered where Marina was, why she wasn't there with Germán....

Then the old man raised his head. One look into his eyes was enough for me to understand the truth. I understood it with the brutal clarity with which dreams vanish. Like a cold, poisoned dagger that plunges without mercy into your soul.

"Where's Marina?" I stammered.

Germán was unable to utter a single word. There was no need. From the look in his eyes I knew that Germán's visits to Sant Pau Hospital had never happened. I knew that the doctor at La Paz Hospital had never treated the painter. I knew that Germán's joy and hope when they returned from Madrid had nothing to do with him. Marina had fooled me from the start.

"The illness that took her mother away," Germán murmured, "is taking her away, Oscar, my friend. It's taking my Marina away...."

I felt my eyelids closing like slabs of stone as the world around me slowly disappeared. Germán hugged me again, and there, in that desolate room of the old house, I cried like a poor fool while the rain began to fall over Barcelona.

From the taxi Sant Pau Hospital looked to me like an enchanted citadel floating on clouds, with its maze of pointed turrets and extravagant domes. Germán had put on a clean suit and sat next to me without speaking. I held a parcel wrapped in the shiniest paper I'd been able to find. When we arrived, the doctor who took care of Marina, one Damián Rojas, looked me up and down and gave me a list of instructions. I must not tire Marina. I must appear positive and optimistic. She was the one who needed my help, and not the other way around. I wasn't there to weep or complain. I was there to help her. If I was unable to follow those rules, I'd better not bother coming back. Damián Rojas was a young doctor and his white coat still had a whiff of medical school about it. He had a stern, impatient tone, and spared very little politeness on me. In other circumstances I would have taken him for an arrogant individual, but something in his manner told me that he hadn't yet learned to isolate himself from his patients' pain, and this was his way of dealing with it.

We walked up to the fourth floor and then down a seemingly endless corridor. It smelled of hospital: a mixture of illness, disinfectant, and air freshener. The moment I set foot in that part of the building I let out a sigh and lost what little courage I had left in me. When we reached Marina's room, Germán went in first. He asked me to wait outside while he announced my visit to Marina. I sensed that Marina would have preferred I didn't see her there.

"Let me speak to her first, Oscar...."

I waited. The corridor was an endless gallery of doors and lost voices. Faces burdened with pain and loss passed one another in silence. Again and again I repeated Dr. Rojas's instructions to myself. I was there to help. Finally Germán peered around the door and nodded at me. I swallowed hard and went in. Germán stayed outside.

The room was a long rectangle where light seemed to evaporate before it touched the floor. From the large window Avenida Gaudí looked like an endless boulevard stretching toward infinity. The towers of the Sagrada Familia sliced the sky in two. There were four beds separated by coarse curtains. Through them you could see the silhouettes of other visitors, like watching a shadow play. Marina's bed was the last on the right, next to the window.

The hardest thing during those first few seconds was to hold her gaze. They had cut her hair short like a boy's. Without her long hair Marina seemed humiliated, naked. I bit my tongue hard, trying to ward off the tears that rose from my soul.

"They had to cut it," she said, guessing. "Because of the tests."

I noticed marks on her throat and on the nape of her

neck. Just looking at them was painful. I tried to smile and handed her the parcel.

"*I* like it," I said as a greeting.

She accepted the parcel and set it on her lap. I drew closer and sat down next to her, silently. She took my hand and pressed it hard. She had lost weight. Her ribs showed through her white hospital nightdress, and there were dark circles under her eyes. Her lips were two thin, parched lines. Her ash-colored eyes no longer shone. With shaky hands she opened the parcel and pulled the book out. She leafed through it and looked up, intrigued.

"All the pages are blank."

"For the time being," I replied. "We have a good story to tell, and I'm only good at bricks and mortar."

She pressed the book against her chest.

"How is Germán doing?" she asked me.

"Fine," I lied. "Tired, but fine."

"And you—how are you?"

"Me?"

"No, me. Who do you think I mean?"

"I'm fine."

"Sure, especially after Sergeant Rojas's lecture...."

I raised my eyebrows as if I didn't have a clue what she was talking about.

"I've missed you," she said.

"Me, too."

Our words were left hanging in the air. For a long moment we looked at each other without speaking. I could see Marina's façade crumbling.

"You have every right to hate me," she said then.

"Hate you? Why should I hate you?"

"I lied to you," said Marina. "When you came to return Germán's watch, I already knew I was ill. I was selfish; I wanted to have a friend...and I think we got lost along the way."

I turned my head to look out the window.

"No, I don't hate you."

She pressed my hand again, then sat up and embraced me.

"Thank you for being the best friend I've ever had," she whispered into my ear.

I felt as if I couldn't breathe. I wanted to run away. Marina held me tight, and I prayed that she wouldn't notice I was crying. Dr. Rojas would take away my pass.

"If you hate me just a little bit, Dr. Rojas won't be annoyed," she said then. "I'm sure it's good for my blood cells or something like that."

"Just a bit, then."

"Thank you."

TWENTY-SEVEN

In the weeks that followed, Germán Blau became my best friend. As soon as my classes were over, at five thirty in the afternoon, I'd run to meet the old painter. We would take a taxi to the hospital and spend the rest of the afternoon with Marina, until the nurses threw us out. Our journeys from Plaza Sarriá to Avenida Gaudí made me realize that Barcelona can be the saddest city in the world in wintertime. Germán's stories and memories became my own.

During the long waits in those desolate hospital corridors Germán shared confidences with me that he had never shared with anyone but his wife. He spoke to me about his years with his teacher, Salvat, about his marriage, and about how only Marina's company had enabled him to survive the loss of his wife. He spoke to me about his doubts and fears, about how experience had taught him that all the things he considered certain were only an illusion, that too many lessons were not worth learning. I, too, spoke to him for the first time without holding anything back. I spoke to him about Marina, about my dreams of becoming an architect at a time when I'd stopped believing in the future. I told him of my loneliness and how until I met them I'd felt as if I were drifting aimlessly through life. I told him how much I feared that I would feel the same way again if I lost them. Germán listened and understood me. He knew that my words were just an attempt to shed light on my own feelings, and he let me talk.

I cherish a special memory of Germán Blau and the days we shared in his house and in the hospital corridors. We both knew that our only bond was Marina and that under other circumstances we would never have exchanged a single word. I always thought Marina became who she was thanks to him, and I have no doubt that what little I am is also due to Germán—more than I care to admit. I keep his advice under lock and key in the coffer of my memory, convinced that one day it will serve as an answer to my own fears and doubts.

That month of March it rained almost every day. Marina wrote the story of Kolvenik and Eva Irinova in the book I had given her while dozens of doctors and their assistants came and went with tests and checkups, and more tests and more checkups. It was then that I remembered the promise I'd made to Marina in the Vallvidrera funicular and began to work on the cathedral. Her cathedral. I found a book on Chartres Cathedral in the school library and started drawing the pieces for the model I was planning to build. First I cut them out of cardboard. After a thousand attempts that almost convinced me I'd never be able to design even a telephone booth, I asked a carpenter on Calle Margenat to cut out my pieces in sheets of wood.

"What are you building, young man?" he asked me, intrigued. "A radiator?"

"A cathedral."

Marina watched with curiosity as I erected her little cathedral on the windowsill. Sometimes she made jokes that kept me from sleeping for days.

"Aren't you in a bit of a hurry, Oscar?" she would ask. "Anyone would think you're expecting me to die tomorrow."

My cathedral soon became popular with the other patients in the room and their visitors. Doña Carmen, an eighty-four-year-old lady from Seville who occupied the next bed, would throw me skeptical looks. She had enough strength of character to destroy an army, and a backside the size of a small car. Doña Carmen seemed to rule the hospital staff with a policeman's whistle. She had been a black marketer, a cabaret singer, a burlesque dancer, a cook, a tobacconist, and God knows what else. She had buried two husbands and three children. Some twenty grandchildren, nephews, and other relatives came to visit and worship her. She kept them in line by telling them that sweet talk was for idiots. I always felt that Doña Carmen had been born in the wrong century. Had she been around at the time, Napoleon would never have crossed the Pyrenees. All of us present—excepting her diabetes—felt the same way.

On the other side of the room was Isabel Llorente, a lady with the airs of a model who spoke in a whisper and looked as if she'd come straight out of the pages of a prewar fashion magazine. She spent the day doing her makeup, looking at herself in a small mirror, and adjusting her wig. Chemotherapy had left her as bald as a billiard ball, but she was convinced that nobody knew. I found out that she had been Miss Barcelona in 1934, and the lover of one of the city's mayors. She kept telling us about a romance with an amazing spy who, any moment now, would reappear and rescue her from this horrible place in which she'd been confined. Doña Carmen would roll her eyes every time Isabel spoke. Nobody ever visited her, and all we had to do was tell her how attractive she looked to keep her smiling for a week. One Thursday afternoon at the end of March we went into the room and found her bed empty. Isabel Llorente had passed away that morning without giving her beau time to come and rescue her.

The other patient in the room was Valeria Astor, a nine-year-old girl who was able to breathe thanks to a tracheotomy. She always smiled at me when I walked in. Her mother spent all the hours she was permitted by her side and, when she wasn't allowed in, she'd sleep in the corridor. Every day she looked a month older. Valeria always asked me whether my friend was a writer, and I'd tell her she was, and a famous one, too. Once she inquired—I'll never know why—whether I was a policeman. Marina would tell her stories she invented as she went along. Valeria had a preference for ghost stories, followed by tales about princesses or about trains, in that order. Doña Carmen would listen to Marina's tales and roar with laughter. Valeria's mother, an emaciated woman, simple to the point of despair, whose name I could never remember, knitted a woolen shawl for Marina in gratitude.

Dr. Damián Rojas came by a few times each day. Bit

by bit, I grew to like him. I discovered that, years earlier, he'd been a pupil at my school and had been on the point of joining the seminary. He had a stunning fiancée named Lulú. Lulú wore a collection of miniskirts and black silk stockings that took my breath away. She visited him every Saturday and would often pop in to say hello and ask us whether her brute of a fiancé was behaving himself. I always went bright red when Lulú spoke to me. Marina would tease me and say that if I kept staring at her like that I'd end up with eyes as big as garters. Lulú and Dr. Rojas were married in April. When the doctor returned from his brief honeymoon in Minorca a week later, he was as thin as a rake. The nurses only had to look at him to start giggling.

For a few months that was my only world. My school lessons were an interlude that I blanked out. Rojas seemed optimistic about Marina. He said she was young and strong and the treatment was producing good results. Germán and I couldn't thank him enough. We gave him cigars, ties, books, and even a Montblanc pen. He would protest, arguing that he was only doing his job, but we both knew that he was putting in many more hours than any other doctor on the floor.

By the end of April Marina had gained a little weight and her color had improved. We would take short walks down the corridor, and when the cold weather began to migrate, we'd step out into the hospital cloister for a while. Marina was still writing in the book I'd given her, although she hadn't allowed me to read a single word.

"Where have you got to?" I'd ask her.

"That's a stupid question."

"Stupid people ask stupid questions. Clever people answer them. Where have you got to?"

She would never say. I guessed that to write down the story we had lived through together had a special significance for her. During one of our walks around the cloister she said something that gave me goose bumps.

"Promise that if something should happen to me, you'll finish the story."

"You'll finish it," I replied. "And anyhow, you have to dedicate it to me."

Meanwhile the small wooden cathedral was growing, and although Doña Carmen said it reminded her of the rubbish incinerator in San Adrián del Besós, by then the spire over the vaulted ceiling was clearly visible. Germán and I started to make plans to take Marina on an excursion to her favorite place—the secret beach between Tossa and Sant Feliu de Guíxols—as soon as she was allowed to leave the hospital. Dr. Rojas, always prudent, gave us an approximate date: the middle of May.

During those weeks I learned that one can live on hope and little else.

Dr. Rojas was in favor of Marina spending as much time as possible walking about and getting some exercise on the hospital premises.

"It will do her good to dress up a bit," he said.

Since he'd got married, Rojas had become an expert on female matters—or so he thought. One Saturday he sent me out with his wife, Lulú, to buy a silk dressing gown for Marina. It was a present, and he paid for it himself. I went with Lulú to a shop selling women's lingerie in Rambla de Cataluña, next to the Alexandra Cinema. The shop assistants knew her. I trailed through the shop behind Lulú, watching her size up an endless display of ingenious undergarments that set my pulse racing. This was far more stimulating than chess.

"Will your girlfriend like this?" Lulú would ask me, licking her rouged lips.

I didn't tell her that Marina wasn't my girlfriend. I felt proud that someone thought she was. Besides, the experience of buying women's underwear with Lulú turned out to be so intoxicating that all I did was nod like a fool at everything she said. When I told Germán, he burst out laughing and admitted that he also thought the doctor's wife was a danger to public health, the way she set one's pulse soaring. It was the first time in months that I'd seen him laugh.

One Saturday morning, while we were getting ready

to go to the hospital, Germán asked me to go up to Marina's room to see if I could find a bottle of her favorite perfume. As I searched in her chest of drawers, I found a folded sheet of paper at the back of a drawer. I opened it and recognized Marina's writing instantly. It was about me. The page was full of crossed-out words and deleted paragraphs. Only these lines had survived:

My friend Oscar is one of those princes without a kingdom who wander around hoping you'll kiss them so they won't turn into frogs. He gets everything back to front and that's why I like him. People who think they get everything right do things wrong, and this, coming from a left-handed person, says it all. He looks at me and thinks I don't see him. He imagines I'll evaporate if he touches me and if he doesn't touch me, then he'll evaporate. He's got me on such a high pedestal he doesn't know how to get up there. He thinks my lips are the door to paradise, but doesn't know they're poisoned. I'm such a coward that I don't tell him so as not to lose him. I pretend I don't see him, and that I am, indeed, going to evaporate. . . .

My friend Oscar is one of those princes who would be well advised to stay away from fairy tales and the princesses who inhabit them. He doesn't know he's really Prince Charming who must kiss Sleeping

Beauty in order to wake her from her eternal sleep, but that's because Oscar doesn't know that fairy tales are lies, although not all lies are fairy tales. Princes aren't charming, and sleeping beauties, however beautiful, never wake from their sleep. He's the best friend I've ever had and if I ever come across Merlin, I'll thank him for having placed him in my path.

I kept the sheet of paper and went down to join Germán. He had put on a special bow tie and seemed more cheerful than ever. He smiled at me and I smiled back. That day, during the taxi ride, the sun was shining. Barcelona was decked out in her best clothes, enchanting both tourists and clouds—for even the clouds paused to stare at her beauty. None of this managed to erase the anxiety those lines had thrust into my mind. It was the first day of May 1980.

TWENTY-EIGHT

That morning we found Marina's bed empty, without sheets. There was no trace of the wooden cathedral, or of her belongings. When I turned my head Germán was already rushing out in search of Dr. Rojas. I ran after him. We found the doctor in his office, looking as if he hadn't slept.

"She's taken a turn for the worse," he said succinctly.

He went on to explain that the night before, only a couple of hours after we'd left, Marina had suffered respiratory failure and her heart had stopped beating for thirty-four seconds. They'd managed to resuscitate her and she was now in the intensive-care unit, unconscious.

319

Her condition was stable and Rojas expected she would be able to leave the unit within the next twenty-four hours, although he didn't want to give us any false hopes. I noticed that Marina's things—her book, the wooden cathedral, and the dressing gown she'd never worn— were on a shelf in the doctor's office.

"May I see my daughter?" asked Germán.

Rojas himself led us to the intensive-care unit. Marina was trapped in a bubble of tubes and steel machines, more monstrous and more real than any of Mijail Kolvenik's inventions. She lay there like a piece of flesh at the mercy of some metal magic. And then I saw the real face of the demon that had tormented Kolvenik, and I understood his madness.

I remember that Germán burst into tears and an uncontrollable force pulled me out of there. I ran and ran, out of breath, until I reached noisy streets full of anonymous faces unaware of my pain. Around me was a world that was unconcerned with Marina's fate. A whole universe in which her life was only a drop of water among the waves. I could think of only one place to go.

The old building in the Ramblas was still standing in its pool of darkness. Dr. Shelley didn't recognize me when he opened the door. The apartment was full of rubbish and smelled moldy. The doctor looked at me with wild, bulging eyes. I led him to his study and made him sit down near the window. María's absence filled the air. It burned us. All the doctor's haughtiness and bad temper had vanished. There was nothing left but an old man, alone and desperate.

"He took her with him," he said. "He took her with him...."

I waited respectfully for him to calm down. At last he looked up and recognized me. He asked me what I wanted, and I told him. He observed me unhurriedly.

"There is no other bottle of Mijail's serum. They were all destroyed. I can't give you what I don't have. But if I had it, I'd be doing you a bad turn. And you'd be making a mistake if you used it on your friend. The same mistake Mijail made..."

His words took a while to sink in. We only have ears for what we want to hear, and I didn't want to hear that. Shelley held my gaze without blinking. I suspected that he had recognized my despair and that the memories it brought back were frightening. I was surprised at myself when I realized that, had it been up to me, at that very moment I would have taken the same route as Kolvenik. Never again would I judge him.

"The territory of humans is life," said the doctor. "Death does not belong to us."

I felt immensely tired. I wanted to surrender—but to what? I turned to leave. Before I left, Shelley called me back.

"You were there, weren't you?" he asked.

I nodded. "María died peacefully, Doctor."

I saw tears in his eyes. He stretched a hand out to me and I shook it. "Thank you."

I never saw him again.

At the end of the week Marina regained consciousness and came out of intensive care. She was moved to a room on the second floor, facing west. She was alone in the room. She no longer wrote in her book and could barely lean over to look at her cathedral—almost finished now—on the windowsill. Rojas asked for permission to carry out one last series of tests. Germán agreed. He still had hope. When Rojas gave us the results in his office, his voice cracked. After months of struggling, he went to pieces when faced with the evidence, while Germán held him up and patted his shoulders.

"There's nothing more I can do.... There's nothing.... Forgive me," cried Damián Rojas.

Two days later we took Marina back to the house in Sarriá. The doctors could not help her any further. We said good-bye to Doña Carmen, Rojas, and Lulú, who wouldn't stop crying. Little Valeria asked me where were we taking my girlfriend, the famous writer. Would she not tell her any more stories?

"Home. We're taking her home."

I left the boarding school on a Monday without letting the school know or telling anyone where I was going. It didn't occur to me that they'd miss me. Nor did I care. My place was next to Marina. We set her up in her bedroom. Her cathedral, now finished, kept her company by the window. It was the best building I have ever made. Germán and I took turns staying by her side around the clock. Rojas had told us she wouldn't suffer, that she would fade away slowly, like a flame flickering in the wind.

Marina never looked more beautiful to me than she did during those last days in the old house in Sarriá. Her hair had grown back, shinier than before, and with silvery highlights. Even her eyes were more luminous. I hardly left her room. I wanted to savor every hour and every minute I had left by her side. We'd spend hours hugging each other without saying a word, without moving. One night, a Thursday, Marina kissed my lips and whispered in my ear that she loved me and that, whatever happened, she would always love me.

She died the following morning, quietly, just as Rojas

had predicted. At daybreak, with the first light of dawn, Marina pressed my hand hard, smiled at her father, and the flame in her eyes went out forever.

———

We made the last journey with Marina in the old Tucker. Germán drove in silence to the beach, just as we'd done months earlier. It was a radiant day. I wanted to believe that the sea she loved so much had dressed up specially to receive her. We parked the car among the trees and went down to the shore to scatter her ashes.

When we returned to the car, Germán, now a broken man, admitted that he felt incapable of driving back. We abandoned the Tucker among the pine trees. Some fishermen who were driving by were kind enough to take us as far as the railway station. By the time we arrived back in Barcelona, at the Estación de Francia, seven days had passed since my disappearance. To me it felt like seven years.

I hugged Germán good-bye on the station platform. I still don't know where he went or what became of him. We both knew we wouldn't be able to look into each other's eyes again without seeing Marina in them. I watched as he walked away, a speck vanishing into the canvas of time. Shortly afterward a plainclothes policeman recognized me and asked me whether my name was Oscar Drai.

EPILOGUE

The Barcelona of my youth no longer exists. Its streets and its light are gone forever and only live on in people's memories. Fifteen years later I returned to the city and revisited the scenes I thought I'd banished from my mind. I discovered that the Sarriá mansion had been demolished. The surrounding streets now form part of a motorway, along which, they say, progress travels. The old cemetery is still there, I suppose, lost in the mist. I sat on the bench in the square that I'd shared so often with Marina. In the distance I glimpsed the outline of my old school, but I didn't dare walk up to it. Something told me that if I did, my youth would evaporate forever. Time doesn't make us wiser, only more cowardly.

For years I've been fleeing without knowing what from. I thought that if I ran farther than the horizon, the shadows of the past would move out of my way. I thought that if I put in enough distance, the voices in my mind could be silenced forever. I returned at last to the secret beach facing the Mediterranean. Beyond it stood the chapel of Sant Elm, always keeping watch from afar. I found the old Tucker belonging to my friend Germán. Oddly enough, it's still there, in its final resting place among the pine trees.

I walked down to the shore and sat on the sand where years ago I scattered Marina's ashes. The sky had the same luminosity as on that day, and I felt her presence sharply. I realized that I could no longer flee, that I no longer wished to do so. I had come back home.

During her last days I promised Marina that if she couldn't do it, I would finish this story. The book I gave her has been by my side all these years. Her words will be my words. I don't know whether I'll be able to do her justice. Sometimes I doubt my memory and wonder whether I will only be able to remember what never really happened.

Marina, you took all the answers away with you.